Three Full Moons

A Galowhisdi Novel

Carolan Dickinson

THREE FULL MOONS
A Galowhisdi Novel

ISBN: 9781533390783

Design by Transcendent Publishing

Printed in the United States of America.

Nothing can dim the light which shines from within

~Maya Angelou

Table of Contents

1

Graveyard Duty

I f I could control my emotions better, I'd never have sent that murder of crows to attack the twins. It probably isn't the most mature thing I've ever done, and yet a part of me feels it's totally worth graveyard duty. This is where I spend my eighteenth birthday, sitting next to my grandmother's headstone, crying. It's not the woman I grieve, though, for I never met her; it's the dream, the dream of someone caring if I'm in the world or not.

Nibs (as in "nibbles like a mouse") Dove and her brother Derrick are from the same village as Grandmother and they tell me stories about her. I think I would've really liked her. Hearing the stories is great, but not the same as having her around to tell me them herself, preferably while braiding my hair or baking cookies. Maybe she didn't even like to bake, but in my mind that's just what grandmothers do.

Nibs and I have a lot in common. Our moms died and our loosely-termed father figures are not in the picture, so here we are at the Sequoyah Boarding School, as the sign says, "A Home for Orphaned Indians." I've been here three years; Nibs and Derrick, two. After my mom died, dear old stepdad couldn't drop me off fast enough. So here I am, and here we are, officially wards of the great state of Oklahoma. At least, for a couple more hours.

As of 12:01 a.m. I will officially enter adulthood. Part of me is excited for a new adventure and part of me is scared to death. I don't know what comes next. I've applied to colleges across the country but haven't heard anything yet. Nibs is like a sister to me, and she already has her entire life planned. After graduation, she'll spend some time in the village working at the free clinic and then she'll be off to Oklahoma City for pre-med. I envy her solid path. I watch a firefly as it goes about its business, knowing that even a firefly has a purpose. Why can't I find mine?

As I sit here pondering the bleak status of my life, a flash of shimmering light catches my eye. I jump up and back away, then stare, wide-eyed, at an apparition floating above my grandmother's grave. I know the name, it's something we share: Nanye'Hi Ward. I see her so clearly. She has the face an artist would paint—olive skin, high prominent cheekbones, huge brown eyes, and thick flowing black hair. She's dressed in a beaded white buckskin dress with matching moccasins on her feet. Sitting on her right shoulder is an owl and in her left hand she holds an intricately carved talking stick.

When her eyes meet mine, I immediately feel a pressure slowly spread across my chest like warm honey, the feeling you get after finally having the sun on your face after days of gloom and rain.

2

My daughter's daughter, she says. *It is time to come home.*

She speaks to me in the language of my people. How I understand her is a mystery since I don't know one word of Cherokee.

"Holy crap!"

I pinch my arms.

I get that sinking feeling in the pit of my stomach because I know. I know that this is yet one more thing to add to my very long list of weird.

I'm still trying to wrap my head around the fact that I'm seeing and hearing my dead grandmother when a rustle in the bushes off to my right startles me. I can't see anything, but I hear it, and it's coming fast. I fight the urge to cover my face with my hands and instead find myself looking for my grandmother. She's gone, and I brace myself to face whatever it is when it breaks through the tree line . . . with a light and voices singing, *"Happy Birthday to you, Happy Birthday to you..."*

"Oh, my God! Nibs, you scared the crap out of me."

"Sorry, White Girl. I thought we'd surprise you."

White Girl. Only Nibs gets to call me that. It'd really stung when my classmates branded me with the name, and Nibs does it to remind me that it is *just* a name. Sticks and stones and that sort of thing.

Derrick stands behind her, looking fidgety as if graveyards make him uncomfortable. I wonder how much she had to bribe him to come out here.

"You just startled me is all."

Nibs looks at me, raising her eyebrow. "You're never scared out here. What happened?"

I'm not ready to tell her about seeing my grandmother. She's my best friend, but still. Am I *sure* that's what that was?

"Nothing happened, I swear."

"Uh huh, sure. Graveyard duty again, Nan, what'd you do this time?"

"Nothing!"

But Nibs is not going to let it go—I have to tell her something.

"You're right. It happened again. On my way to class, the twins started calling me White Girl and you know how I feel about that. I started getting mad and couldn't control it. A murder of crows was hanging out on the fence line, and... It just sort of happened."

Derrick's laughter bursts out of him, accompanied by some small snorting noises.

"That was *you*?" he says incredulously as more snorts escape him. At my nods, he turns to Nibs. "It was the best laugh I've had all year. The twins were running down the sidewalk, long black braids flying in the wind with their hands over their heads while the crows were flying all over and peckin' at them. It was hilarious."

I give him a quick smile.

Trying to stifle a laugh, Nibs says, "I guess it wasn't too serious. Really, Nan, you need to learn how to control it or you're going to hurt someone for real. And this wasn't about the twins, either. You've been majorly cranky for days."

She's right. As much as I'd like to blame graveyard duty on the crows and the twins, I can't.

"We'll figure it out, I promise," Nibs says with a reassuring touch to my shoulder. She always calms me down. She has that effect on most people. It's one of her many gifts and one of the many reasons she'll make a great doctor.

"What else is going on?" she asks.

"Nothing."

"You'll tell me when you're ready." Nibs nods decisively. She knows me so well.

"Cake?" Derrick asks.

"There's cake?"

"Strawberry, of course," Nibs says.

Nibs always remembers. I'm so lucky. I'll try to remember that the next time I send a murder of crows to do my dirty work. It might help me stay calm.

We celebrate my birthday next to Grandmother's grave. I keep a watchful eye, but nothing else happens. Everything looks totally different as the sun comes up and we head back to the school. Two more weeks, that's it, and then what?

The question no sooner flashes through my mind when a voice over my right shoulder says, "Nanye'Hi, come home." I jump and look in the direction of the voice.

Nibs and Derrick both stop and scan the cemetery for some threat.

"What is it?" Nibs asks.

"Nothing, I . . ."

"*Right.* When you're ready."

———◦◦◦———

Grandmother, my *dead* grandmother, has been talking non-stop for two weeks. I'm starting to lose it. She is annoying, resilient, stubborn and an overall pain in my backside. Last night she even followed me into my dreams. She always appears to me the same way she did that night in the grave-yard: white buckskin dress, owl on her shoulder and talking stick in her hand. She keeps repeating the same thing: *It's time to come home.* I'm so over it. Why now and why me?

When Mom was still alive we moved from crappy apartment to seedy flophouse every couple of months. The longest I've ever lived anywhere has been here at Sequoyah. I try everything I can think of to block Grandmother's voice. I find myself singing songs in my head and counting constantly. I don't how much longer this will work, but for now I'll use whatever I can.

I'm in homeroom when my teacher, Ms. River, gives me a note.

Great, called to the headmaster's office, *again*. I seriously can't think of anything I've done.

I make the long walk to the front office, ignoring my classmates' calls of "White Girl" as I pass by. I don't get it. No one is one hundred percent anything anymore. I know I look different, but my blond hair truly is the only thing that sets me apart. The rest of me looks like them—same olive skin, high prominent cheekbones, and brown eyes. I may be curvier than most . . . but still.

Of course there was also the weird squirrel incident. I still cringe whenever it replays in my mind. No matter what I did, or where I went, squirrels followed me like a gaggle of baby ducks after their mother. That day "White Girl" got a sister nickname, "Squirrel Lady," though it didn't end there. Since then I've been trying to ignore them, praying, hoping and pleading that they would just go away. That *it*—whatever it is-would just go away. I just want a normal life, and to feel like I belong somewhere.

"Enter," a voice booms from the other side of the headmaster's door. I dread going in there. Two more weeks and I'm gone, no matter what he says. I can handle anything for two weeks. The headmaster is sitting behind his huge oak desk. Creating a frame around his large body on the wall behind him, and on every available space, are antique Indian artifacts.

"Nanye'Hi."

"Nan, please, Mr. Brock."

"You should be proud of your heritage."

I stare down at my hands clasped in front of me.

"Very well, Nan. I have something for you. A couple of things."

"I'm not in trouble?"

"Not this time," he says, looking at me over the top of his glasses. Reaching into his drawer he pulls out two envelopes and hands them to me. I stand there staring at them.

"Well?" Mr. Brock asks.

I grab both envelopes and head out the door, barely remembering to say thank you. I can feel his eyes locked on me as I leave. I need some space and head for the one place I know no one will bother me.

Sitting on the red clay dirt next to Grandmother's grave, I stare at the envelopes. One is from UCLA. The other is handwritten and addressed very formally to Nanye'Hi Ward. My hands are shaking as I tear open the envelope and start reading.

Grandmother?

How is this possible? My eyes find the date, written several years ago. *At least,* I think wryly, *she was alive when she wrote it.*

My daughter's daughter, on her eighteenth birthday,

Happy Birthday. I wish there had been time to spend with you. I cannot prepare you for what is to come, this you must do on your own. I know that you have many questions, and they will be answered at exactly the right time and place. Trust in that. If I could have shown you a better world in your early years, I would have done so. The Great Mystery calls me to be of service and in this, I have no choice. All of this you will understand one day. You will be asked to make a very important decision soon.

The cabin and land are yours now, as it should be. All that I ask is that you go to Galowhisdi and stay three full moons. Then you must decide. Your decision will affect many, and for generations to come. One of my goals in this lifetime was to leave the world better than I found it. With your help that can still be accomplished. Learn from the Elders, pay attention to the animals, listen to the ancestors and to your intuition. We will be together one day, in the old way. I love you with a heart as big as the sky.

Love, Grandmother

More than anything I would love to know *what* Grandmother is talking about. It would be wonderful if I could just have a normal conversation with her, one where I asked questions and she gave answers. Instead, the mysteries keep piling up and there is no one to ask. I *could* ask her, but that would just start the whole "Go to Galowhisdi and stay three full moons" routine all over again. Just thinking about Galowhisdi makes my stomach hurt. When my head feels like it might explode from all the questions, I give up and tear open the second envelope—my acceptance letter to UCLA. It's hard to be excited about it now. I'm more confused than ever and a little surprised to find more tears for a woman I've never met.

The next morning, the sun is shining, and the birds are singing—extremely loudly—outside my window.

"Please, not again."

About twenty robins sit perched in the tree directly outside my bedroom window, giving me a private concert. I look over at Nibs's bed to see if the noise is disturbing her, but she's already gone, most likely to the library.

Considering that Sequoyah's been around since just after the Civil War ended, they've done a pretty good job at making it livable. I've always loved the look of the buildings, with their sturdy red brick and white trim. If you didn't know better, you'd think this was a college campus. Most of my classmates have a room just like Nibs and I, except we're on the coveted second floor, giving us a great view of the courtyard. Our dorm room has two beds with a shared living room and bathroom. I look over at her side of the room, and at the drawings over her bed. They're all body parts and body part systems. That girl eats, drinks, and sleeps medicine. Over my bed are pictures of animals, the beach, and places I've never seen, but dream of seeing. The robins are getting louder.

I go to the window and open it. "Quiet. *Please, please* be quiet."

It's too late. My classmates are already beginning to gather and watch the show. The robins are unconcerned about my humiliation.

What am I going to do? Not only about the birds, but about everything?

In the fall, Nibs will go to the University of Oklahoma for pre-med and then on to medical school on a full scholarship because she's that smart. My grades aren't bad, but hers are better. She's more motivated and has a plan. I'm in awe of how focused she is. Then she'll intern and do her residency and end up back at the one place I'm desperately trying to avoid ever seeing: the Indian village of Galowhisdi.

Nibs invited me many times to come with her and see where my mom grew up and my grandmother lived, but I haven't been able to bring myself to do it. Every time I've gotten close to going, something stops me. It's a foreboding, a feeling that screams *danger* and plants a pit the size of a basketball in my gut. I know it's not logical, but is anything in my life? You would think I'd want to see it, but I don't. I don't want anything to remind me about losing my mother or my grandmother. Instead, I've stayed at Sequoyah the last three summers, working in Tahlequah at Sam and Ella's Chicken and Pizza Palace. I've also been lucky enough to snag a part-time gig at Sam and Ella's Floats, as a tour guide along the Illinois River. Now those two envelopes had brought me to a crossroads and I'm not sure about anything except getting the heck out of here. Don't I deserve a fresh start, a new life?

Finally, graduation arrives. Everyone around me seems excited to see their families, yet for me it's a bit lackluster. I watch people I've never met surround Nibs and congratulate her. She gives me a look that lets me know, as always, how well she understands how I'm feeling. After graduation, I load up my truck with my meager belongings and say goodbye to Sequoyah, Nibs, and my old life. It is bittersweet, for though I'm thrilled at the prospect of never having to hear "White Girl" again, I am, without Nibs, truly alone in the world.

Praying the craziness won't follow me, I head west to California. I know I will pass the turnoff to Galowhisdi soon, the mere thought tying my stomach in knots. As I approach the turnoff, Grandmother appears next to me in the passenger seat. I'm so startled I jerk the truck off the road and onto the shoulder.

"Nanye'Hi, you must come home," she says.

I pound on the steering wheel. "I almost made it; I was almost out of here!" Should I pretend I don't see her? I should've known it wouldn't be this easy. "Sorry, Grandmother, I just can't."

When I pull back onto the highway, Grandmother vanishes.

There's nothing for me in Galowhisdi. I need to get as far away from here as possible.

UCLA isn't far enough.

I drive to Tahlequah and find the nearest Air Force recruiting office.

2

Meeting Myself

Seven years later, they give me a purple heart. They shouldn't have.

I look past the women seated around the table and out the window to gaze at the beach scene outside. There are worse places to be than San Diego, California. If only I were here on vacation. Instead, I've been ordered here to attend the Women's Trauma Recovery Center. Looking around the table, I see their faces and hear their stories. I know I don't belong here. None of these women caused the death of their crew like I did.

It was my second tour in Afghanistan, at a tiny airbase with no name. My fellow airmen and I called it Hades, a tent city out in the middle of the Registan Desert, between Helmand and Kandahar. The land of extremes. A constant source of sand, wind, heat, and fleas. At any given time of the day I could take a bite of food and feel the grit of sand between my teeth. Our official presence in Hades was supposed to foster peace, but, like many of our assignments, we will never know the true reasons. Shortly after we arrived, Hades became a beacon in the desert for every radical and insurgent group in the desert. We were on perpetual combat alert.

Captain Michael Lane, a decorated and dedicated military officer, was my superior. Lane was gorgeous, charming, smart and, as it turned out, demented, cruel, and evil. It started innocently enough, with little comments here and there about my appearance. Some of it I let slide. Then his "innocent" comments turned into suggestive innuendos, leering, and blatant sexual harassment.

One day after a crew briefing, he followed me into the rear of a supply truck and backed me into a corner. I was shaking with rage.

"Sir, I have taken all the crap from you I plan on taking. Now back off. "

He moved forward and pressed himself against me.

"Oh, come on, Nan, you know you want this. I see the way you look at me."

"I said, back the hell off." I pushed him as hard as I could. "And if this ever happens again, I *will* report you."

His face turned bright red, which I took for embarrassment and, seeming genuinely contrite, he stepped away.

As far as women in the military have come, we still have a few hills to climb before reaching equality. If I had reported every time a supposed "comrade" hit on me, I'd never have been taken seriously. Instead I tried to handle it on my own, which was absolutely the worst decision I could've made.

About a week later, after most of the camp had called it a night, a one-striper came to my tent with a message from Captain Lane to report to the operations tent.

I entered the tent and stood at attention. "Sergeant Ward, reporting as ordered, sir." I saluted only because it was required, then looked over his head at a blank spot on the wall. He began to pace.

"Sergeant Ward, I've been thinking."

Uh oh.

"I have an assignment for you. Consider it professional development, and an opportunity for a much-needed attitude adjustment. Take your crew and patrol the borders of the camp, especially along the southern border. There's been intel that insurgents are trying to breach camp."

Apparently, Captain Michael Lane didn't get turned down too often.

Whatever his motivation, I had no choice but to follow the order. I gathered my crew, all five of whom were under twenty years old, and we headed out–the senior airman and three one-stripers in one Humvee, myself and the other one-striper in the other.

We began patrolling along the fence line in opposite directions. I don't even know why they bothered with the fence. It was chain link with posts set into cement buckets to keep the wind from blowing it over. There was a five-inch gap at the bottom, and the rest of it was covered with camouflage netting. Beyond the fence were miles and miles of sand dunes of varying height, excellent for hiding behind. The lights in tent city made it clear viewing for anyone wanting to see inside, while the darkness on the opposite side created opportunity for clandestine movement. That night, the wind was blowing as usual, and the sand with it, adding to the lack of visibility. I was feeling edgy.

A crackle of noise hit my radio.

I keyed up and said, "Airman Zeek, this is Sergeant Ward, repeat your last transmission." What I got was another garbled message of static along with something that sounded like shouting.

I transmitted in the blind, hoping the other crew would hear me.

"Airman Zeek, I'm heading in your direction."

I spotted their headlights and headed straight for them. They were stationary. Were they having engine trouble? My headlights illuminated the Humvee in front of us just in time for me to see my crew being pulled from the vehicle by armed rebel forces.

"Call Command!" I yelled, as I grabbed my rifle and, using the door as a shield, began to fire. It felt like everything was happening in slow motion, then I was engulfed in the unmistakable blinding flash and roaring boom of an explosion.

My crew.

I opened my eyes to nothing but white, a strange beeping noise and a blistering heat along my entire back.

"Welcome back, Sergeant," a female voice said.

I tried to turn my head but something was stopping me. I reached up and touched something soft but firm wrapped around my neck—a brace? I finally cut my eyes in the direction of the voice and saw the nurse standing next to my hospital bed.

With a hoarse and gritty voice, I asked, "Where's my crew?"

The nursed paused. "I'm sorry, Sergeant, they didn't make it."

"None of them?"

"I'm sorry."

The rest of my days at the hospital were spent in a haze, partly from the drugs they were giving me, and partly because I couldn't face the world, or myself. After several days of lying in bed wishing I'd died with my crew, I heard *him* talking to my nurse outside my room.

"I really need to see her."

"She doesn't want any visitors."

"I'm not a visitor, I'm her superior officer."

"That doesn't apply here. Right now, she's my patient and not your subordinate. Understand, Captain?"

"Yes, Major."

For once I was thankful that rank had its privileges. Captain Lane was the last person I wanted to see. My instincts were telling me that he had a lot more to do with what happened that night than the reports would say. Those reports wouldn't tell the truth, that much I was sure of. For the sake of my crew, and for the safety of the men and women under his command, I had to make sure the truth was told.

As soon as I was physically able to get out of my hospital bed, I made my way to the unit commander's office to find that he had been prepared for me, courtesy of Captain Lane. Spread across his desk in an impressive display were Lane's personnel reports. The highlights? *My* "inappropriate behavior" and "delusions of his advances." Through his reports, the captain had created a behavioral profile consistent with that of someone suffering from post-traumatic stress disorder.

"Sergeant," he says as he hands me report after report. I began to read, my shock quickly turning to rage. The blood rushed to my face, and by the time I got to the last report my hands were visibly shaking. It took every last bit of self-control to hold in the unholy wrath that wanted to rip out of my body. Looking back, I think the shock might have been the only thing keeping me standing.

The commander was sympathetic . . . sort of. "PTSD isn't a character defect, Sergeant. It's real. They're making medical advances in this field all the time. You're tough, you'll make it."

"Sir, this isn't PTSD. What you're looking at is revenge, because I had the nerve to turn down the sexual advances of my commanding officer. Please, sir, talk to the captain's assistant. He was there that night. He'll confirm what I'm telling you."

"I did talk to him, Sergeant, under oath. He saw nothing that would indicate anything but the total opposite of what you have accused Captain Lane–who, I might add, I know personally and hold in high regard–of doing."

I know how crazy all of it sounds, but I had to try . . . for my crew. Lane had set us up to be ambushed that night and he was going to get away with it. Shock of a different kind hit me, and I was stunned into silence. This was a betrayal of all I thought sacred. The world I believed in, where I felt safe, secure, and proud to be a part of, was gone. Gone as fast as the blinding flash and roaring boom that had killed my crew.

The commander's recommendation: transfer to a treatment facility for a mental health evaluation.

There was nothing left. I had no one in my corner, and no one to help me fight for those who had died that night.

I should have, is my mantra these days, right along with, *What if?*

"Sergeant Ward."

I blink at the sound of my name, my gaze flickering around the table again before returning out the window to the beach.

San Diego, I'm in San Diego.

I can see by the look on their knowing faces that it's happened again. I'd gotten lost in the past.

"Sergeant Ward, can you tell us about it?" Dr. Davis asks. Her voice helps pull me back to the present.

I know it's *group therapy*, but I can't bring myself to say it out loud. That would make it too real. There is no going back from it, once you say it. I'm not ready. I don't belong here, not with these honorable women.

"Not yet," I say. But I can't stop the words that come next. They feel foreign, like someone else is saying them.

"It was my fault. They died because of me. Don't you get it? I should have died that day. I wish I *had* died that day."

A woman sitting directly across from me asks, "What are you waiting for?"

Stunned, I feel the heat of anger rushing up the back of my neck then continue to my face where it blooms on my cheeks.

"What . . . did . . . you . . . say?"

"I said, what are you waiting for? If you truly want to die, then why aren't you dead?"

I stare at her for a moment with my mouth open. Then I wonder . . . I should have . . . what if?

I take a deep breath. Dr. Davis interrupts before I have a chance to say something I'm sure I'll regret later.

"I think what Cheryl is trying to say is there must be a reason you haven't done it. Do you truly want to die, or do you want things to be different, and to feel differently?"

"All I know for sure is that right now, my crew should be going home to their families. The rest, I'll have to get back to you on."

I have no idea what I feel, or what I want.

Depression, nightmares, anxiety, and panic attacks become my new norm. Sometimes they come one at a time, but mostly they come all together, like a tsunami. Then, slowly, the PTSD symptoms seem to lighten up. The days meld into one another, and I find myself feeling a little more grounded each day.

Everything inside the Recovery Center reminds me of a spa; even the colors—soft beachy blues and greens and various shades of white—are designed to soothe and heal. Each of us has our own room that opens to a hallway that leads to the common living room and kitchen. All the rooms have full-length sliding glass doors that open to individual patio areas with access to the beach. The staff encourages us to get outside daily and walk. In these moments of peace along the beach, I manage to write in my journal and get a letter or two off to Nibs. They're rather cryptic, though, because I haven't been able to tell her what's happened. I haven't been able to tell anyone. Not even my group. Until I do, I doubt very seriously that they'll let me go. I don't have a clue what my next assignment will be, or where. I don't even know if I care.

It's early enough in the spring that the air still has a bite. There's no hint of June gloom, and the sun shines brightly every day. I shiver from the cool misty ocean breeze, feeling my cheeks sting and my nose run. I pull my hoodie around me, zipping it up tight. After Hades, it's a welcome change. Nibs will laugh when she reads that I've fallen in love with yoga. When we were at Sequoyah, she was always trying to get me to try something that was centering and naturally stress-reducing. After a while, she quit talking about it but would leave articles on my bed about the benefits of yoga and meditation. Seven years later, I'm doing both.

The sun, the ocean breeze, and walks on the beach do as much for my recovery as my women's group and therapy sessions. I don't know exactly how it happens but at some point, I take up the practice of praying. My prayers always begin the same, "Dear God, guides, and angels, please help me." I haven't prayed like this since I was a little girl.

Today, as I'm sitting deep in meditation, I feel a familiar warm energy wrap around me like a blanket. A sense of deep peace, safety, and serenity fills me completely. Emotions flow out of me in the form of tears. I feel like they'll never stop, but eventually they do. The next morning when I open my eyes I'm energized. I feel as though a fog has lifted from my soul.

After about a month of group therapy, my story pours out of me. It feels unstoppable. The women around the table envelop me in compassion, strength, and a sisterhood I've never experienced before. We share a common goal—to survive—to heal.

Then the final word comes down from headquarters: Honorable Discharge.

The following day, and several more after that, I find it difficult to leave my bed. I wonder if it's because I've lost my purpose for getting out of it.

Is this it—is this my life now? Do I have the courage to keep putting one foot in front of the other? Maybe courage can be counted in seconds, like breath.

After a particularly bad night, I wake drenched in sweat. I feel a sense of urgency, then a sensation I haven't felt in seven years spreads across my chest like warm honey. Directly above me floats a ghostly apparition. I start to scream, but the apparition puts her finger to her lips, and softly whispers, *Nanye'Hi, come home.*

"Grandmother?" I whisper.

I don't wait for an answer; I just close my eyes, place my hands over them and say a short, silent prayer that she goes away. When I open my eyes, no one is there.

Why is this happening again, now, after I've successfully blocked it out all these years?

I'm so deep in thought that when I hear it again, I nearly jump out of my skin.

Nanye'Hi, it's time to come home.

Crap.

I don't know whether to hope it's her or not. Then I decide . . . *Oh dear Lord, please let it be her.* On top of everything else, I cannot be batshit crazy. That would be too much, even for me.

I'm sitting on the bed, rocking back and forth with the bedcovers pulled up tight under my chin.

"Okay, girlfriend, get it together," I tell myself, trying to find some intestinal fortitude.

The next morning begins the avoidance phase, which basically means I try to brush it off and make myself busy by working out, meditating, praying, and watching endless reruns of Friends. Nothing works. Every day, morning and night, I get the same message: *Nanye'Hi, come home.* The only thing that changes is the way the message is delivered. Sometimes it comes accompanied by the apparition of my grandmother, and other times it flows through like a whisper on a breeze. In that deep place in the pit of my stomach I know it's her. She's annoying and relentless—is—was—*whatever*.

The craziness that has become my life keeps me from thinking about everything else. The next day the nurse brings me a letter, a letter addressed to Nanye'Hi Ward. Not Sergeant Ward, or Nan, but Nanye'Hi.

With my hands shaking, I tear open the envelope and begin reading. Instantaneously I flash to my eighteenth birthday, sitting next to my grandmother's grave at Sequoyah. Except for the date, I'm reading the exact same letter.

That awful ball of fear takes root in the pit of my stomach. The moment of truth has arrived. I can continue to be driven crazy by my dearly departed grandmother, or I can face what I've been avoiding for seven years. What other *good* option do I really have? I need answers, and the only place I will find them is Galowhisdi, Oklahoma.

3

Galowhisdi

G alowhisdi is seventy-five miles south of Fayette-ville, Arkansas, and ten miles to the north of Tahle-quah, Oklahoma, the same tiny village where I'd worked those summers jobs while at Sequoyah's. It is sur-rounded by Forest Service land, beautifully nestled in the foothills of the Ozark Mountains. This part of Oklahoma has four distinct seasons; my favorites are fall and spring. Every-thing is so alive with color then, especially the leaves on the trees and the dogwoods when they bloom. I remember the stories Nibs used to tell me about Galowhisdi, which is the Cherokee word for "pathway." Now I find myself wondering where this pathway leads.

My mother named me Nanye'Hi, or *One Who Goes About with the Spirit People,* after my grandmother and all the grandmothers that came before her. The original Nanye'Hi was born of the fiercest clan in the Cherokee Nation—the Wolf Clan. The tribe migrated from Tennessee in the 1830s during the Indian Removal Act. The Cherokee call it the Trail of Tears. You won't find it on any map. It's tucked away and hidden from most. That's it, that's all I know of my family and my heritage. Mom wasn't big on sharing. Drugs and men were her highest priority.

The free-floating fear that has crept into me almost constantly since Afghanistan starts to roar as I approach the turn-off. Though it has gotten much better, thanks to a daily practice of yoga, journaling, meditation, and prayer, it's still a full-time job keeping that fear at bay. Whenever I allow my mind to get quiet, everything that happened starts repeating, over and over. I start sweating, my breath races, and my heart jumps around in my chest. What's worse is the fog that creeps over my brain. It's almost like temporary amnesia. I'll forget where I am or what I'm doing. It's exhausting.

I distract myself by looking for the little turn-off onto the dirt road. And, just like Grandmother told me, there's a beautiful hand-carved totem pole atop an old tree stump, marking the spot. I'm still surprised to see it. None of the grass or bushes have grown around it as you would expect in the spring.

Nanye'Hi, says a voice, *You are home.*

And here she is.

I almost give myself whiplash turning my head in the direction of the words. Grandmother's form and voice are as corporeal as I am. I turn onto the dirt road feeling lightheaded and dizzy. I stop the truck and get out. As soon as I put my feet on the red clay earth, the dizziness stops.

"Grandmother, please stop doing that. Can't you see that I have *a thing*? Please consider that before you decide to scare the crap out of me again."

She's gone.

Somewhat apprehensive, I climb back in the truck and continue down the dirt road that leads to Galowhisdi until I'm stopped by the scenery in front of me. I don't know what I expected, but it isn't this: a beautiful field of tall grass mixed with wildflowers. They seem to go on forever, as if the field flows directly into the clouds on the horizon. As I draw closer, however, I see that it drops off into the Illinois River. The current is strong, and the water roars as it splashes across the rocks.

Grabbing my backpack, I get out of the truck and fall exhausted to the ground, landing splayed out, snow-angel-style on my back. I look up at the blue sky, letting the smell of sweet grass wash over me and the earth support my entire body. Time does not exist at this moment—I allow myself to feel this place.

I have no idea how long I laid there. I might have fallen asleep. After taking a few minutes to breathe in the fresh air, I realize that I'm putting off the inevitable. I need to see the condition of Grandmother's cabin. I prepare myself for the worst. Feeling a physical nudge from Grandmother, I start walking and soon see the cabin across the field and into a clearing. I stop for a moment and stare at it. The cabin's pine logs are shining as though someone had just waxed them. I remember Nibs's description of Grandmother's place, which was, "more like a shack." What I'm seeing makes no sense.

An older, sort of red, sort of brown Chevy pickup with rust on the hood and a dent in the right front fender is parked toward the rear of the cabin.

Is it squatters? Since when do squatters make home improvements?

"Crap." I'd almost forgotten my pistol.

Squatting down in the tall grass, I reach into my backpack for Bernice. I fell in love with her the first time I placed her in my hand. She fit perfectly in my palm. There's just something about the nine-millimeter Beretta that speaks to me. The weight is completely balanced. Not too light and not too heavy. She racks easily and has little to no recoil. I never go anywhere without her. The military gave me a badge for sharpshooting. Whoever is living in Grandmother's cabin will be making a quick exit.

Crouching low and moving silently through the grass, I move closer to see if I can spot anyone. What I see through the corner of the window makes no sense. Who brought in new furniture?

Trailing my hand along the pine logs of the cabin, I can tell by the feel and smell of them that they've recently been stained and sealed. Crap, there are even flowers on the dining room table. I'll just sit here and wait out whoever's in there.

"Hey, White Girl, what'cha doing?" someone says.

I jump back from the window, spinning, and fall face first into the dirt, Bernice flying out of my hand. Jumping up quickly, I try to recover, whipping around, crouching low, with dukes up ready to fight. Standing two feet away from me is a beautiful Cherokee woman who is laughing so hard she has to sit down.

"What . . . who?"

"Oh, White Girl, you're hilarious. What did they teach you in the Air Force, anyway?"

Slowly, recognition catches up with me.

"Nibs? Oh, my god, I almost shot you. You're almost taller than I am. How did that happen?"

Nibs shrugs. "Dunno. Guess I'm just a really late bloomer. Come on, White Girl, let's have some tea and get caught up."

"Well you look amazing. And forget the tea; I need coffee. Very strong coffee."

"Great, you have both. Come on, let's go inside."

We don't try to force conversation. Instead, I look around, trying to take everything in; it's impressive, but puzzling.

"I'm hoping that the days of the outhouse and fetching water from the outside pump are gone?"

Nibs nods her head. "There have been some improvements. I think you'll like them."

And I do. Yes, it's a log cabin, but an updated one. A place you would expect a couple from the city to buy for weekend and holiday getaways.

Nibs hands me a cup of coffee. "This is a gift from Grandmother. She knew you'd come back here one day."

"Thank you for this, Nibs, and for being here." I pause. "Why *are* you here?"

"I live here most of the time."

Nibs hands me an envelope with *To Nanye'Hi from Grandmother, with a heart as big as the sky* scrawled across it in the now familiar handwriting. I look at her, puzzled.

"How and where did you get this?" I ask, my eyes filling with tears.

Doing a little squirming and sniffling of her own, Nibs asks, "Why don't I come over for breakfast in the morning, and we can get caught up then. The kitchen's stocked, including dinner for tonight."

"Okay. Thanks again, Nibs, for everything."

She gives me a hard hug and says, "Have a good sleep. I can't wait until tomorrow. I'll want all the details, especially the juicy ones."

"Wait—how did you know I was coming?"

"Tomorrow?"

I nod my head in agreement.

"I'm thrilled you're here," I tell her.

"Me, too." Nibs gives me another hug on her way out the door. Wow, how long has it been since I've had anyone hug me?

After she leaves I take closer look around. In the kitchen are all new stainless-steel appliances, with a replica of an old wood-fired stove, except this one burns clean with electric energy, and beautiful white pine cabinets with the same painstaking care given to each one.

All the interior doors are closed. I don't know where to start so I open the first door I come to. The master bedroom is filled with handmade log furniture including a queen size bed, two nightstands, a dresser, and an armoire. They are gorgeous, gleaming pieces. Around another door, I instantly fall in love with an enormous claw foot tub and vow to become acquainted with it as soon as possible.

Someone has gone to a lot of trouble for me, and it makes me feel very uncomfortable.

I don't deserve it. This beautiful cabin and all the handmade furniture in it were built as if the person knew me, and intimately. I don't like that feeling, but I admit I love this cabin and everything in it.

"Thank you, Grandmother," I say quietly.

Welcome home, Nanye'Hi."

I jump.

"Grandmother, please quit doing that!"

The rest of the two-bedroom, two-bath cabin is equally as beautiful. The smallest details have been taken care of, right down to the flat screen television. Everything built in, and in its place. I end up back in the living room and start looking over the books that line the shelves.

My childhood favorites are all here: The Twilight Series; The House of Night; all the Harry Potters; The Vampire Academy Series; and The Hunger Games, just to name a few. Where did they come from, and who knew me well enough to put them there?

My eyes flick to a picture of Grandmother and me hanging over the fireplace. Wait a minute. That's not me–could not be me. But such a likeness! I move closer to the old black and white print. Yes, that's definitely Grandmother—I'd know her anywhere, *now*. But who is that woman next to her who has my face, cheekbones, and eyes? Aside from her dark hair, she could be my twin.

Grandmother had the best smile, I think, and I'm once again surprised by the heaviness of grief in my chest. I know it doesn't make sense that I would feel this kind of loss for someone I never met, and yet the feelings persist. Instead of dealing with the onslaught of emotions threatening to surface, I do what I always do—get busy.

As the evening starts to settle in, I go on the hunt for wood for the fireplace and find a door that leads into the kitchen and from there a small mudroom that opens outside to the deck. Right outside the door is a craftsman-style wood box stocked with perfectly sized logs for the fireplace and another smaller box stocked with kindling.

Once the fire is going I decide on a soak in the claw foot tub. I run the water and set out my most comfortable pajamas, all the while knowing I am just prolonging the inevitable. I stay in the tub, which is indeed heavenly, until the water has turned tepid and my fingers and toes are wrinkly; then I reluctantly drag myself out, slip into the flannels and settle into the handmade rocking chair to open yet another letter from Grandmother.

My daughter's daughter,

If you are reading this letter, then you have found your way home. At least, I hope you will be at home here. I could not be prouder of you. This cabin and land are yours now, as they should be. Know in your heart that you will always be welcome here. The People will love you. Strange days are ahead for you. Although you are no stranger to service, you must focus even more on what service means to you. It will bring pain, sacrifice, and honor. It will also bring joy, love, and purpose. I know you would not have it any other way. The day will soon come when this will all make sense. I know you, Granddaughter, better than I know myself.

Pay attention to your dreams, surroundings, and intuition. We will see each other again, in the old way. There is nothing that you could have done, or think you have done, that would change the fact that I love you with a heart as big as the sky.

Love, Grandmother

I lower the paper and close my eyes. *Strange days ahead of me...?* I don't know how they could be stranger than what I've already experienced, yet I don't doubt it for a minute. I feel the fear tickling the edges of my mind, but suddenly I am too tired to care.

I don't know if it was the relaxing bath or plain old exhaustion, but I barely remember slipping between the sheets of my new bed.

I wake disoriented, trying to remember where I am as the sun begins to make its way into the bedroom. The enticing aroma of freshly brewed coffee mingled with the delicious smell of bacon cooking has me jumping out of bed.

What a thoughtful thing for Nibs to do.

I scramble around and throw on fresh clothes. After washing my face and brushing my teeth, I head into the kitchen.

"Nibs, you should have woken me. I would've cooked –"

I stop short, frozen in fear. There is a stranger—a man— in my kitchen, cooking.

"Okay mister, step away from the bacon," I say, slowly making my way to the bookshelf where I'd hidden Bernice. "You can quietly leave out the back door, and no one gets hurt, okay?"

The stranger turns to face me, and a powerful jolt of electricity courses through my body. I freeze for just a second, noting the look of surprise written all over his chiseled face... surprise that quickly turns into laughter.

"Really? You're going to laugh at me while I have Bernice in my hand, with a bead directly between your eyes? Mister, you're either insane, or you have a death wish. Which is it?"

"Neither, actually."

"Would you explain to me who you are, and why in the hell you're in my kitchen making breakfast, and why in the hell you're in my cabin at all? Now that I think about it, how in the hell did you get in here in the first place?"

"I invited him," a familiar voice says from behind me.

"Nibs, you almost got your friend shot!"

"On that note, I think you better make introductions before she shoots both of us," he says.

My hands shake uncontrollably, yet I manage to place Bernice back on the bookshelf and sit in the rocker with my head between my knees. I try to breathe normally, but each inhale is ragged, unfulfilling.

In through the nose, out through the nose. In through the nose, out through the nose...

I know that if I just concentrate on my breath eventually the shaking will stop. The fear will move through me.

Suddenly I feel a large hand in the middle of my back. I hear the stranger begin to breathe with me, then his soft chanting of a Cherokee prayer.

"May the warm winds of heaven blow softly upon your house. May the Great Spirit bless all who enter there. May your moccasins make happy tracks in many snows, and may the rainbow always touch your shoulder."

Crap. Here we go again. The man is speaking in Cherokee, which I shouldn't be able to understand.

Except I do.

I try to speak, but nothing comes out of my mouth. Instead, I close my lips, shrug my shoulders, and shake my head.

Nibs kneels on the floor in front of me, holding my hands. "My God, Nan," she whispers, "What happened to you?"

The stranger, who has in the space of few minutes gone from threatening intruder to some sort of shaman, takes his hand from my back and places it on my shoulder.

"I know who you are," he says, "You are the infamous Nanye'Hi Ghigau Ward of the Cherokee, whose ancestors come from as far back as the Wolf Clan from the hills of Tennessee. You prefer Nan, or in some cases White Girl, though I have no idea why."

"It seems you know more about me than I do. What's Ghigau?"

I make a mental note ask him about the *infamous* comment later.

He is about to say something when Nibs cuts him off. He gives her a look.

"Nan, this is my cousin Brayden."

"It's nice to meet you, thank you for the assist, and for making this excellent breakfast."

"Hey, White Girl, I helped," Nibs says.

"What, with the toast? I remember how you cook. No wonder you brought your cousin along."

It will be nice to have friends again. Would they still want to be friends if they knew what I had done?

While listening to the easy banter across the table, I get a better look at the two of them. Both have high prominent cheekbones and dark brown eyes, and though Nibs's skin tone is deeper than Brayden's, their facial features are so similar they look more like siblings than cousins. They both have jet-black hair too, but Brayden's is somehow darker, giving it almost a bluish sheen I have never seen before, and very short, close to a military high and tight. He probably has two to three inches on Nibs, which would make him about six feet, and he is very muscular, but not overly so. He wears a hand-beaded friendship bracelet on his left wrist and notices me looking at it.

"Your grandmother made that for me. She was very kind." He looks down and away.

"Okay, cousin, out," Nibs says with a good-natured shooing motion. "It's girl time, and I know you don't want to be included in that."

Brayden is out the door before I can even say goodbye.

As my eyes follow him, I decide I'm going to start a list of all the weird and strange things that are happening. At this rate, I better get more paper.

4

Village Square

Nibs doesn't have to ask me twice to go to the village; the idea of fresh air and exercise sounds incredible. It's the beginning of June, and still chilly here in the foothills of the Ozark Mountains. Blooming dogwood trees and a scattering of oaks line the red clay road we walk, creating a canopy dense enough to partially obscure the sun. I look down and see my sneakers covered with red dirt; yep, I'm definitely in Oklahoma. The knot in my stomach continues to plague me, though I've yet to discover the cause. I hear the screech of an eagle and watch it glide in front of us. Down the dirt road are smaller ones that veer off in seemingly random directions. Instead of street signs, each road has a single carved animal on top of a tree stump. All of them appear to be the same style as the larger one at the turn-off to Galowhisdi. The next road we come to has a bear on top of a tree stump. It's as detailed as some of the pen and ink drawings I've seen.

"What are these carvings for?" I ask.

"You didn't pay attention in school, did you?"

"What are they?"

"This road goes to Brayden's House. This carving is what his family, and now he, has chosen for their animal totem. Each person claims their family symbol, or 'totem,' they feel a connection to."

She points out the turnoff to her place where a carving of a dove stands.

It makes sense, since Dove is their last name. What doesn't make sense is that there is no carving at the turnoff to Grandmother's cabin.

"Remember all the nights we spent in the graveyard?" Nibs asks.

"How could I forget?"

My mind flashes to my eighteenth birthday, when Nibs and Derrick brought me a cake to celebrate. It was the first time I ever saw Grandmother; she just happened to be floating over her own grave.

"Tell me about your life. What's happened other than what you wrote about in your letters?" I grab her hand and squeeze. "Those letters saved me, by the way."

"Other than medical school and residency in Oklahoma City, there isn't much to tell. I was splitting my time between a medical group in Tahlequah and the clinic here, but eventually I realized my heart was at our clinic. I'm there fulltime now."

Then Nibs gets quiet and glances and away. I know that look, and I don't push. Whatever it is, she'll say it when she's ready.

"Congratulations, Dr. Nibs. Can we go see the clinic?"

"Yes, but let's have coffee and do some shopping first."

As we walk from the tree-lined dirt road into the village, I'm stunned. When we were in school, Nibs would tell me stories about Grandmother and the village. I had formed pictures in my mind about what it would look like–a poor village with worn-out buildings, a shanty post office and a general store. Instead, I see a quaint, artsy village full of unique clothing and jewelry stores, coffee shops, an organic food market, and a huge bookstore. When Nibs tells me that there are little nooks throughout the store where you can grab a coffee, sit down with a book, and read, I make a mental note to come back and get lost in there.

No, this is most certainly not the same village Nibs described to me. Every building has been constructed and tended to in the same way as my cabin—with love, thought, and care. Even the sidewalks are finished with small benches and flowers in hand-painted clay pots. Native American artwork is proudly on display everywhere.

As we walk along the sidewalk, people are noticing us. Some I recognize as former classmates, but most I can't place at all. Everyone greets us with, "Hey, Doc" or "Look, there's White Girl," which, oddly enough, doesn't bother me. Probably because I am in awe of this place, so upbeat and clearly thriving. It reminds me of Sedona, Arizona, with its quirky New Age shops, boutiques, and unique restaurants, only instead of red rocks it is framed by the trees towering in the background. Although I've never been here, I have a sense of familiarity and vaguely wonder if it's from Nibs's stories.

In a place where Nibs once played stickball, we stop to have lunch in an upscale bistro. We sit at an outside table with a great view of the village and are served the freshest, most exquisite food I've had in a very long time. How they managed to create such a place here is puzzling. And how did all these people find their way here? Was it because they had embraced their heritage, rather than running from it as I had?

I scan the shops again. "What, no yoga studio?"

Nibs stops mid-chew. "Open one."

"Maybe, but I don't know if I'm staying yet, past the three full moons, I mean months—three full months."

Nibs gives me the "side eye," which grabs my attention immediately. It's a gesture left over from our days at Sequoyah. The "side eye" means something odd is occurring, while the "side-eye-plus- sideways glance combo" means that something very odd, maybe even magical, is at work.

"Let me guess, dreams–really vivid ones–and a message from Grandmother?" She stops and gives me the side-eye-plus-sideways-glance.

"Yes–why, are you having dreams too?" I ask her.

"I guess you could call them dreams. Anyway, you just can't ignore Grandmother and get any peace. She will wear down your resistance, even from the Great Mystery."

"You're preaching to the choir, sister."

Nibs gives me the combo again, but this time I don't answer her, I just clumsily change the subject. I know she isn't fooled, just being patient.

When we finish our extravagantly large pieces of peanut butter and chocolate fudge, we end up at the clinic. Warm *hellos* seem to come from everywhere as Nibs introduces me all around. I know I won't remember everyone's name.

Nibs turns to me. "Sorry, Nan, can you give me about a half an hour? I need to see someone."

"Of course."

Time to explore. I feel a sort of sensory overload as I look at everything and start walking. I have a lot more to add to my "weird list." I'm drawn to a corner store with a colored flag out front. The store stands out to me from the others. When I get closer, I realize I'm looking at the flag of the Cherokee Nation. For a moment I just stand on the sidewalk staring at it, trying to see what I remember of my Cherokee history. The seven-pointed star represents the seven clans of the Cherokee Nation: The Bird, Wild Potato, Deer, Long Hair, Paint, Blue, and Wolf. The wreath of leaves and acorns surrounding the star represents the sacred fire of the Cherokee, maintained for hundreds of years by spiritual leaders. Surrounding these elements are the words, "Seal of the Cherokee Nation," followed by "Tsa la gi hi A ye li," which in the language of the People means "Cherokee Nation." In the upper corner of the flag is a large, black, seven-pointed star honoring all that died on the Trail of Tears. Though I have never been able to say, "my people," I realize I remember more than I thought I did. I continue to stand there, staring. I feel a flood of tears pooling in my throat and swelling in my chest. I don't understand why I'm experiencing them now, and I don't try. For once, I just allow them to be what they are—grief and pride, meshed into one.

I feel more than see a powerful presence behind the shaded windows of the store. I'm riveted. It's different from grandmother's warmth; it feels more masculine and powerful, if that even makes sense.

———◦———

"It took her long enough," I say to the empty room.

Although I haven't heard her voice or seen her in several months, I know Grandmother's here. I feel her presence often as she helps me to keep an eye on the People and this village.

I pass by the mirror and do a double take. Taking my finger and thumb, I pinch my right cheek just to make sure it's me. Wow, where did the time go? The truth is, I've had the gray since I was thirty, and it has served as a constant reminder not to get too cocky. Back then I thought I knew it all. Until he came the first time. The next morning my hair was completely gray. The People gave me a new name that day, and it has been with me since.

I keep telling myself that I look wise and distinguished, but really, I'm just getting old. I know it, the People know it, everyone knows it. I just hope when they look at me and see all that gray hair and wrinkles, they see the wisdom and maturity of their medicine man. Right now, though, my main concern is with one person in particular.

"She should have been here long ago," I say in a slightly reproachful tone.

When I told Grandmother I'd help her, I didn't think I'd have to wait seven years. Then again, you'd think I'd know better than to make such a promise to a crafty old sorceress like her. And as for young Nanye'Hi, she is powerful and full of potential, but untrained and wild. As her energy washes over me, it feels familiar, and also foreign. Strong yet vulnerable, and a tad fragile. Interesting; her energy is akin to Grandmother's but there's something else too. I can't identify it, at least not yet.

I wonder, what is young Nanye'Hi's character? I hope she's not hardheaded like her grandmother. Let's hope by the Great Spirit that she's not ruled by her emotions, like her mother. That was a shame. She had all the talent and promise to be a powerful leader–and what a looker she was too, with those haunting brown eyes and a mess of unruly blond hair. But she chose the glittering path that led to bad men, drugs, and more bad men. We might have had a little something, but she chose a different life. One that didn't include me, this village, or my work. The Great Mystery has a reason for everything; most of us spend lifetimes trying to figure it out.

Shifting my eyes to where I feel Grandmother's presence, I tell her, "Well, it looks like it's time for me to keep my promise. I will do my best, but the rest, as you well know, is up to her."

———◦◉◦———

"Well, are you just gonna stand there and gawk, or are you coming in?" a raspy, gruff voice asks. I turn in the direction of the question.

"Well?"

I don't know what to say. I just stand there, staring at him with my mouth half open.

The raspy voice belongs to an average-looking, middle-aged Indian man with large brown eyes that crinkle at the edges and long silvery hair that falls to his shoulders and is secured by a hand-beaded headband. He wears a colorful shirt and jeans with black boots and walks slightly bent and with a stiffness that only comes from age, hard living, or a combination of both.

"Hi," I say, resisting the urge to look behind me to make sure he's not talking to someone else.

The sign on the door says Trading Post. He opens the door wider and points inside. He has that Commanding Officer sort of timber and stance. Like all good soldiers, I do as I'm told.

The walls are full of pictures, old black-and-whites as well as paintings by local artists. The shelves and cases are full of antique Indian artifacts, and the outside wall holds books about Cherokee history and folklore. He doesn't say a word, but I can feel him watching me as I absorb everything.

"It's about time you got here," he says.

I draw back in surprise. "What? What do you mean?"

"It took you long enough. Seven years is a long time to wait."

Just when I'm about to ask a bunch of questions, I notice a picture of my grandmother and my look-alike hanging on his wall. In this photo, they are in a circle of women around a fire. Each is holding a drum. I'm frozen in place, staring at it.

"You look just like her, you know."

"I'm sorry, I think you're mistaking me for someone else."

"No mistake, you're Nanye'Hi Ghigau Ward of the Cherokee, aren't you?"

"I don't know about the Ghigau part, what is that?"

"You are looking at a photograph of your great-great-great-grandmother," he continues with his eyes closed, remembering. "Your hair is lighter, your eyes and skin coloring a little different, but you are the spitting image of her. You will find the answers to your questions. Pay attention to the animals, your intuition, and your heart. They will keep you on the Red Road."

Stunned, I pay for the photograph. He adds a book in with my purchase.

"I'm sorry," I say. "The book is not mine."

"It's a gift from Grandmother. It will help you with your totem animals and your journey."

He steps away for a moment, then returns with a rattle decorated with native writings, leather, feathers, and beads. I watch, wide-eyed, as he begins shaking and moving the rattle over my head and down along my back. He continues along the periphery of my body, speaking in Cherokee as he does so, and once again I understand every word.

"May the warm winds of heaven blow softly on your house, may the Great Spirit bless all who enter there, may your moccasins make happy tracks in many snows, and may the rainbow always touch your shoulder."

"Why did I understand everything that you just said?" I ask; then, remembering not to be rude, I thank him for his blessing.

"It has begun. When you return, bring me a giveaway, and I will tell you my name if you don't know it by then. Your grandmother is right; you are entertaining."

"Wait a minute, *what* has begun? What's the Red Road? What's Ghigau? Did you know my grandmother?"

Before I know what's happening, he's ushering me out the door and locking it behind me.

Crap, I think, my stomach tightening. So many questions, no answers. I'm starting to think I've made a huge mistake coming here.

After leaving the Trading Post, I head back to the clinic to meet up with Nibs. As we begin the walk back down the path leading home, I start to feel uncomfortable, like suddenly I don't have enough clothes on or something. I slow my pace and put my hand out to stop Nibs, placing a finger to my mouth and give her "the eye." Standing very still, I close my eyes, trying to sense rather than see where it's coming from. Pointing to the forest off to my right through the thicket, I feel the faintest fluttering of something. I almost have it, whatever it is, but then it's gone. Strange fluttering things, check. Weird old man, check. More Cherokee stuff I don't know about, check. Just a few more things to add to the Weird List.

I grab Nibs's arm. "I'm losing my mind. Yep, that's it; I think you better have me committed or something because I'm almost positive I won't be able to care for myself. You can put my stuff in storage. I'll sign everything over to you. Please, Nibs, will you? Will you do it?"

"Okay, White Girl, let's get home. You need to tell me everything, and no squirming your way out of it. Once I hear the whole story, if I think you're crazy I'll commit you myself. Deal?"

"Deal."

It's almost dark by the time we get back to the cabin. When the sun sets the air is on the chilly side. I make myself busy starting a fire.

"Okay, White Girl, no more stalling. Dish!"

I do, although I can't look her in the face. I still feel so responsible and guilty about everything. She doesn't say anything for a long time and then she just grabs my hands in support.

"You know what scares me the most?" I ask.

"What's that?"

"That this is going to be my life now, just trying to get over what happened. It almost feels like I have something contagious and I don't want to infect anyone with it."

"I can tell you that everything you just said is absolute nonsense. You don't *really* believe that, do you?"

"I'm always wondering if I had done something different, would they still have died, if I had made a different choice?"

"Nan, you are not responsible for the death of your crew. Hate, war, and maybe the captain, did that."

"Maybe."

"What else is going on?" Nibs asks while giving me a familiar look. The one that tells me she already knows something.

"Nothing."

"Uh huh. When you're ready my friend, I'm here."

"Thank you."

Nibs leaves the room and comes back with a box of tissues, a bottle of wine, and a couple of glasses. We warm up leftovers from lunch and polish off a bottle of wine. For dessert, a couple more glasses of wine. We stay up most of the night talking, laughing, crying, and sincerely getting to know each other as adult women. This is the first time since the "incident" that I feel like I have a right to feel as I do.

I don't know if I will ever be able to accept what happened as the wreckage of war. There's just too much stuff that makes no sense. I feel it in my bones. At some point, the truth will surface.

With Nibs tucked away in the guest room, I do the bare minimum getting ready for bed. I barely put my head on my pillow when—*whoosh*!—I feel my spirit leave my body. I have no control over what's happening.

I open my eyes and feel myself become more stable. My feet touch the earth beneath me, and I look around. This world is ancient. I know I'm dreaming, yet I'm able to direct where I'm going. As I check things out, I discover I can move and direct myself. I start exploring and find a familiar-looking forest next to a flowing river. To test my theory, I step away from the river and into a stand of trees. The air is sharp and clean, smelling of pine. I hear birds, crickets, and the crunching sounds of animals walking on dry brush.

Soft chanting and drumming are coming from upriver, and I follow the sounds leading me to them. Around the next bend, I see a group of Cherokee, drumming and chanting around a fire. Kneeling behind a pine tree, I watch. One woman appears to be leading them. She holds her hand up, and everything stops. The only thing left making a sound is my breath and the nervous thumping of my heart. The native woman turns in my direction, and I see myself.

I am the one leading the group.

What the hell?

Rather than be discovered I hold my breath and duck my head. As I get ready to pass out from lack of oxygen, the drumming starts again.

As silently as I can, I make my way. Once sure that I'm in the clear, I stop and sit down by the river.

What is this supposed to mean? There is something I need to know, but what?

It's happening again, and *whoosh*, I'm forced from my body one more time.

Damn, I hate that feeling.

I hear the drumming first and follow it down the path leading to the river. It's evening and very close to sunset. I arrive at the source of the drumming and find a circle full of people.

Nibs and Brayden, what are they doing here? Wait, it looks like them, but it's not. I realize that I'm seeing their ancestors as well as my own.

I sit down and start drumming with them. Everyone takes turns introducing themselves and saying what brought them to the drum circle. When it's my turn I start to panic but instead take a breath.

"I am Nanye'Hi. I've been sent here to be of service, and to learn the ways of my ancestors."

It takes me a minute to realize that I'm speaking in Cherokee. When the drum circle ends, each person hands me an entirely smooth, gleaming gemstone; I count seven. I place all of them in a white medicine bag and hang it around my neck. After thanking everyone in the circle, this world fades.

I wake as the sun is just beginning to filter in through the trees. As I lay there stretching, I replay my dreams. I can't ever remember having dreams this vivid.

I swing my feet over the side of the bed and there it is on the nightstand . . . a beautiful white leather medicine bag. My hands shake as I lift it. The beading is exactly like the one in my dream. When I open it, I discover they're all there, seven gleaming gemstones in all the colors of the rainbow.

"Oh, my God, I have gone completely off the deep end. They say that most people who think they're crazy aren't, and I wonder if the opposite is true as well. If it is then I'm in trouble, because I don't feel crazy at all."

The words have barely left my lips when the sensation of warm honey falls around me. My grandmother appears before me.

Nanye'Hi, she says, *it is a gift of balance and protection. Wear it at all times.*

"Protection from what, Grandmother?"

I don't get an answer but slip the medicine bag around my neck, grab my robe and slippers, and get a fire going in the fireplace. On the table is a note.

It's clinic day, White Girl. Thanks for everything. Talk to you soon, Nibs

5

The Truth

I dress and grab my yoga mat, then head for the deck. Since San Diego, yoga has been my saving grace, helping me find my center no matter what kind of crazy is going on. With all the crazy going on these days, I figure I'd better keep up the practice.

"Okay," I say, thirty minutes and several sun salutations later, "Now that that's done, I can think."

I grab a fresh cup of coffee and fire up my laptop. If Nibs, Brayden, and the cranky old man at the Trading Post refuse to answer my questions, I'll turn to my trusty friend, Google. Google has never failed me yet, but I do find myself wishing I'd paid more attention in school as I type in "Ghigau" in the search field.

The now familiar sensation of warm honey starts spreading across my chest, and I automatically look around for Grandmother. I don't see her, though, and she's uncharacteristically silent.

Still, I feel like I'm onto something. I wait for a moment as the computer does its work, then, sure enough, I am looking at a picture of my great-great-great-grandmother. The article, entitled "The Beloved Woman of the Cherokee," talks about her life and the amazing things she did for the tribe. She sat on the council of elders and held the responsibility of deciding the life or death of all prisoners; she was also instrumental in keeping her people from many battles. She was credited for introducing cattle into the tribe and learned from an English settler how to milk them and churn butter. Eventually she married French Trader Bryant Ward, and I wondered if he was the contributor of the blond hair gene.

The warm honey sensation across my chest keeps building until I find breathing to be a little uncomfortable. Continuing to read, I see a list of Great-Great-Great Grandmother's descendants, including my grandmother's name, my mother's and then my own, though since we all have the same name we're distinguishable only by the birthdates. Underneath that is a link to the Cherokee Nation website. I follow the link and click on the page for the Ghigau.

"What the hell?" I jump up and start pacing back and forth across the living room floor, trying to make sense out of what I've read. Finally, when I'm able to take a full breath, I go back to the computer. On the screen is my picture along with a very old document written on a tattered patina-colored paper with little dots of ink and flowing letters.

Ghigau Covenant, November 1756

On this date, Chief Atakullakulla, (Little Carpenter) makes a covenant:

For all the generations of Nanye'Hi Ward. The first-born female of every generation shall, on her eighteenth birthday, serve as Ghigau to the People for the duration of her life or when the next generation reaches eighteen years old.

Nanye'Hi.

"Not now, Grandmother, please not now."

I find a spot on the floor and curl my legs underneath me. I need to feel grounded right now. My arms and legs start feeling kind of tingly and numb.

I remind myself to breathe. *In through the nose, out through the nose. In through the nose, out through the nose.*

When I can think and breathe without telling myself to do either, I once again return to the computer, looking at everything in front of me. Bits and pieces seem to fall into place, though none of it is logical. It would've been great if someone had told me something—anything—sent up a flare or a fricking smoke signal.

What does that even mean? Surely it can't mean anything anymore, right? It's probably nothing. Probably. Then I remember Grandmother's letter.

I dig up and reread the letter I'd received on my eighteenth birthday. Okay, so maybe it means something. What now?

There's someone I think I can get to talk, if I can just remember how to get there. I splash some cold water on my face, run a comb through my hair, and head out the door.

I start looking for the road marked by a bear carving sitting on a tree stump. Once I find it, I continue walking in a northeast direction for about a mile and reach a clearing. The smell of sweet grass and clover are almost overpowering. There, sitting in the middle of the meadow, is Brayden's place—a sprawling two-story ranch, one side of which is roof-to-floor windows and a wraparound deck. It looks regal.

I hear someone talking and follow the sound of the voice toward the back of the house. When I turn the corner, I find Brayden standing in a fenced pasture with a brown and white paint horse, talking to it in soft, reassuring tones. My heart starts racing and I begin to feel slightly queasy, like I need to run. The rush of feelings startles me. I look up to find both the horse and Brayden staring at me, then the horse runs off, leaving a slightly wide-eyed Brayden standing there.

"What are you doing here?" he says.

"I'm sorry, I didn't mean to disturb you. I'll just leave," I say, stomping my way to the front side of the house.

"Nan, *Nan* . . . wait. I'm sorry, you just startled me. Please don't leave."

He seems sincere, and I am unannounced, which apparently is a thing here. I hate it when I get angry because I always seem to end up crying.

"Nan, I'm sorry… Geez, are you crying? I feel horrible. Stop—come back, please."

"I'm not crying," I say, wiping tears from my cheeks.

He then says the magic words. "I have coffee. Please, let me make it up to you."

While Brayden's putting on a fresh pot of coffee and eating some humble pie, I look around, noticing the smallest details of his house. Books fill the built-in bookshelves. The fireplace mantel is hand-carved wood and gleams like my kitchen cabinets. Old and now-familiar photos are hanging on the walls. Artwork, tastefully placed, is a mixture of Native American paintings and drawings. I stand up to get a closer look at one of the photos and almost throw up on his handmade rug. It's the same woman in the picture from the Trading Post and, according to the cranky old man, my great-great-great grandmother. The one that's me but not me, standing in the middle of a circle of Native Americans, dressed in a beautiful beaded white buckskin dress. On one shoulder is an owl and in the opposite hand, a very intricately carved talking stick.

"Okay, Nan, sit down and start talking. What's going on?"

When I can speak, I answer his question with a question. "What do you know about the Ghigau business?"

"Here, drink this," Brayden says, handing me a cup of coffee.

"Tell me what you know."

Looking at his face and into his velvety brown eyes, I have the same sense with him that I have with Nibs, that I can trust him. How much I can trust him is yet to be determined. I feel like the gorgeous brown and white paint horse in the pasture, ready to run off at the slightest motion.

"I have questions for you, can we start there?"

He nods.

"Why do all the cabins and businesses in the village look so much alike, how well did you know my grandmother, how much about me did my grandmother tell you, why do you wear your hair that way, and why do you have that eagle tattoo on your bicep?"

Brayden sits back in his chair, arms crossed, leaning a little as he smiles and frowns. He starts to answer, but I interrupt.

"And, what were you trying to do to that horse?"

"You noticed my bicep?"

I feel color flush my face and lower my eyes, suddenly fascinated with the contents of my coffee cup. When I glance up at him again he is looking at me with his deep brown eyes and blue-black hair, still frowning and smiling at the same time. I pretend to ignore him and wait for the awkward silence to end.

"That's just too many questions that require very long answers for one day. How about we start with the easy ones?" He drops the frown, leaving just a hint of a smile. "I started cutting my hair in basic training and like it short. I served in the 181st Airborne, Fort Campbell. I saw very little of Kentucky when I was in the army. Got up close and personal with the sand fleas of Iran, Iraq, and Afghanistan, mostly, and a few locations I still can't talk about." His eyes fall and he looks away.

I instinctively reach out my hand to touch his, pulling back before he sees. I nod my head and listen to his war stories about how he went out and got a "little tipsy" with his buddies and found a tattoo parlor. All five of them got matching tattoos. After his last tour, he and his friend wanted to find somewhere to put down some roots. He remembered coming here with his father when Nibs and her brother lived here. He had fallen in love with the land, the trees, and the people. His friend came with him. Brayden's eyes fall again, and his shoulders start to droop.

"I'm sorry, that's as much as I can do today, let me walk you out. Thanks for stopping by," he says, almost shoving me out the door.

"Crap," I mutter as I walk away from the house, "I'm such an idiot." I feel horrible, not sure what I did but certain I had done something.

I'm still talking to myself when I reach the fork where the carved bear meets the road. Looking at my watch, I see I have plenty of time to make it to the village and home before dark. *Somebody* better start talking.

I enter the village with Brayden's dismissal weighing on my mind, but I don't have time to dwell on it. It seems with every step along the sidewalk some other person I've never met before is waving or saying hello. I assume it's because they had seen me with Nibs the day before.

I knock on the door of the Trading Post, which is locked with the lights off and shades drawn. It's only three in the afternoon. Where could he possibly be? Puzzled and more than a little irritated, I choose a new priority: find coffee and chocolate. That's where Nibs finds me, sitting on a bench in front of the coffee shop, deep in thought.

"Hey, White Girl."

"Hey, Nibs."

As we walk home together, Nibs starts telling me about her day, which unfortunately began with a killer hangover from all the wine we'd had the night before. It's not long before I'm laughing at her stories of quirky patients, which are even funnier because she was dealing with them with a sour stomach and a pounding headache. I then tell her about going to Brayden's and how I'd left things with him.

"It's not my story to tell," Nibs said.

"I knew you were going to say that."

"As far as the man at the Trading Post goes, well, welcome home, White Girl. The rest of the story sounds pretty . . ." She trails off, giving me the eye and sideways glance combo.

We come to Nibs's turnoff marked with a dove.

"Hey, White Girl, since tomorrow night is Friday, why don't you come for dinner and I'll invite Brayden?"

I have the feeling she wants to say something else, but she doesn't, and I'm too tired to push it.

"Yes, and I'll be ready to talk."

This time, Nibs just raises an eyebrow at me, as if having second thoughts about the invitation.

I ignore it. "What time, and should I bring wine?"

"Six, and no wine, yuck."

6

The Covenant

I make a fire to get the chill off the room. After changing
into comfy clothes, I grab the book the man at the Trading
Post sent home with me. Reading is a nice break from the
chatter and worry that, though less and less these days, still
sometimes run rampant in my head. How often I've wished
I could just forget that awful night in the desert and focus on
happier memories. That hasn't worked, but losing myself in
a book, in someone else's story, does the trick for a while.
I sit down to read, and that's when I notice that the book is
locked.

I snort in frustration. I'm so *over* being kept in the dark.
I look through the cabinets in the kitchen, laundry room, and
then along the insides of the built-in bookshelves in the living room.

"Focus, girlfriend."

Maybe it will be clearer after a nice hot bath.

Doing something normal sometimes helps me feel normal even when things are most certainly not. While brushing

my teeth, my mind flashes on the walk-in closet in the master bedroom. I hadn't looked in there much since arriving at the cabin and figure now's as good a time as any. After rinsing my mouth I pad over to the closet and open the door, deeply inhaling the earthy smell of cedar. This closet is thoughtfully put together, with places for jewelry, shoes, and handbags. As I look closer into these cubbies, I keep getting the feeling that I need to move to the back panel of the closet. I don't want to miss anything. I make sure I check everything along the way.

Even with the light on it's dark, so I feel more than look my way across the panel. As I get to the upper right side, my fingers find an indentation about two inches long, and I head into the kitchen cabinet where I had seen a flashlight.

A few minutes later I return to the closet, flashlight in hand. I shine it on the two-inch groove and realize it's an *N* engraved into the cedar panel. I begin tapping lightly on the top, along the sides, and then directly underneath. I touch something just right, and a tiny drawer lined with blue velvet opens. Inside are two keys on a small key ring. I take the keys out, close the box, and return to the living room. With hands shaking I grab the book and put one of the keys in the lock. The lock clicks open, but I can't find the courage to open it and place it back on the bookshelf instead.

"If you were here, Grandmother, you and I would have a serious discussion about communication!"

I am here, Nanye'Hi.

I jerk my head up and bang it into the top of the bookshelf.

"Owww. Grandmother you have got to quit doing that. Now you decide to pop in? I don't know how to do this Grandmother; I don't."

You will learn, my daughter's daughter.

That feeling of warm honey stays with me. Again I regret not paying attention in school and tuning out Nibs's stories about my grandmother and Galowhisdi. My mind initiates a data dump, overflowing with information since I came here. In my mind's eye, I begin seeing images of the buildings, this cabin, the village, Nibs, and Brayden. I do the only thing left I can do. Go to bed and pull the covers over my head.

———◎———

After coffee and yoga, I sit on my mat and meditate. There is just enough sun showing through the trees to warm my face and shoulders. I give thanks to the Great Spirit, my grand-mother, and my teachers, then, with palms touching at my heart center, say, "Namaste."

Before opening my eyes, I feel the softest touch, almost like a whisper, on my right cheek and then at the tip of my nose. Slowly, I open my eyes and gasp with surprise as I look cross-eyed at the butterfly sitting there. Quietly and softly, I place a finger in perch position next to my nose and the but-terfly transfers there. It's a monarch, adorned with magnifi-cent colors of yellow, gold, and orange all traced in black. I silently give thanks to the butterfly. After it flies away, I run into the house to find my notepad to record the encounter. My pen seems to keep flowing with words as I tell myself, "Today I will conquer at least one fear, even if it's a tiny one."

I start a new list:

Things I'm afraid of
Being alone

Being crazy

Never finding love

Having no purpose

Being broken

That I can't take care of myself

That I will get hurt again

That I will never find peace

Odd noises

The unknown

I then read the list out loud to whomsoever may be listening so as to take power away from the irrational fears that live in my head. I ask myself another question:

What am I afraid of today?

Being alone.

I send Nibs a text to let her know that I'm going on a hike on one of the trails that surround the village. I know I'll be back in plenty of time for dinner. Just as I'm getting ready to send another text, Nibs replies, "Cool. And definitely no thank you on the wine. I still have a headache!"

I gather my camera, pen, notebook pad, water, snacks and, most importantly, Grandmother's book and keys. I put everything in my backpack, and after arguing with myself for several minutes, I decide to leave Bernice. Today is a day to conquer at least one fear, *without* training wheels. As I'm leaving the house, I start to feel panicky and shaky. I begin mindfully breathing and focus on being present. As I walk down the trail, I look at the trees and notice how green the leaves are, and how the sun feels on my face. I pass Brayden's bear carving and turn at the next path that leads north. I take mental notes of the animals I see. Soon, my breathing is easier and my body feels more relaxed.

Letting my mind wander, I continue at a steady pace. The trail leads me through a stand of trees to a clearing. The grass is lush and green here, and I find the perfect spot to read Grandmother's diary. Ignoring the nervous fluttering in the pit of my stomach, I put the key in the lock and open it. The musty smell of an old book hits my nostrils, and a calmness flows over me, further relaxing my body and calming my mind. I am no longer surprised that I can understand the Cherokee words; I just feel a profound connectedness as I read the entries written not only by my grandmother, but by every Ghigau, beginning with Nanye'Hi Ghigau Ward, dated on Covenant Day in 1756.

Spring 1756

Fort Louden, Tennessee

My husband makes a heart-wrenching sound. I try to find him as quickly as I can through the smoke of musket fire and the deafening sounds of battle. Kneeling on all fours, I feel the grass; it's wet and sticky with blood. I feel my way up to his leg until my hands find his face. He is alive but will be with the ancestors soon. We speak our truth and our love to each other as he gives me messages for our son. The light in the world goes out for me. I am a widow at eighteen.

The world around me is gray. In my mind, there is only the face of my dead husband with his blood spilling into the earth. There is no fear, only hate and the overpowering urge to seek revenge on our enemy. I grab the musket and fire, then reload and fire again, until no enemy moves.

As I crouch on the ground with the musket in my hands, someone comes up behind me placing a hand on my shoulder, "Nanye'Hi, it is over. The enemy is dead."

I can't move or speak. Breathing is difficult as I struggle to remain a part of this world. The face of my son flashes into my consciousness. I take a breath and then another and then stand. Now is not the time for grieving, these warriors will not welcome my tears.

One of the women comes to look me over; there is so much blood. Looking down at my hands and feet, she asks, "Are you injured?"

"It is not my blood," I tell her.

All I can see is the face of my dead husband with his blood spilling into the earth.

She is searching my face, looking into my eyes to see if I have come back to myself. Satisfied with what she sees, she takes my hand and leads me to the water. "You do not want your child to see you looking like this. He will have enough to face this day."

She continues leading me past the creek, walking farther away from our village. We arrive at a hot spring. When we reach the water's edge, she helps me get out of my blood-soaked clothes. I ease myself into the water and allow the hot spring to wash away any evidence of battle and death.

The tears fall silently at first, then I hear something that sounds like a wounded wolf and realize that it's coming from me. The racking sobs begin, and I cry until the tears no longer fall. This is our way—our very private way—the way of the Cherokee.

The woman from the village returns with clean clothes for me to wear, fussing over me until no outward signs of battle remain. I must be strong and brave for my son. Today he lost his father; he will not lose his mother.

When we return to the village, the warriors are already counting coup. They are chanting, drumming, and singing around the fire. I walk toward the circle with my head held high and proud.

Everything stops.

Why are they doing this? Why are they honoring me? They remain silent as I make my way to my cabin and my son.

In the morning, though I thought it impossible to do so, the sun rises. My son is still sleeping as I offer prayers to the Great Spirit and greet this day. No matter how heavy my heart, my son must be tended to. I open the front door of the cabin to get water, and I'm stopped by a pile of blankets, food, and pottery. This is a sign of honor; surely someone has made a mistake.

The Chief of the Cherokee Nation calls the people of our village to the center fire. "From this day forward, Nanye'Hi shall be the Ghigau, Beloved Woman of the Cherokee."

He must be speaking of someone else.

The Chief makes a motion for me to come forward. I walk slowly because I cannot feel my feet touch the earth. My heart races and my breathing is too fast. When I am standing directly in front of him, he speaks. "In the battle with the Creeks, Nanye'Hi killed more of our enemy than any other warrior. She speaks with the ancestors and the spirit animals. Her first daughter and all the first daughters to come shall forever be, the Beloved Woman. I have spoken, and so it is, and will be."

I have no voice. My feelings in this matter are not important.

The Chief's declaration creates my destiny and the destiny of my daughters and their daughters. What does it mean to be the Beloved Woman of the Cherokee?

I'm overwhelmed with emotion as I consider what my ancestors endured in their lifetimes. Instead of feeling inspired, it seems to highlight all the places in my spirit that are lacking and wounded. The last time I was responsible for people they died. I can't be responsible for the death, or even the possibility of death, of another human being. I can't.

An eagle crying overhead draws my attention. I watch as he circles the meadow above me. I'm mesmerized by his outstretched wings that are wider than I am tall. I reach into my backpack to grab a bottle of water, then sit down in the grass to sip it and watch the magnificent bird's graceful glide. Something falls from the sky; I run over to see what it is and find one perfect eagle feather. I send gratitude to the eagle and place the feather between the pages of my notebook for safekeeping.

I focus in on the eagle and feel myself shift in awareness. I feel odd, nauseated almost. My vision is blurry, and I close my eyes. When I open them, I see through the eyes of the eagle, seeing as the eagle sees. I look down and see myself in the meadow, backpack by my side. Suddenly, my spirit is slammed harshly back into my body falling like a concrete brick. As soon as I'm able to focus, I look overhead and watch the eagle as it glides from my view, giving one last cry.

I write down the experience in the blank pages in the back of the diary that I know is meant for me. Then I flash back to my life at Sequoyah and all the weird animal stuff, and I begin to put things together, maybe.

Shouldn't I be freaked out?

I continue to write it all down and take in my surroundings. I realize that I've been here longer than I thought. I pack up my things and head back the way I came. As I'm leaving the forest to step back onto the path, I hear the faint hoot of an owl. It's odd for an owl to be active in the middle of the day. The feeling of warm honey spreads across my chest and Grandmother says, *Pay attention to the animals; they will bring you signs and messages.*

I follow the hooting sounds to a branch midway up a pine tree and spot a small white and gray owl looking back at me with huge eyes. I immediately know the message he's bringing me. I thank him and promise to look up the meaning of owl medicine when I get home. For now, it's time to get back and get ready for dinner with Nibs and Brayden.

Once I'm on the trail, I have the feeling of being watched. I look around but don't see anyone. On instinct, I crouch low in the brush. Sweat forms on my face and runs down my back. I hear a noise off to my right like someone is taking slow, careful steps on dry leaves. Every instinct I have is screaming at me to run. I fight it. As suddenly as the feeling comes over me, it is gone. It's like a light switch is flipped. My heartbeat and breathing return to normal. Realizing that I have my eyes shut, I open them. At the edge of the forest stands a whitetail deer with her two babies, all of them looking at me with big wide eyes.

In that moment I realize those feelings of panic and fear didn't belong to me.

Nanye'Hi, in time you will learn to tell the difference between your feelings and those of another. Practice.

"Grandmother, please don't be in my head."

You are entertaining, my granddaughter.

The way she says it makes me feel that an eye roll accompanied the statement.

Once back home, I sit in my rocker, writing about the trip I had taken. My experience with the animals had rocked my sense of reality, and yet it felt familiar. How can I feel both at the same time? How can I feel, sense, and see what they do? How is that even possible? It seems I have new mantras these days, each of them a question. A flood of guilt washes over me, and I think about my crew. I don't know what to do with the guilt. How do I remember them, release the guilt over what happened to them, and forgive myself in the process?

So many questions, and I don't have an answer for any of them.

Today, however, I'd survived my fear of being alone—outside by myself, nobody around for miles—without Bernice. I mentally give myself a high five and head for the bathroom to start getting ready for dinner.

I take extra time in the bath, adding jasmine to the water, allowing the fragrance to mix with the steam, cocooning me. This is magic, a unique form of magic that releases tension and soreness out of my body and allows my mind to rest.

In this still and quiet space devoid of thought, something shifts in my consciousness. *Whoosh,* I'm pulled from my body and transported to a place deep in the forest. It's so dense that the sun barely shows through. As I come to a clearing, it's here I see her for the second time. I have come to know her from pictures and my dreams as Ghigau, the Beloved Woman of the Cherokee and my great-great-great-grandmother. She stands with her arms stretched to the sky, chanting a prayer. After her prayer, she faces me.

Daughter of my daughters, soon it will be time for you to choose.

"Choose what?" I ask, knowing full well what she wants from me.

To lead the people as Ghigau, the Beloved Woman of the Cherokee.

"What does it mean, to be the Beloved Woman of the Cherokee?"

I receive a vision of the lives of many ancestors who have been the Beloved Woman. Each served as the spiritual guide and protector of the Cherokee people; each had a unique spiritual gift with a particular purpose for that lifetime. In this space, I can feel and intuit *my* purpose in this life. I am to keep vigil over the sacred place, Cherokee lands, and the People. What I don't know is how.

"What makes you think that I, of all people, would be worthy of such an honor, of such a responsibility? I am not special. I don't have any gifts. I am broken and damaged. I have a *thing*!"

Daughter of my daughters, it is not for me to say what you do, or do not have, or even if you are worthy. This is something you must know and discover for yourself. I can only hold this space for you for three full moons; soon you will need to decide.

"What happens if I choose not to be the Ghigau?"

Before I get an answer, I am deposited back in my body.

After finishing my bath and getting dressed, I hop in my truck and head to Nibs's. Her cabin is about the same size as mine, and I can tell by the craftsmanship that the same person built both of them. Hers feels snug, safe, and homey, with a décor that can only be described as eclectic. The furniture is all warm colors with oversized cushions, and there's a sort of order in the chaos, as if she'd chosen something from every place she ever lived or visited. The light from the fireplace and the candles give the room a soft, inviting glow.

"Nibs, this is so you."

"Yes, different than the Sequoyah days for certain. Brayden is a very talented carpenter."

"He did this?"

"Yes, and all the carvings around town. They're great, right? Speak of the devil, here he is."

Brayden walks in the door, appearing to be back to his happy, charming self. His eyes are full of mischief, like someone you need to keep an eye on so he doesn't short-sheet your bed or something.

"Please tell me we have more interesting things to talk about tonight than the devil," he said.

"How come there is no carving at Grandmother's place?" I ask.

"Grandmother wanted it to be your choice. I'm waiting on you."

Nibs frowns at her cousin as he hands her a bottle of Mercato. "Um...thanks?"

"Wow, I can take it home. You've always been kind of a princess, you know."

He sounded mean, but it didn't reach his eyes. I can see how close the two of them are.

"Okay then, this will be the hair of the dog," he says, opening the bottle of wine. "It will either cure you or kill you. I'm hoping of course for the first option, but one never knows."

Nibs narrows her eyes at him but accepts the drink, and by the time dinner is on the table she announces herself cured.

I want to tell them of my conversation with Great-Great-Great Grandmother and ask them about the Ghigau stuff, but

I know how crazy it's going to sound. I am debating how to broach the subject when I look up from my dinner plate and notice something unspoken pass between the cousins.

Nibs catches me. "Okay, White Girl, what's going on with you?"

I pause for a moment. "This may sound a little strange, so please just let me get it all out before I lose my nerve."

The cousins place utensils down and give me their undivided attention. I feel a sense of calm wash over me as I begin. I tell them the entire story, some of which Nibs already knows, starting with Sequoyah and meeting my grandmother for the first time, the animal stuff, why I joined the Air Force, the death of my crew, PTSD, and why I came to Galowhisdi. I tell them about everything that's happened since I got here, including finding out about the Beloved Woman and my grandmother's covenant. Then, realizing that I have my head down, I slowly pick it up to see the cousins s*miling* at me. Of all the reactions I had expected, this is not one of them.

Nibs comes over and hugs me. "Thank God you know. Now we don't have to hide stuff anymore."

"You mean, you knew all this time?" I'm looking back and forth between the cousins as they nod their heads.

"Why didn't you tell me?" My voice starts to rise in volume, and I feel a warm rush of energy that climbs up the back of my neck.

"We couldn't say anything, Nan," Nibs says quickly. "There's so much to all of this, and I'm afraid we are bound both by honor and energy to not lead or influence you in any way."

"What are you talking about?"

"There are forces at work here that we have no control over."

The feeling of warm honey spreads not only across my chest, but I feel it expand through the room.

"Grandmother?"

"Yes," Nibs says.

"Okay, what can you tell me?"

"That you are not alone. Brayden and I, along with the others, will support you. But you must make the journey and the decision on your own."

"What journey?" I ask, hoping now that the cat's out of the bag information will flow.

Instead of a response, the cousins just shake their heads and shrug their shoulders.

"However, we are both well-versed in weird, so bring it on," Brayden says, then I feel the warmth of his hand as he clasps my shoulder in support.

Now it's my turn to shrug. "Well, the good news is I'm not bat shit crazy."

7

Mister White Owl

Fortified by a dreamless, no-spirit-traveling night's sleep, I grab a cup of coffee and spot Grandmother's book and the keys sitting on the bookshelf. I take one step toward my target and stop. Okay, maybe yoga on the deck first. As I lay my mat out and prepare to start my practice, something bright flashes from under the top step of the deck. It's an abalone shell filled with fragrant sage and other herbs. Next to it is a box of matches and lying across it is a feather. They did smudge ceremonies at Sequoyah all the time, but I didn't pay attention to those either. I decide to just follow my instincts and hope I don't get it wrong and have some creepy, dark, Cherokee spirit rain down on my head.

I light the mixture of sage, tobacco, cedar, and sweetgrass and allow the heady fragrance to wash over me. Prayerfully and with intention, I allow the smoking contents to waft over my body, starting at my head and finishing at the bottoms of my feet. It's cleansing and purifying. I sit preparing for meditation and enter the Dreamtime. The feeling of warm honey spreads across my chest. Grandmother rewards me with a visit.

My daughter's daughter, you must trust someone.

"What do you mean?"

Trust those around you to help you. They are here to guide you on your journey. I cannot interfere, only guide.

"Grandmother, I have so many questions, I don't know where to start. How can I make decisions when I have no answers?"

You must learn to listen with all of your senses.

I receive a mental picture of the cranky man with the silver hair.

"Thank you, Grandmother."

Please remember that you are never alone, especially when you feel most alone.

I can't deny this connection to my grandmother. It feels as if we've been together forever, and I am grateful for that relationship. I send her love, and as I do, I feel the warm honey spreading across my chest, as if she is replying to me.

Each person in your circle has a personal journey and path. Part of their journey is to help you, Nanye'Hi. There is no such thing as a lone wolf, for every wolf has its pack.

I'm making my way to the Trading Post when I remember that I'm supposed to give the man a "giveaway," whatever the heck that is.

No sooner do I pose the question in my mind when my grandmother answers in my head.

It is a present or gift. Stop. Look to your right and under that pine tree. See that speck of blue?

"Yes, Grandmother, I see it." I reach down and pick up a half of Robin's eggshell. "Really? Is he really going to want this?"

I hear her quietly laugh and feel it as lightness in my belly.

When I arrive, the door is locked and the shades lowered. I knock again and again. I look at my watch and see it's only three in the afternoon. Where is this guy? I am turning around to leave when I hear the click of the lock.

"Yes?" he says as he barely opens the door.

"Hi, it's me, Nan. You know, from the other day?"

"Yes?"

I feel Grandmother nudge me from behind. "I have a giveaway for you, Mister White Owl."

He opens the door fully and gestures inside. "Well, let me see it. How did you discover my name?"

"A little birdie told me."

"Not bad, not bad at all. I see there's some potential here."

"What do you mean? Before you start answering questions with questions, please get that I've had it up to my eyebrows with secrets! I'm done being polite, and I want some answers."

"Good, let's get to work. And it's just White Owl, no mister. Mister just sounds weird."

"Mister sounds weird? There's a whole lot of crazy going on, and *mister* sounds weird."

I look directly into his eyes and realize that they remind me of someone. I'm trying to figure it out and pay attention at the same time and not having much luck.

"I can't make up for your lack of training, education, or talent," he is saying, "But I made a promise to your Grandmother, so I'll do what I can."

Gee thanks.

I open my mouth, ready to go down my list of questions, when he jumps in.

"Have you read that book I gave you?"

"Yes," I say while pretending to look at some painting on the wall.

He cocks his eyebrow at me.

"Well, some of it."

He shakes his head and starts to stand up but then sits back down. "Read the book."

It's not a question.

"Yes."

"I know you want answers. I can try to teach you the things about herbs, spirituality, and energy medicine, and help guide you with your gifts, but the rest will be revealed when it's time. Do you understand Cherokee yet?"

"Yes."

"Good, then we are at least that far along."

"What does that mean?"

"It means that the Great Spirit has not given up on you yet."

A question quickly forms in my mind, and before I know it, it's past my lips and in the air. "Did you know my mother?"

"Yes."

"What happened to her?"

He shakes his head. "It's not my story to tell."

I try to stare him down with one hand on my hip. It doesn't work.

"You will know when it's time for you to know." At least this he delivered with some softness in his voice.

Then it's back to business. He shows me around the building. Behind the storefront of the Trading Post is a series of rooms that connect from a round room in the center of the building. It has benches all around a central firepit with graduating heights, like a small amphitheater. A small fire is crackling in the firepit and there is small air vent in the roof.

"This is a hothouse. Anyone wanting a warm place to sleep or safety, for whatever reason, is welcome here," White Owl says. "We keep a fire going at all times, to honor the Great Spirit and create a sacred circle."

He then takes me through the rooms surrounding the center, each of which is occupied by young people learning various aspects of Native American medicine and spirituality. In one room, a young woman is working with plants and herbs. In another, young men and women are engaged in painting, beadwork, and pottery. I hear soft, lovely flute music and my body instantly responds; I follow it to the next room.

White Owl follows behind me, muttering, "Hmmm, good to know."

I don't say anything because all I want to do is find the flute music. On the other end of the flute is a handsome young man about eighteen. He never looks up or even notices me. He continues to play. The flute music carries me out of my body and into the forest. I am part of the trees, the earth, the sky, and the animals. When the flute music stops, I open my eyes feeling rejuvenated and renewed. Grounded.

White Owl introduces us.

"Wind Song—Ghigau. Ghigau—Wind Song."

"Wait a minute. Are you *the* Ghigau? I mean, nice to umm . . . I don't know what to say."

White Owl waves his hand in dismissal. Wind Song is undeterred.

"Ghigau? Is it really you? I thought they were just making up ole Cherokee fairy tales."

I fight the urge to run out of the room. "It's nice to meet you, Wind Song. I love your flute music. Thank you."

"Really? Did you like it? It's such an honor —"

White Owl steps in. "Okay, kid, that's enough. Hit the trail."

"Okay, but wow! I can't believe it's her."

"You too, Ghigau, hit the trail. Read the book, and I'll let you know when we'll meet for your training."

Again, it's not a question.

———⊙———

I grab Grandmother's diary and head outside to the deck. There is a heavy scent of pine in the morning air, and I breathe it in as I look up to see fluffy white clouds flowing across the sky. I take my position on the deck and settle in, deep in thought as I read about animal totems and their medicine.

I'm deep in concentration when I'm startled by the fast thudding of heavy footfalls coming in my direction. A beautiful palomino stallion gallops straight to me and skids to a stop beside the deck. I reach out to touch the white star on his forehead. When I do, he jumps and sprints away from me about half the length of a football field. I take a deep breath and walk toward him, speaking in what I hope is a soothing voice. After only a few moments, he lowers his head and snorts, standing perfectly still. That's when I see the large tear on his right side from his hip down to his foreleg. I run inside and grab a towel and my phone.

While silently praying for Brayden and the vet to get here, I gently placed the towel on the wound. It surprises me that the palomino is so calm, especially since he's injured. While I'm tending his wound, I talk to him like he's my best friend. He looks back at me, chuffing and grunting like he wants to tell me something.

Brayden shows up with the vet and a halter. While showing me how to put it on, he says, "Well, it looks like you have yourself a horse."

"What?"

"He obviously doesn't want to go anywhere, and I don't recognize him."

The vet nods his head in agreement. "I don't either, but minus the injury he's in excellent shape. The cut's not serious, but it'll need to be cleaned with a fresh dressing twice a day. He'll need antibiotics and pasture for safekeeping for at least a couple of weeks. The wound needs to heal from the inside out. In the meantime I'll put the word out and see if anyone is missing a horse."

While the vet shows me how to clean and dress the wound, I discover I have no fear of the palomino. I just know I'm safe with him and I *think* he feels the same way about me. Brayden offers his pasture for the horse and to keep Daisy company.

"*Daisy*, the brown and white paint?" I ask.

"Yeah, Daisy. What's wrong with that? I'll bet you're going with something really obvious, like Star."

"No way, that's definitely too obvious. I haven't asked him his name. I'll wait until he tells me." I ignore Brayden's raised eyebrow. "For now, I think Buddy's good."

I put Buddy's halter and lead rope on him the way Brayden showed me, though I sense he would have followed me without it. We start walking toward the ranch, Buddy behind me with the butt of his head against the back of my arm; he's happy to let me lead. When I quit walking, he gently bumps his forehead into the back of my arm until I start moving again. At his touch I start seeing a series of pictures. It's amazing how clear and detailed they are. I see him walking through a tree line around the banks of the river when something startles him. He breaks into a panic, running into a branch from a deadfall that had a razor-sharp edge. I stop for a moment, shaking my head. Could this be one of my gifts?

I feel Buddy tense, and he turns to face me, throwing his head high and tossing it from side to side. I feel his panic starting to grow and try to calm him down by talking to him. I don't know what he's so frightened of, but whatever it is, it makes the hair on the back my neck stand up; goosebumps trickle down my arm.

"Okay, Buddy, we're just going to pick up the pace a little."

I'm relieved when I see Brayden's house. He's waiting for us on the front deck, a furrow between his brows.

"What happened?"

"I'm not sure. We felt something off. I don't know what it was, but something."

"What do you mean by 'we'?"

"Buddy felt it too."

Brayden is looking in the direction we came. "Well, whatever it was, it's gone now. Let's go have some coffee and we'll leave your friend here to get acquainted with Daisy."

"Wait, how do you know? Did you feel it too?"

Brayden just looks at me, shaking his head.

"It's another one of those things you can't tell me, right?"
He nods.

That's fine because I don't think I'm ready to know yet what that was. One thing's for certain, it's incredibly dark. Darker than I'd ever experienced before, and that's saying a lot.

While Brayden settles Buddy in the pasture with Daisy, I head inside to make the coffee. I rummage around in Brayden's kitchen looking for cups, spoons, and crème and sugar; it doesn't feel awkward, as I would expect it to, but comfortable and easy. When Brayden joins me a few minutes later our conversation flows in the same way. We have more in common than I would have imagined; I'm enjoying his company.

I look at Brayden and watch him intently as his voice fades into the background. I try to stay present. It's tough, though, when all I can think about is how nice it would be to step into his arms and put my head on his shoulder, just for a minute.

Brayden catches me staring. "What? Do I have dirt on my face or something?"

"Sorry, I'm just worried about Buddy."

We move over to the window to watch Buddy and Daisy nibble on each other's withers.

"Well, it looks like Daisy has a new friend," he says, and I nod, grateful the attention is off me and the strange new direction my thoughts have taken.

Walking home, I try to let everything go and not over-think it. The answers seem to come easier when I don't push. If I only have "three full moons" I want to make sure I have all the information. Allowing my inner thoughts to melt away, I focus on the trees, placing one foot in front of the other, and allow myself to feel the ground and connect with

Mother Earth. I listen to an eagle screech overhead, watching as it glides above me, and on my next inhale I am flooded with the feeling of warm honey.

My daughter's daughter, you must go to the Sacred Place.

Great. So much for peace and calm.

"Hi Grandmother. And just where is this Sacred Place?"

8

The Sacred Place

I pinch the bridge of my nose and rub my temples. I have been reading this diary from cover to cover and still can't find where the Sacred Place is, and how one goes about getting there. And of course Grandmother won't tell me, no matter how many times I yell for her. I'm so frustrated I want to stomp my feet and scream like a two-year-old. Instead, I give myself a time out and I try again.

"Grandmother, would you please help me understand about the Sacred Place? Where is it, and why do I need to go there?"

My daughter's daughter, you must ask those in your circle for help.

"I'll ask, but so far they haven't been able to tell me anything."

Nanye'Hi, look at the date.

The first full moon is only one week away. I start to feel myself slide into a panic, but I catch myself before I fall and instead pull out my phone and text Nibs and Brayden:

Can you two come over for dinner? There will be food and margaritas.

Looking at the pile of nachos and tacos on the counter, I wonder if I have gone a little overboard. Then I remember Brayden's appetite. Over the roar of the blender, I hear Nibs walk in with Brayden right on her heels.

"What's going on, White Girl?" Nibs asks without preamble.

I point to the diary on the table and pour three giant margaritas. "That's what's going on. Oh, and Grandmother."

"Uh-oh," Brayden says.

"Okay, you two, what do you know about the Sacred Place and please don't tell me you don't know anything because Grandmother told me to ask you."

Brayden stood. "Umm, I should probably go now, and let you two talk."

"Oh, no you don't."

He froze.

"What do you know? Have a seat and start talking, both of you."

Nibs starts talking first. "What is written on those pages is for your eyes, Nan. You get to choose."

"In *theory*, I have a choice. There is so much I don't understand, and I know that every decision has consequences."

Brayden steps to my side and puts an arm around my shoulder. "No pressure, right?" he says, half-jokingly, but I fail to see the humor.

"Nan, we know where the Sacred Place is," Nibs says, "and have been there many times. Part of your initiation and journey is to trust that spirit will lead you where you need to go."

"We can't tell you," Brayden says, "We'd like to, but . . ." He trails off, frowning, smiling, and pointing towards the ceiling.

My friends are getting ready to leave when Nibs turns and says, "We will help you any way we can."

"But that's just it. You're *not* helping me," I snap, feeling the heat of frustration rise to my face. "You're not helping me at all."

Nibs gives me an apologetic but resigned look, then the two of them file out the door. After they leave, I settle into my chair in front of the fireplace, trying to release my annoyance at them and focus on the problems at hand–those being that I still don't know where the Sacred Place is and the time for me to make a decision about becoming Ghigau is fast approaching.

"I told you they wouldn't help, Grandmother."

The feeling of warm honey envelops me.

Nanye'Hi, go to the Sacred Place, it will be revealed.

"Okay, Grandmother, okay."

Next week is my first test. It will take place on the full moon at the Sacred Place, and part of the trial is finding it.

The good news is, I now have a job description. The Ghigau's primary duty is to hold space for her tribe by creating a prayerful intention of protection and safety. She is also responsible for maintaining the natural balance in the four directions, above and below. But the most important part of being Ghigau is acting as an intermediary between the Great Spirit and the People until all are united in a circle that includes all tribes, as the Great Spirit intended.

I didn't ask for the job, and yet here I am. I could just walk away, but the consequences of doing that are too profound. I made it through basic training and then combat training, so surely I can do three full moons. I know I'll have to dig deep. I just don't know if those places are deep enough. I suppose that's why there's this whole three full moons thing in the first place.

In the meantime, the questions continue to pile up. There are historical events written in the diary, and gaps in that history where there was no Ghigau. What does that mean? Did one or more of my ancestors say no, and what happened to the tribe then?

I meet with White Owl at our scheduled time.

"Are you wearing your medicine bag?" he asks gruffly.

"Yes, why?"

White Owl touches the beaded headband across his forehead and says, "Always wear it, young Nanye'Hi."

"What can you tell me be about the Sacred Place and my initiation?"

"Nothing. I can tell you nothing except you will remember everything."

When I arrive at Brayden's, Buddy is standing at the pasture fence waiting for me. As soon as he spots me, he whinnies and starts running up and down the fence line—showing off. Whether it's for my benefit or Daisy's, I'm not sure. The pasture fencing is just like everything else that Brayden's hand touches, finished with craftsmanship and flair. The post and rail fencing are all wood, painted white and about five feet tall. The horizontal slats are just far enough apart that a person could shimmy through, but not far enough apart for a horse or other large animal to maneuver. I stand here a minute to take in this lush green meadow surrounded by towering oak trees. Brayden even built the horses a covered stall so they have a place to get out of the weather. Buddy continues to show off, trying to get my attention.

"Hello, gorgeous," I tell him, and he prances a little higher.

I study him as he trots back and forth. His bandage is off and the wound looks completely healed with only a small scar. He's sturdy and strong with rippling muscles and a shiny coat. After a few moments he stops directly in front of me and puts his head over the fence. I place my hand in the middle of his forehead, touching the place his white star sits.

"How is this possible?" I ask him.

"He's a fast healer," Brayden says as he comes around the corner of the house.

"This has to be a record." I turn to Brayden and study his face. There's something he's not telling me. I'm not going to push it, not after last time. I know as usual there's more to the story. A wound that large and deep could not heal that fast without a little mystical help.

"I hope you don't mind, I wanted to check on him. I also want to know how I can help, since he's staying at your place."

"Now that you mention it . . ."

We walk the fence line of Brayden's five acres, mending it where necessary. Mostly, I hold the tools. He makes small talk as he works, making me think he's trying to mend more than the fence before us. Buddy and Daisy follow our every move. I'm bending over, handing Brayden some wire thingy when Buddy stretches his neck over and nuzzles my ear. He gets tangled up in my hair and snorts.

"Ewww, Buddy, that's *so* gross."

"Come on, I know while there's a hair emergency happening I'll get no work out of you." Brayden takes my hand and leads me to an outside water pump. "Bend over, it's going to be cold, but I know you don't want horse snot in your hair."

"That's not cold, it's freakin' *arctic*. Geez, hurry up. Is it all out yet?"

"Let me see . . ." I feel his warm hand on the back of my neck trailing down to my ear and then through the rest of my hair. I'm glad I'm bent over with hair covering my face so he can't see how flushed it is.

"Thanks."

"You're welcome, now let's get back to work."

We finish the fence, fill up the horses' water tanks and put out fresh hay. Brayden shows me where he keeps the horses' grain and how much to give them.

"Come over anytime. I'll show you where I stash the extra key."

"I still want to know how Buddy healed so fast."

The look on his face told me he's done talking about it.

"Do you think Buddy's well enough to go for a trip in the mountains?"

"He's ready, when are you going?"

"On the full moon."

"Of course." Brayden raises his eyebrows. "I'm not sure I like the idea of you going off on your own. Why don't I go with you?"

"Thanks for the offer, but you know I have to go alone."

We're standing close together, looking eye to eye, with Brayden doing that smiling and frowning thing he does. Today his eyes look almost amber instead of dark brown.

I look away first. "Thanks for taking such good care of Buddy."

Later that day I head for the Tribal Library in Tahlequah, hoping it will have some of the answers I'm looking for. I take the road along the river; I love how the dogwood trees line it. In narrow places, the trees bend over the water, creating a perfect frame. I know this river by heart, and should, after working on it three seasons in a row. Between float guiding and Sam & Ella's Chicken Palace, I made decent money.

By mid-summer, the dogwoods will be in full bloom with brilliant red and pink flowers. Then the river will be filled with college students and tourists "floating." In the fall, tourists will come armed with cameras, wanting to capture images of the migrating bald eagles. One season, I counted twenty on one run. I never grew tired of seeing them.

I park my truck in the library's parking lot, but instead of going inside I feel pulled in the direction of downtown Tahlequah. I'm sure there are other places like this in the country, but none *just* like this. I take a big breath in and my stomach growls in response to the scrumptious, spicy smells coming from Sam & Ella's.

Tahlequah reminds me of Sequoyah, with its big brick buildings, white trim, and cobblestone streets. I walk around, looking through the windows of art galleries and boutiques, and eventually find myself in front of the Cherokee Nation's Cultural Center. A familiar energy is nudging me to go inside.

"Hi, Grandmother," I say as I walk through the door. There are several Native American women in the room, and they're all staring—at me.

I start to turn around and leave, and that's when I see it: a display in the middle of the room and a life-sized picture of the original Ghigau, Nanye'Hi Ward. Engraved on a bronze plaque next to her photo are the words, "The Famous Indian Woman from Tennessee." All eyes are on me as I read them, and it's no wonder, considering the uncanny resemblance between me and the woman in the photo. Finally, a young woman wearing traditional Cherokee apparel approaches me.

"Osiyo."

"Osiyo, hello," I say, looking around the room at the others.

"They are old school and tradition dictates speaking when spoken to," she says.

"Well in that case . . . Osiyo," I say to the room. That's all it takes, apparently, for within seconds several women surround me and start talking at once; mostly, they're asking questions about the woman standing before us in the photo. I try to field them as best I can, then they lead me out to the back patio. As they pour coffee the questions begin again.

"Give her a chance to catch her breath," the young woman says, "Geez."

"I wish I could answer your questions, but that's one of the reasons I'm here. I didn't know about my grandmother until recently..." My voice trails off and I give them a sheepish look. "... I didn't even know about me."

"My name is Rayna," the young woman says warmly, "How can we help you?"

I introduce myself and before I know it I'm telling them about finding the diary, learning about the covenant, and my initiation into becoming the next Ghigau. I tell them that my concern over the gaps in history where there was no Ghigau.

"I'm trying to discover what happens to the tribe in those times."

Everyone in the group looks to an older woman, whose eyes remind me of Grandmother's and are full of wisdom.

"There are always periods of darkness when there is no Ghigau," she says.

"What kind of darkness?"

"It's different every time."

"What do you mean?"

"Look at the dates when there was no Ghigau and check Cherokee history."

"Thank you."

"Your grandmother was a great woman."

"Yes, she was."

After parting with my new friends I return to the Tribal Library and check out as many books as I can about Cherokee history. I have one more stop to make: Sam & Ella's for two large pizzas. By my calculations, Brayden can probably eat one all by himself. When it comes to doing research, I am not above bribery. I can use all the help I can get.

———◉———

I replay the surreal experience at the cultural center and realize the women hadn't really told me anything new. Of course, I had been so overwhelmed by their attention—not to mention seeing the life-sized Ghigau—that I had forgotten to ask the important questions.

I get back to my cabin just after dusk. No sooner do I have dishes and napkins put next to the pies on the counter when Nibs walks in with Brayden right behind her.

How do they do that?

Nibs immediately gives me a huge bear hug but Brayden stops short, offering me a fist bump instead. He sniffs the air, then opens one of the pizza boxes and dives right in.

"Hey, what'd you find?" he says.

I'm amazed he can say anything with all that pizza in his mouth.

The cousins think it's hilarious when I tell them about meeting the life-size pinup of my great-grandmother. When I tell them what the Cherokee Elder said Nibs's face scrunches up in concentration.

"I know that look," I say, eyes narrowing. "What do you know?"

"You're right . . . It's not what I know, but what I suspect. Part legend, part guesswork."

Brayden nods his head as he swallows the last bite of crust and reaches for another slice.

"Do you agree that the Ghigau's most important job is to protect the tribe against the dark?" Nibs asks.

"Okay . . . yes, and I had a dream about it." I give her the eye and sideways glance combo.

Nibs nods her head. "I think when there is no Ghigau to protect, shield, and balance the light, some darkness—in the name of disaster or tragedy—falls over the tribe."

Not what I wanted to hear.

When the pizza is gone, the three of us tackle the research, checking the names of the Ghigaus in the diary against the library books. According to the diary, the first period with no Ghigau began in 1830 when Catherine Ward, daughter of the first Ghigau, chose instead to marry a British army officer.

Brayden flips to the back of one of the history books and begins skimming the index, then goes to a page about halfway through. "After the enactment of the Indian Removal act of 1830," he reads, "the Cherokee Nation of 17,000 were forced from their ancestral homelands in Tennessee and Arkansas to the newly designated Indian Territory in Oklahoma. Along the way over 6,000 thousand Cherokee died from exposure to the weather, disease, or starvation. Surviving Cherokee named this forced march The Trail of Tears."

"I remember my mother telling me about it. Crap, what's the next date?" I say, and I feel the warmth spreading across my chest.

My daughter's daughter, you must go to the Sacred Place.

"Okay," I say.

"Okay, what?" Nibs asks.

I just shrug my shoulders. I'm not in the mood to translate for Grandmother.

Neither of them comments; they just ignore me and get back to work–business as usual. I glance at the both of them, shaking my head. Once again, I'm the only one who finds all of this to be anything *but* usual.

9

The First Full Moon

Per Grandmother's instructions, I pack her diary and just enough supplies to last me a few days. The whole time I'm saddling Buddy, Brayden keeps trying to talk me out of going alone.

"Why don't you let me go with you?"

"I have to go alone."

"Why?"

"You know why," I say, pointing to the sky.

Brayden nods his head and has a look on his face I can't identify. Maybe after we've known each other longer, I'll be able to understand all his facial expressions. Of course I'd like him to come along. I'd also like to have this so-called journey of mine spelled out on a piece a paper with clear and absolute instructions. I'm learning this is not how spirit works, though, at least not as far as I can tell. I have no choice but to trust that I'm going in the right direction.

I feel the excitement oozing from Buddy as we hit the trail. He has a smooth gait, and his calm demeanor is contagious. He is surefooted and steady, and I fall into a nice rhythm on his back.

Watch for the signs, Nanye'Hi.

"What signs, Grandmother?"

You will know.

Since we're talking, I take the opportunity to ask Grandmother some questions. "What happened to my mother and father? Why all the secrets?"

You would not understand, not yet, Granddaughter.

"I would really like the answer to those questions, Grandmother. It's important to me."

I feel an incredible darkness creeping up on us from behind. Buddy feels it too and tenses beneath me. I immediately send a prayer to the Great Spirit for protection, surrounding both of us in brilliant white light. We become hyper-vigilant, looking and listening for anything.

An eagle cries overhead and Buddy stops. I look around. There it is, half-hidden by brush.

"Okay, let's go."

I squeeze my knees slightly, urging Buddy forward. He turns onto a path mostly obscured by branches and leaves, and as he does I feel tiny electrical pulses throughout my body. The energy of this place is like a rhythm, traveling through Buddy and into me, but it doesn't feel foreign. Like a thunderstorm or the trees, it's just there. The trail is steep and narrow, barely wide enough for us to get through. The eagle glides overhead, leading the way.

"Any reasonable person would be afraid of going out in the wilderness alone with only her horse. No offense, Buddy. Then again, we aren't reasonable, are we?" I pat his neck.

Since being diagnosed with PTSD, my emotions can go from zero to sixty at the drop of a hat. Despite, or even because of, the magical, mystical world that I now call my life, my symptoms have been better. I allow my mind to wander and it latches onto a picture of Brayden working in the pasture. He is shirtless, and I can see his nicely tanned back, his muscles bunching up in the sunlight. Now that's a beautiful picture. That's all it will be, a dream in my head. It's hard for me to imagine anyone would want to be tethered to someone as damaged as me. I start doing an internal inventory of my emotions and discover that I'm mostly happy and content. Here I am on a gorgeous, golden palomino, going off on an adventure. When I woke up in the hospital, not that long ago, life as I knew it was over and I was certain it would never again have any redeeming aspects. Yet, here I am with Buddy, on this trail that leads to a sacred place, a majestic eagle screeching and gliding overhead, guiding us. What could be better?

I decide to stop for a break; it's been a long time since I've sat on a horse and my backside is feeling it. Just then, the sound of nearby running water piques my interest, and Buddy's too, apparently, for he turns toward the sound and steps off the path, in through the trees. When we come to the stream I bring Buddy to a stop, then climb off him and look around, marveling at the scene before me. Giant oak trees stand at attention around this lush, park-like meadow with grass so green it looks a tinge blue.

You are here; this is the Sacred Place. You will stay three moons.

"Yes, Grandmother."

How'd you do that?" I ask Buddy.

Buddy sends me a picture of him unsaddled, and I comply. Around one stand of trees, next to the water is a large circle made of rocks on raised ground; it's a medicine wheel. There are a couple of logs sitting next to it, and a firepit.

I no longer feel the darkness that stalked us on the trail. Buddy releases any remaining tension from his body, as do I. I take my time exploring this place and, like many things since I've been in Galowhisdi, it feels familiar when I know there isn't a logical reason for it to feel that way. I follow Buddy to the stream where we both drink clear mountain water. I look at my watch and discover that it quit working. On a hunch, I pull out my phone, no signal. I start to feel a little panicky when Buddy steps over putting his forehead in the middle of my chest. I take a deep breath in and let it out, doing that a couple more times. I relax.

"I've trusted this far. I can't stop now," I tell him.

This place is alive with energy, feeling as ancient as it does new.

When I close my eyes, I feel my ancestors close by and hear their voices chanting with the rhythm of the Mother Drum in their circle. This is a sacred place of ceremonies gone by, of the gathering of the Elders, and moon lodge ceremonies. It feels so real to me. I can almost smell the sage mixed with cedar and sacred tobacco offerings. Grandmother brings me back to the present as she tells me, *With a heart as big as the sky.*

There must be something about the number three, or things that happen in a series of threes, but I don't know what it is yet. First Grandmother had guided me to Galowhisdi and told me to stay "three full moons." Now that I have finally arrived at the Sacred Place, it seems I'm to remain here for "three moons." Three nights.

Guided by Grandmother, I set up camp by the stream. In the days that follow, I walk the land and breathe the fresh air, drinking water from the pristine mountain stream. At night, I sit by the fire, remembering the teachings of my ancestors. Little by little I feel an expansion in my awareness and *remember* the stories written in the diary. I remember the ancient medicine teachings of White Owl, and where they came from. I remember everything I never knew. I pray, offering a smudge ceremony for gratitude. When cleansed and purified, I enter and walk the medicine wheel. I am wholly connected here; part of the earth, and part of the sky.

The third night, I dream vividly and receive a gift, a vision of my great-great-great grandmother; the Ghigau. She is wearing white buckskin with her raven black hair shining through the firelight. An Owl sits on her right shoulder.

I am pleased, young Nanye'Hi. You have faced each challenge and found the strength to rise above it. Soon you must decide.

"I am not worthy," I reply.

All before you have walked the earth as humans. To serve the People, you must understand all that it means to be human, both the light and the dark. You rise every morning in prayer, you love, you give thanks, even in the face of adversity. This is truly the meaning of being the Ghigau. You must serve, even when faced with sadness and pain. You, my great-great-great granddaughter, have a warrior's heart. Allow yourself to be healed, the animals will help you.

I wake with tears streaming down my face and the fire smoldering. My time at the Sacred Place is done. I know that

I have passed the first initiation of the first full moon. Buddy looks up from grazing in anticipation.

"Yep, time to go home."

The Sacred Place is again part of my soul. While packing my belongings, I begin to feel queasy and make my way to the mountain stream. I cup cool clear water in my hand, splashing my face, hoping to clear whatever is causing the queasiness.

My reflection looks back at me, but it's not my reflection. It's my hair, face, and body, but I'm dressed in clothes of my ancestors. The reflection moves her hand when I move, but the hand I see in the reflection is adorned with jewels. I have none. The hair in the reflection is dark and braided. Mine is blond and loose, yet the reflection moves as I move, exactly.

I sit on my knees at the edge of the bank and cover my eyes. I just need a moment. Why would I see this other version of myself in the water? Slowly I look through my fingers, and my reflection self is doing the exact same thing.

Then my image changes to a vision. I watch myself walking down the path that leads to Brayden's house. Buddy is walking behind me with his head pressed firmly against the back of my arm. I feel it all over again. The same darkness that Buddy and I felt so strongly that day on the way to Brayden's.

Is this a warning?

I stand, and when I look into the water I no longer see my mirror self. The queasiness is gone as well. I have trusted the Great Spirit and my ancestors. Now is the time to start trusting myself. Still, when I return to camp I allow my grandmother and great-great-great grandmother to guide me as I gather my tools for ritual. I smudge for purity, clarity, and to ask the ancestors for their guidance and direction, then I step into the center of the medicine wheel and take a seat. I give thanks to all and everything that has allowed me to arrive this moment. To the Great Spirit, I pray that I may know what is right.

A few slow, deep breaths later I enter the Dreamtime. In the vision I am walking the medicine wheel, beginning in the East. Here I am met by Eagle, who tells me that I am grounded on my path. Eagle offers his medicine to help me rise above the mundane and find that place within that dares to dream. I am being challenged to find my courage.

In the South, I am offered the medicine of Dragonfly to remind me to enjoy life and play. When harnessed, dragonfly medicine can help you embrace the joyous moments when they're given.

As I continue walking to the West, I find Horse waiting for me. Horse offers power and empowerment in a balanced way, knowing how much power to exude and when to use it.

In the North position, I am greeted by my trusted totem, Bear. I am told by my ancestors that Bear has been with me since birth. Bear medicine is where all things begin, and all things end. Bear medicine is the wisdom to go inward to seek the Great Spirit, first and always. I close the circle and give thanks to all directions, the Great Spirit, and the Spirit Animals.

As I leave the Dreamtime, I wonder why the answers are so veiled and mysterious? Why can't everything be straight-forward and clear?

What fun is there in that, my child?

We're supposed to be having breakfast together, but my cousin is anywhere but here. He is here physically, but not present in his body. It's annoying trying to have a conversation like that.

"You know she's not even close to being ready for any kind of relationship, right?" I say, feeling how deeply he cares for her.

"No fair, cousin, keep your feelers to yourself."

"I can't help it if you're broadcasting them. Does she know?"

Brayden shrugs his shoulders. "I have no idea what you're talking about. I think she likes me as a friend, and as you well know, that is the relationship kiss of death. Hell, now I sound like some lovesick teenager, and a girl at that. The next thing I know I'll be asking you if she *likes me,* likes me."

"You both have a lot going on, and I would hate for either of you to get hurt."

"I want to be ready—for her—and I'll do whatever it takes. Hey, wait a minute. Do you know something? Is there anything you might want to tell me?"

I wag my eyebrows at him, knowing him well enough to know that he would never cross the line intentionally. Brayden is just now starting to get the hang of his gift and still gets things mixed up. It's easy to do at first, discovering whose feelings belong to whom. I'm lucky, because I've always had the gift; discernment is like breathing to me.

"When are we going to tell Nan?"

"Not until we have to. Have you felt anything weird around here lately?"

I cut my eyes at him. "What kind of weird?"

He tells me about the darkness he felt when Nan brought Buddy to his place. He didn't want to spook her, but he felt it too.

I nod my head. "Yes. I felt it at the clinic, and a few of my patients mentioned their animals were acting a little odd. Then it was gone."

"I'll feel a lot better about it when Nan gets home."

"Oh, cousin, you've got it bad."

"Knock it off."

It's not that I don't want to see my cousin happy. It would be a miracle if the two most important people in my world ended up together. But while he knows about Nan's trauma, she does not yet know about his. I'd like to think she can handle it, but after all she has been through I cannot be sure. Sometimes the secrets weigh heavy.

10

The Darkness

As soon as Buddy and I are back on the trail leading home, I feel it. The darkness is waiting for us. Buddy's body tenses under my seat, and I watch his head lift higher and higher as he cranes his neck, looking for the threat.

"Whoa boy, we can't outrun it; it's here."

The darkness steps out of the shadows and onto the trail in front of us; it's standing on two legs and pointing a gun at the spot between my eyes. When I see it I'm shocked and yet at the same time I realize I had felt this energy, this darkness, every time I was in its presence, masked as it was by a handsome face.

Captain Michael Lane.

"Climb down. Don't do anything stupid and I'll *try* not to shoot your horse."

Placing one hand on Buddy's withers, I step between him and Michael, creating a barrier. I whisper to him and slap him on the butt for good measure. He turns on a dime, running too quickly for Michael to get a clean shot. Michael is knocked sideways and fires in the air. He turns to take another shot, but he's too late. Buddy's gone.

He will kill me. I see the hate in his eyes. I just don't know how long he'll toy with me first. The last thing I see is the handle of the gun coming fast, aimed at the spot between my eyes.

———◦◉◦———

I hear it before I see it, a fast-galloping horse coming in my direction. I turn to give Nan hell for riding that fast when I see Buddy, barreling home with no rider.

"What the–Buddy, where is she, what's happened?"

After checking Buddy for injuries, I call Nibs.

"Buddy's back, sweaty and frothy, no Nan. Come take care of him; I'm going to find her."

By the time I have Daisy saddled, Nibs arrives. She takes Buddy into the pasture, softly talking to him as she walks him around, trying to calm him and get him cooled down. It doesn't work. He won't settle.

I see the look on Nibs's face. "What'd you get?" I ask.

"You've got to find her, Brayden. She's terrified, and Buddy is beside himself."

I swing my leg over Daisy, and we're gone. Daisy is fast and light on her feet. As soon as we get on the trail, I feel it, the evil permeating everything.

"Careful girl, we won't be any help to her if we get hurt."

I don't have a clue where to look, but sense from the way she is flaring her nostrils that Daisy might. I loosen the reigns and let her have her head. She steps through a small opening marked by giant oaks and obscured by brush. It's a trail I haven't been on for years, the kind of trail that's hard to find unless you know what you're looking for. Last night's rain has made the trail dust free, and the earth packed. I feel a sense of urgency flowing from Daisy into me. Everything in this forest feels like it's whispering the same thing.

Find Nan.

———◈———

The first thing I'm aware of is the brutal throbbing of my head. I open my eyes just enough to let some light in and instead see the Ghigau standing before me.

He has come, she says.

Yes, I reply, *he wants to finish what he started.*

My granddaughter, he is more than you know. He is an evil so old that he doesn't even know what he is. This evil does not want our line to continue. This evil has been around since before my lifetime.

How do we fight it? I ask.

You must fight it, Nanye'Hi, as Ghigau. I cannot interfere. This evil has taken the form of Michael in your lifetime.

Fight it alone? I can't do that! I no sooner have the thought when I hear Great-Great-Great-Grandmother's reply in my head.

Then evil will overcome the People, as it has before. We have not always been successful.

Suddenly I am filled with a few fleeting, happy memories of my mother. A shadow then falls over the village in the form of an epidemic of drug and alcohol addictions. That was the evil of my mother's lifetime. The People crumbled into poverty and all the trappings that addictions bring with it. I experience the People of that time and how alcohol and drugs had overtaken them. The village was not like it is now.

My mother?

Now you see, Nanye'Hi. The evil of your mother's time lured her. She was not strong. You must fight, and as Ghigau. You must decide. My spirit cannot remain here much longer.

Grandmother, how do I fight this evil?

You must see beyond the physical realm. Trust that all you need is within you. Ask. I may guide, but I cannot interfere.

The first thing I do when I come to is throw up. Nothing reduces me to feeling like a two-year-old quicker than puking.

He kicks me right in the ribs. "Wake up!"

"Hello…Michael," I manage in between gasps, "I would say… I'm happy… to see you again… but you know how I hate liars."

———◦◉◦———

Daisy and I search everywhere. Darkness is so close that we'll need to be very careful getting back. I feel like absolute shit. Once before I failed to protect someone I care about; that cannot happen again.

Please, Nan, please don't give up.

I'm not normally a praying man–White Owl and the circle have that part covered–but if it helps I'll start right now. I'll do whatever it takes to get Nan back. I thought we were close to finding her a couple of times. I found a pool of blood and followed it, but it disappeared. The trail just stopped—no blood—no tracks—nothing.

I don't have a choice but to go home, regroup, and begin again at sunrise.

Nibs is waiting for me.

"How is she?" I ask, knowing she's connected to Nan empathically.

"She's alive, that's all I know."

"Let's pray she stays that way."

As I settle the horses down for the night, Buddy reaches over the fence, nudging my shoulder with the flat part of his head.

"Buddy, it's you and me tomorrow. I have a feeling about you."

I rise before dawn and find Nibs curled up in a blanket at the end of the couch. I make a pot of coffee, pack food, a first aid kit, and go to feed and water the horses. Buddy's gone. Must've been damn motivated to jump a five-foot fence.

Where'd he go?

———◉———

I'm in and out of consciousness a few times until I wake for good. I'm so grateful he finally passed out; I take a moment to thank everything holy for cheap whiskey. All I know for sure is that it's cold, dark, and I have, at the very least, a head wound of some kind. There is a small fire burning in a pit, and it is my only light source. I know from the small rocks digging into my body that I'm sitting on dirt. I manage to grab some with my tied hands and let it pass through my fingers. It's moist and thick like clay. The tall shadows surrounding us are most assuredly trees. Nothing looks familiar, but this is a campsite. Hopefully, we're still on Forest Service land somewhere around the village. How far out, I have no clue.

For a moment, I just watch him sleep the slumber of the drunk. He is an entirely different Michael from the one I'd known before. Gone is any resemblance of a clean-shaven, put-together military man. Now his outside matches the inside: dirty, smelly, and rotten. I'll never be able to forget this stench—rotting garbage mixed with cheap whiskey, urine, and stale tobacco, like the back alley of a big city. Along with his being psychotic, there is something else here, and it's driven purely by instinct, hate, and survival. *Whatever* it is, it's telling him I need to die. I'm going to do everything I can to make sure that doesn't happen.

I need to get out of here before he wakes. I try to remember what the Ghigau said; it's time to test her theory out about Buddy.

Trust yourself, Ghigau says.

Closing my eyes, I send a prayer: *Great Spirit, hear my prayer, help me to feel and connect with the four-legged and the winged.* In my mind's eye, I center myself and send mental images to Buddy and the eagle. I hope I'm connecting.

A searing pain roars across my face. "Wake up, Bitch. It's time for fun." I hear something like a snarl. "At least for me."

He unties my feet, leaving my hands tied behind my back. He stands me up, putting his right leg in between mine. I'm so nauseated all I want to do is throw up, but I force myself to choke it down, knowing it would earn me another slap, or worse. I keep trying to connect with Buddy and the eagle while Michael *tries* to assault me. Try is the key word as Michael's attempts fail; I send another grateful prayer for cheap whiskey.

I don't say a word, refusing to plead, beg, or cry.

"Don't you worry, Bitch. I'll have what I want right after a little nap." He passes out again.

He left my feet untied.

I curl up on my right side and bring my knees up to my chest, shimmying my arms around my legs and bringing them in front of me.

Thank you, yoga Gods.

As soon as I stand up, I fall. The whole world starts spinning, and this time I do throw up. The only reason I don't make any gagging noises is that I don't want to die. Carefully, I pull myself onto my hands and knees and slowly start making my way away from the camp and Michael. It's almost dawn. The sun will be up soon, but not soon enough for me.

Please don't let him wake up.

When I'm a few feet away, I again try to get to my feet. Sweat starts running down my back and with my vision swimming, I struggle to remain upright. My breathing starts to get ragged and uneven.

I remind myself to breathe *in through the nose out through the nose, in through the nose out through the nose.* When that feels relatively stable, I put one foot in front of the other until I remember how to walk. I continue feeling my way through the bushes when I hear a horse snort.

Buddy!

I make my way to him.

"Okay, boy, I can't jump." I send him a mental picture, and he kneels on his front legs so that I can get on his back. I'm bareback with no bridle and my hands still tied, but that's the least of my worries. Michael comes crashing through the bushes. I tighten my legs around Buddy and grab a part of his mane.

"Let's get out here, boy."

I can hear Michael cussing and throwing threats in my direction, but he's too late and too drunk. With each step Buddy takes, it feels like my right eyeball is coming straight out of the socket. When I'm sure Buddy's put enough distance between us, I relax my knees and fold over his neck, retching because there's nothing left to vomit.

"Let's go home, boy." I send Buddy a picture of Brayden's cabin. It probably isn't necessary, he knows what he's doing, but I send him the picture anyway.

———◦———

Daisy and I are halfway down the trail as sunlight hits the top of the trees. I hear an eagle cry and watch it circle overhead while it continues to screech. I pay attention, *feeling* that there is something different about this eagle. It stays in the same pattern, continuing to cry out. I follow it, and that's when I see them.

My heart is hammering in my chest as I squeeze Daisy into high gear; Buddy nickers in response. I'm there in an instant, but it feels like an eternity. Not bothering to dismount, I grab Nan off Buddy's back and into my lap, then turn Daisy toward home. I'm hoping Nib's empathic connection to Nan is still strong, and that she knows we're on our way.

"Nan! Nan, please don't die."

"I'm not going to die," she gasps, "but if you don't slow down, I will puke on you."

Sweeter words have never spoken to me, ever.

"He is right behind me."

"Who, Nan ... who did this to you?"

She doesn't open her eyes or move her head from the crook of my neck. Blood is continuing to flow down both of us and onto Daisy. I've seen enough head wounds to know they often look far worse than they are; I hope it's true in this case.

"Michael," she says finally, then loses consciousness. I keep a watchful eye out for the evil, but my passenger is my primary concern. I will deal with him later. Revenge is not high moral ground, but it has its place. I will take my time getting it, for her.

11

Recovery

I'm awake, but I don't open my eyes, not yet. I want to relish this perfect space of warmth and softness. Carefully, I open my left eye; my right one refuses to comply at first. After some more coaxing, I'm able to open both eyes to a room that has a Native American blanket and flute on the wall. I instantly recognize the bed, dresser, and high back rocking chair as Brayden's work and, in here, decidedly masculine. Nibs is curled up in the rocking chair, and Brayden is sitting in a chair next to me, his hand protectively over mine. Both are sleeping. It feels perfectly natural to have my hand under his, warm and tingly.

I have an I.V. in my arm and one mother of a headache. I don't want to wake either of them, but I need to move my legs. When I do, they both jump like they heard a gunshot.

"Shit, Nan," Nibs exclaims, "You scared the crap out of me! Don't ever, ever do that again."

I raise an eyebrow at her and say, "Promise." I then shift my eyes to Brayden. "Thank you for coming for me.

I don't know what I would have done if you hadn't found me." I busy myself straightening the covers and clearing my throat, then attempt a joke. "At the very least I probably owe you a new shirt, so let me know where you like to shop."

He's doing that half-smile, half-frown thing as he looks intently at my face. "Just focus on getting better, okay? Coffee?" I nod slowly and look up into his brown eyes.

I see Nibs barely shake her head and Brayden nod in response like they're having a private conversation.

Nibs asks me, "How do you feel?"

"Confused, tired, sad, hungry, scared, and very grateful."

"I'd be more concerned if you didn't feel those things." Nibs nods her head at Brayden.

"I'm going to check on the horses." He leaves the room.

"You were seriously dehydrated, with a major gash between your eyes and you have a pretty significant concussion."

"Nibs, I'm so sorry about all of this…"

"White Girl, quit apologizing."

"Do I do that a lot?"

"All the time."

"Now what?"

"Brayden already called the Park Rangers and the Sheriff's Department. They'll probably want a statement and a description of that *bastard*."

"Why, Dr. Nibs, I'm not used to you using such foul language."

She shoots me a humorless look.

"So, not in the mood for jokes, huh? Then why don't you tell me what's going on between you and Brayden."

"What do you mean?" Nibs gets up from the chair and starts fidgeting with my I.V. and checking my pulse.

"You know what I'm talking about."

I am about to probe her further when we're startled by a small knock at the window next to the bed. Nibs reaches over and opens it.

Brayden is there, grinning like a Cheshire cat. A second later, Buddy sticks his head in the window.

"He was going to break down the front door if I didn't let him see you."

I carefully reach over and scratch him between the ears, softly running my thumbs over his eyelids, his favorite spot.

"Oh Buddy, you're such a good boy, I don't know how to thank you."

Buddy neighs softly, which I take to mean, *Anytime, my friend.*

I'm on bedrest for at least twenty-four hours. I'll let Nibs win this time because frankly, I feel like crap! I do feel a little stronger after a cup of coffee and a bowl of soup. I settle under the covers, and one day turns into three.

"I never would have thought you were crazy," Nibs says as she checks my bandages. "You know, about talking to Grandmother." She pauses. "She's even visited me a time or two."

"What?" I ask, then I remember her vague comment about vivid dreams when I first arrived in Galowhisdi.

She shrugs. "Grandmother makes periodic drop-ins, though I can't say that I'll ever get used to it. How do you think I knew when you were coming home?"

Nibs leaves me to rest and, no doubt, talk with her cousin, who aside from delivering me food and drink has made himself scarce. I wonder if he's annoyed that he had to rescue me, or if he just prefers to stay away from damaged goods.

Whatever the reason, I'm left alone much of the time, with little to do but sleep and think. First, it's mostly scary stuff, about what happened with Michael and even worse, what could have happened; but after a while my thoughts wander back to my time in the military, before he ruined everything. Feelings of pride to have served my country, to have been part of something bigger than me, rise to the surface for the first time since Afghanistan.

For years, I felt like I belonged in the military which, after years of being the blond-hair outsider at Sequoyah was like a salve for my self-esteem. Until Michael, I'd been fortunate when it came to supervisors. I'll never forget Major Johnson. He's a no-nonsense guy, very gung-ho military, and by the book, but he also saw things that most people didn't. He would have stood in my corner when things went sideways.

I'd been a "golden girl." My military career flowed with great jobs, early promotions, and easy camaraderie. It seemed that military life and I were destined. One day, Major Johnson and I were having a heart-to-heart when he told me, "One *Aw Shit* can wipe out a whole lot of *Atta Girls*." It was a prophetic statement.

The same questions are set on replay whenever I think about Michael. Is it my fault? Could I have stopped it? That's the real question, isn't it?

What if I'd reported him right away? Would that have stopped my crew from getting ambushed? What if I heard the warning bells and whistles?

What if?

I shake my head, as if to rid myself of the questions. Mentally, I know that there isn't anything I could have done differently that night, except disobey a direct order.

Maybe there isn't anything else I need to know. At least I didn't go into a full-blown meltdown thinking about it. Just the fact that I can think about it at all reassures me that somehow, even without any intervention, professional or otherwise, healing is happening.

The next morning I awake knowing I'm ready to go home. I take this as a good sign. After getting dressed, I find Nibs in the kitchen and pour myself a coffee.

"Where's Brayden?"

"He was gone when I got up this morning, Daisy too."

"I wanted to thank him for his hospitality, and to tell him I'm going back to my cabin today."

"Are you sure you're ready?" Nibs asks.

"I need to . . . I can't hide out here forever."

"If you start feeling shaky, physically or emotionally, call me." Nibs hugs me before heading off to the clinic.

I go to the pasture and step inside the fence to talk with Buddy. I tell him I'll be back in a day or so. He never takes his eyes off me. I feel like he's trying to tell me something, but I'm not getting the mental picture. I turn and start walking to the gate. Buddy steps in front of me blocking my path. I move to the side, and it happens again.

I start to cry and throw my arms around his neck. I don't know how long we stay like this. Finally, when the tears of despair and sadness are replaced with tears of gratitude, I know with certainty how glad I am to be alive. I have a second chance to make a difference and to live entirely without apology. I get an opportunity to love with all my heart, to belong and be of service, right where I am. Yes, I am indeed very, very grateful. Buddy snorts and sends me a mental picture of me placing my left hand on his heart space and the other hand at his withers. I follow the images I'm given, and as I do, I feel unconditional love course through me. There are no judgments, only acceptance and love. Buddy could not care less what my life's circumstances are, where I've been, or what I've done. He sees my essence, the core of who I am, and wants to be with me anyway. After loving him right back, I start to turn around and leave. Buddy turns his body in front of mine, to stop me.

What is happening here?

As I place my hands back in position on Buddy, I feel the energy course from his body into mine, instinctively giving what I need most. I've felt for so long that I'm broken, damaged, and flat-out unlovable. I've believed that no one of character could love me. At this moment, I know that Buddy "sees me"—the truth of me and the sum of my experiences.

Maybe, just maybe, there is hope for me yet.

When I get home, I make a pot of tea and grab Grandmother's diary. On these pages, I get a sense of what she was feeling when she found out that my mother did not choose to become Ghigau. Grandmother wrote about my mother's death and what happened to the tribe and the village because of it. As I read my grandmother's words, despair and grief over the loss of my mother ooze from these pages. I was five years old when my mom died. I never knew who my birth father was. No one talked about him and whenever I tried to bring him up I was immediately shut down.

Grandmother spoke more quietly than I've ever heard her before.

We did not talk about it, she said.

"Why, Grandmother?"

She doesn't answer. Apparently, our genetic dysfunctional communication skills go back a few generations. Probably from the very beginning.

I wonder how the tribe and village can be flourishing with no Ghigau in place; it doesn't make any sense.

"Grandmother, I wish you were here."

As big as the sky, Nanye'Hi, that is how much I love you.

The more I read, the less I understand. There's just so much to learn. I'm grateful for White Owl, Grandmother, and the People. If only… and there it is again. My old mantra is raising its ugly head. What I need more than anything are straight answers given directly, without riddles or platitudes. I feel myself drifting off from the warmth of the fireplace as the light it sheds envelops me in a warm, soft glow. I take a deep breath and sigh it out, feeling relaxed, despite all the unanswered questions.

I'm acutely aware that I'm dreaming and find myself in a pasture with four horses. They welcome me by nickering and throwing their heads from side to side. I walk into the center of these magnificent beings as they form a circle around me. I jump up and grab the withers of a palomino with a star on his forehead and a black and white paint. We are running as a group when we finally lift and begin flying through the night sky like it's the most natural thing in the world. When I wake, I look up the meaning of horse in Grandmother's diary. It reads, *Horse is a symbol of personal power and empowerment. When Horse comes to you, expect a test of your strength.*

Great, now what?

Mornings are spent on the deck, drinking coffee and doing yoga, meditating, and holding smudging ceremonies. When I finish, I hear a horse snort and without looking I know it's Buddy. This morning, however, he is joined by a huge black and white gelding with a white star on his forehead. The same one from my dream.

"Good Morning, Buddy. I see you have brought a new friend with you."

Both horses snort and shake their heads.

"What is this all about?" I ask, and Buddy sends me a mental picture of me connecting with the gelding, much the same way I connect with him.

"Well, I'll try, but that's kind of up to him."

I fetch some grooming tools, then carefully move around the black and white paint, whispering gently to him. I then start brushing and silently ask his name. He shows me a picture.

"Magic, what a great name."

I continue communicating with him in pictures like I have with Buddy. I relax deeply, as does the knot in my chest that I didn't even know was there. I look at Magic's face and see his lower lip quivering, the sight of it bringing tears to my eyes and flowing down my cheeks. Geez, again? Magic takes my pain and this frightens me; I don't want to hurt him.

He is one of your totem animals, I hear Grandmother say, *and will not be harmed. Trust yourself, and him.*

Magic moves directly in front of me, placing the front part of his head in the center of my chest, then rubs his head up and down from my heart to my solar plexus. I don't understand what he is doing and start to break the connection with him when Grandmother says, *Feel what he's doing, and where he's rubbing.*

Magic is taking my pain and healing my heart. Whenever I start to shut down or move, he moves. The minute I settle into a connected space with him, he becomes still. Finally, we hit the sweet spot of a heart-to-heart connection and find a sacred space that's meant only for the two of us. For the first time as an adult, I feel the joy of being able to give love unconditionally. It is so pure and gracious.

When he finally steps back, I run to the refrigerator and get carrots. After giving Buddy and Magic their treats, I send them both on their way with a mental picture of Brayden's pasture. I then send Brayden a text: *A new friend showed up today, his name is Magic. I hope you like him. Be over at 5:00 p.m., if that's okay. We need to talk about the horses.* I worry this is becoming a burden on Brayden's hospitality.

A second later, my phone dings with his reply: *K*

He is a man of few words, or in this case, few letters. Well, too bad, I think. Brayden and I need to have a conversation, one that does not involve him walking away when things get real.

I gather my tools for smudging and enter the Dreamtime. In my mind's eye, I see myself in a beautiful meadow with soft rising hills and offer prayers of gratitude for my friends, my life, and well . . . everything. A voice I have come to know as the Ghigau speaks to me.

I am very proud of you, Nanye'Hi. On the second full moon, you will face a new test. Be ready. Continue to work with your totems, be at peace and know that all will come in its own time.

After a relaxing day, most of it spent on deck, I head inside to shower and dress. I try to ignore the fact that I change shirts three times and fuss more than usual with my hair. On the way to Brayden's, I worry again about all the extra work Buddy, and now Magic, have created for him. By the time I get there I'm convinced Brayden's not going to want anything to do with me or my animals. My fears are quickly laid to rest as I walk to the back side of the house to the pasture and find him practically swooning over Magic.

"Hey Nan, you didn't tell me he's part draft horse. He's amazing."

"Oh, is that what he is? I only know he's big. What's the other part?"

"Paint."

"Paint and draft." Leaning over, I whisper in his ear. "That's what makes you so special, huh, boy?"

"No fair keeping secrets," Brayden says, looking at me from across Magic's wide back.

I feel it so strongly, like the day in my kitchen. An electric shock that runs into my core and down to my toes. I start to feel something else, but it shuts down, quickly.

"I could say the same to you."

Brayden starts putting stuff away. "You wanted to talk about the horses?"

12

Magical Healing

All I can think about as I'm getting ready for bed is Brayden and his great big doe eyes. I caught him looking at me a couple of times tonight with a look I had never seen before. It's a little disconcerting that I'm beginning to know his expressions so well. I sit down as something I'm feeling starts to overwhelm me, catching in my chest. He has been kind, caring, and thoughtful, but that doesn't mean anything. It's probably just his nature. He can also be aggravating, surly, and a smartass. Then again, I kind of like smartass. He has just the right amount of it, mixed with charm, plus he looks great without a shirt on. I could swim in his beautiful brown and amber eyes and would have fun running my fingers through his incredibly thick black hair. And I have paid good money for eyelashes that long and dark.

A wave of sadness washes over me as I realize that I can't have him, or anyone else for that matter. Even if Brayden is interested, it doesn't mean love and a family would be in the cards for me. It sounds like the stuff of fairytales and rainbows, and I'm not a rainbow and fairytale type of person, never have been. Then again, reality for me these days is subjective. I'm learning there is way more to life than meets the eye. I am beginning to see new possibilities, but do I dare dream them? If I somehow pass the initiation, will being Ghigau be enough for me? Then there's Michael and all the horrible things he is capable of to consider.

Just thinking about him makes my skin crawl. I feel the darkness slowly invade my cabin and immediately call upon the Great Spirit for protection. The Great Spirit answers my call by shifting the energy and replacing the darkness with a lightness in the air, and a calmness that wraps around me.

As soon as my head is on the pillow and I close my eyes, the Ghigau and my grandmother greet me. We're standing in the center of a beautifully sparkling medicine wheel that looks like it's coated in diamonds. The sky is a sea of glittering stars against an indigo backdrop.

Nanye'Hi, the Ghigau says, *your initiation is at hand. On the second full moon, you will journey on a vision quest through the power of the ancestors. If you are successful, you will walk the medicine wheel.*

I feel her essence start to dim. "Ghigau, please don't go. I have so many questions. What if I'm not successful, what then? How do I do this? I've never done a vision quest before. Where do I need to go and what will I need?"

Oh, daughter of my daughters, you are entertaining. Do not worry; you will have everything you need. Trust and listen to the still small voice within, and the voice of the ancestors. All will be revealed.

This time I'm sure I hear the Ghigau laugh.

Trust, Nanye'Hi.

In the morning I wake up cranky, having dreamt about bats and, oddly enough, butter. I know what to do to fix that and head outside with my yoga mat. After practice, prayers, and meditation, I begin to feel more like a person. On any given day, I can read something inspirational from the Christian faith, conduct a smudge ceremony, flow through yoga, meditate, and enter the Dreamtime.

Over time, I have come to understand the diversity of my beliefs and have incorporated what I like about each into a spiritual practice that works for me. I appreciate that about Galowhisdi. There is a sense of freedom and acceptance of everyone beliefs and how they choose to participate, or not participate, for that matter.

Someone knocks at my door, and even without looking I know it's Brayden.

"Just a minute," I call out, then I run to the kitchen and fix his coffee as he takes it—loaded with cream and sugar.

I open the door and hand it to him, pleased by the look of enjoyment on his face when he takes a sip.

"How do you do it?" he asks; then, noticing my puzzled expression, he adds, "Connect with the horses like that. I would love to be able to do that."

I smile. "I think it would be better to show you rather than try to explain it. What do you say?"

"I'm willing to give it a try. We'll need to go to my place though."

"Never mind, I see they once again are one step, or several, ahead of me." Brayden looks over my shoulder out the window to see Magic, Daisy, and Buddy grazing on some overgrown grass along the deck line.

"How are they getting out? I check that fence every day."

"I'm learning that there are some questions better left unanswered."

"So how does this work?"

"You need to create a sacred space with them, so put your right hand on Buddy's withers and your left hand at his heart. But first, let's burn some sage."

I retrieve my smudge bowl and light the contents, maneuvering the smoke mixture so it flows over Brayden and Buddy, from head to feet. As it does, I see Brayden's shoulders lower onto his back and his jaw relax.

When Brayden makes the connection, Buddy immediately drops his head, relaxes, and his bottom lip begins to quiver. His eyelids are relaxed, and half-closed.

Quietly, I tell Brayden, "Imagine your heart opening and then just relax. Let him in."

Brayden nods almost imperceptibly. I feel more than see when they connect and step back. My heart wants to burst open with love when I see that Magic and Daisy are turned facing out, helping to create sacred space and protection. I've seen mares do this when they have a young one in the herd. They are such loving and compassionate beings. Just another gift of the Great Spirit.

Brayden and Buddy stay in this space for what seems like an hour. When horse and human disconnect, Brayden throws his arms around Buddy's neck and whispers, "Thank you," and "You're such a good boy."

Then, with his back still to me, he lifts his t-shirt to wipe his eyes. Sensing he wants a few moments of privacy, I slip back inside the cabin to get some coffee and carrots.

When I return I hand him a steaming mug. "Here it is, sweet as a candy bar. For the record, I've never seen anyone take their coffee like this."

I decide I won't ask about his experience with Buddy; that is personal, between him and his healing partner.

He accepts the mug from me. "I don't know what to say."

"You don't *have* to say anything."

"I want to, if you don't mind?"

My heart quickens, and I nod.

"I had a friend, a very close friend, who I grew up with. We joined the army together, went to boot camp, and got stationed together. On our second tour in Afghanistan, he got hit by a roadside IED and lost his right leg from the knee down. Developed PTSD as a result. He didn't want to take medication or go to therapy. He just kept thinking that he was going to be able to muscle his way through it. Everyone tried to get him to get help, but . . ."

Brayden shakes his head and for a moment I think he won't say anymore.

"One day he couldn't take it anymore and took his life."

"Brayden, I'm so sorry. I know from experience that when you're in the middle of all of that emotional upheaval it's hard to see a way out. It feels like you're trapped, and sometimes it just feels hopeless. If you can get past that one horrible moment, hang on a second, and take a breath, that breath can mean the difference between life or death." As I say the words, I realize, perhaps for the first time, how truly blessed I am.

Brayden doesn't respond or even look at me; he just turns and walks off. I'm wondering whether I should go after him when his pace slows. I realize that he needs a minute, not only to digest what we just talked about but also his session with Buddy. When he comes back, I put my hand on his shoulder.

"Maybe this wasn't such a good idea?"

"No, it isn't that. It was absolutely a good idea. It's just that, well, it made me sad, and I didn't want you to see me being a wuss."

I raise an eyebrow at him. "A wuss? Really? C'mon, let's finish our coffee on the deck."

We've just sat down when the back door opens and Nibs steps through it.

"What's going on? I felt it all the way in the village," she says, but she's smiling.

"Our girl has discovered another gift," Brayden says.

"Really?" Nibs says, raising an eyebrow at him. "Has she... 'our girl'?"

I ignore the inuendo and gesture toward an empty chair. Nibs takes a seat.

"Buddy showed me," I tell her. "The horses—our horses—are brilliant, loving, and compassionate beings with the ability to heal."

Nibs sits up straighter in her chair. "Go on."

I tell her how we can connect through the horse's heart and be healed thoroughly and on many different levels. The horses know exactly what needs to be healed and where. It's different from Brayden's physical healing ability, I'm hopeful that at some point he will share that with me.

"Wow," Nibs says.

"It's incredible, especially for someone who has experienced trauma. The horses already know so you don't need to tell them about any of it. That alone is a miracle, as just talking about the source of the trauma can be nearly impossible for someone going through it. Since my work with the horses, I haven't had a panic attack or a flashback. It's amazing."

I glance at Brayden to see him slowly nodding his head in agreement. Nibs looks excited yet puzzled, squinting and darting looks between Brayden and me. When she looks at Brayden again, he shakes his head very slightly, but I catch the motion. What is going on here? I open my mouth to ask but am interrupted.

"Do you think I can send some patients out here to work with the horses?" Nibs asks.

"I say absolutely, what do you think, partner?" I ask Brayden.

"Yes, absolutely!"

I've never heard him sound so excited about anything.

Nibs is acting very strange. It's *almost* something I can identify but not quite. At some point, she'll tell me, and if she doesn't, I'll find a way to squeeze it out of her.

———◈———

Peering into her window and hiding in the shadows won't be enough; it won't satisfy *him* long at all. He is not patient. He is not calculating. He just takes and destroys. It's what he does and has always done. I've held him back for a long time, longer than I ever thought possible. The doctors, and certainly my parents, all thought he was gone. I *knew* he wasn't. I've always felt him in there but kept him at bay. Now, nothing will contain him. He was just sleeping, waiting until the time was right and he was at his full power.

She'll get what's coming to her and more. It's her fault he awakened anyway. This time she will not get away. *Damn,* I had her all tied up in a neat little bow, but lust and whiskey fouled everything up. That cannot happen again.

The little girls used to get away from me, and then I would have to be satisfied with their pets. A poor second, indeed. A laugh comes from somewhere deep within that raises the hair on the back of my head. It's not mine; it belongs to him. He's getting stronger. Everything before this moment was child's play. This is the stuff created by nightmares. I will have my moment, I think, and am rewarded with stabbing pain in my temple. No, this moment belongs solely to him. He will take, claim, and satisfy his hunger whenever and however he wants. I had deluded myself into thinking that I could control him, until *she* came into my life.

I look down at the lifeless form lying at my feet. For now, this one will have to do. She was lovely enough with her long dark hair falling over her forehead, but she's not Nan. Soon, I will get to feel my bare hands wrap around *her* throat; squeezing, until I get the ultimate gift of seeing the life vanish from her eyes. This is the only thing that will quiet the monster within.

13

Death At My Door

Coffee, then to the deck to do my yoga flow. The sun's not quite up yet, just barely reaching the tops of the trees. I freeze in my tracks as I open the back door. There is something in a heap in the middle of my deck. Is it an injured animal?

I step gingerly toward whatever it is, speaking softly so as not to frighten it. My whispers become a full-throated scream when I realize what it is.

I run back in the house and go from door to door, locking them. It is only after I've pulled Bernice from her hiding place that I call 911 and with shaking hands text Nibs and Brayden.

Oh God, Oh Great Spirit, that poor woman.

I know I should wait for the cousins and the deputy, but I feel pulled toward the deck. As soon as I open the back-door fear catches in my chest, accompanied by heaviness and the familiar stench of rancid garbage and stale liquor. *Michael!*

It had never occurred to me that he would harm anyone else. Or that he is still stalking me.

My heart starts to race and my breath is coming in rasps as I shut the door, lock it and step away. I am still standing there when Brayden arrives with the deputy right on his heels. I don't remember seeing Nibs come in, but suddenly she's here, standing right in front of me. Gently, she places a hand on each of my shoulders.

"Nan . . . Nan, we're here."

"Michael," I gasp, and for a minute I'm transported back to that night in the woods. "The smell..."

I feel a slight pressure on my shoulders. "Nan, look around, where are you? Look at the clock, what time is it?"

Slowly I find myself coming back to the present. I take a few deep breaths and return solidly back into my body. Brayden puts a blanket around me while Nibs goes to the deck, where the deputy is crouching over the woman.

"Thanks, Brayden. I'm alright."

"You are most certainly not alright. How could you be?"

I give him a grateful smile and move to head for the deck, but Brayden stops me.

"Just give it a minute, Nan, let Nibs and the deputy do their jobs. Okay?"

I nod and look up to meet his gaze, seeing the concern there.

Nibs returns and shakes her head no, and I realize she had been holding out hope that the woman was still alive.

"Do you know her?"

"Shasta, from the coffee shop."

"I'm sorry just doesn't cut it," I say, and Nibs gives me a look that says, *we'll talk about it later.*

"Bastard," Brayden says as he begins pacing the floor, clenching and unclenching his hands. "What he did to that poor girl, and from the looks of things he didn't make it fast either."

She had been sliced diagonally, from her right shoulder to her left hip, but not deep enough to kill her. He'd duct-taped her mouth and wrists, and her legs were restrained with zip ties.

"There's something else..." Nibs trails off as the deputy comes into the house.

He introduces himself as Deputy Daniel Gaston. I think that's what he says. He hands me a bloody note with two words.

I read them aloud: "You're next."

I'm surprised when rock-solid Nibs quickly lowers herself into a chair. Brayden lets out a string of words I haven't heard since basic training.

I may be in shock because all I can do is stare at the deputy—a tall drink of water with sandy blond hair and brown eyes. He might be a little older than me and has a mixed ethnic look—part this, part that, like most of us. Large dark eyes, caramel-colored skin. He's handsome enough, I suppose, but there is no attraction. Something else has me homed in on him.

"Nan, right?" he said, and I nod, unable to speak. "I'm going to need to ask you a few questions."

I nod again, unable to take my eyes off him. I can feel Brayden and Nibs staring at me, trying to figure out what's going on. I don't know what it is either, but something about the deputy is grabbing my attention, and I won't ignore it.

Brayden steps forward. "I can answer your questions, most of them at least. Can we let Nan rest a bit?"

I finally find my voice. "Have we met before?"

"I don't think so," Gaston says, peering at me curiously, then he turns to Brayden. "Sure, we can start with you."

"Thank you," Brayden says, then with another strange look at me he moves the deputy out of my view and to the kitchen.

When they're clear of us, Nibs asks me, "What is it?"

"I'm not sure, but it's something."

"Yes, it is. I can feel it. Doesn't feel like attraction, though."

"No, not at all, but it's strange, like I know him from somewhere." I look at her. "How well do you and Brayden know him?"

"Not well at all. I've only met him a couple of times, when he's brought someone to the clinic," she says. "And Brayden probably knows him from around town." She looks at me curiously. "But how would you know him?"

I shrug. I have no idea, and besides, we have bigger problems to face right now, including telling Shasta's family. The deputy said that he would do the family notification, but I feel like I have to go with him. It's the least I can do.

I say as much to Deputy Gaston when he and Brayden return to the room. For a minute I think he's going to say no—something to do with protocol—but then Nibs jumps in.

"I'll go too. I've known the family many years."

The deputy nods, then says to me, "I think it would be wise not to go anywhere by yourself until we catch this guy. In fact, all of you may be targets."

"You're right," I say, "We should have a plan."

"The family will want to see her body," Nibs tells him, "but please make arrangements with me so that I can have her cleaned up beforehand. It's one thing to know how she passed and quite another to have that image burned into your memory forever. Do you agree with that, Deputy?"

Gaston nods again. "Of course. As soon as the autopsy is finished." He then calls an ambulance to transport Shasta's body to the nearest medical examiner, a few towns away.

An hour later we're standing at Shasta's parents' front door. Thank God Nibs does most of the talking—I just stand there as they scream, my legs nearly buckling beneath the weight of my guilt. Shasta died because of me, because of Michael's sick vendetta. As long as he is out there, no one is safe.

I need to end this before he kills someone else.

In the meantime, we create a plan to try to keep everyone safe. Once again Gaston says that sticking together is the best bet.

"Since I'm the one with the biggest house," Brayden suggests, "I think you two should stay with me until this is over."

"What if I have an emergency and get called out?" Nibs says, "One of us would be left alone."

"We need a fourth person," Brayden agrees. He turns to the deputy. "What do you say, Daniel?"

"I can be on call to make sure that Mary is never alone," Gaston says, and it's interesting that I can't read his expression. He's also the only person I've ever heard call Nibs by her given name.

Secretly, I'm glad not to be alone with Brayden right now. I'm feeling a little vulnerable, and that along with already being attracted to him would probably be a recipe for heartache for one, if not both, of us. I'm not willing to risk it. If there's something more between us, it deserves the time to develop naturally, without any psycho killers on the loose threatening the People, or my newly found family.

The others stay with me while I pack a bag, then we go to Nibs's so she can do the same before heading to Brayden's. I get settled into one of his guestrooms–the same one with the flute and the blanket on the wall, where I stayed after the kidnapping. I love it, and find I'm just as comfortable here as in my own home. I relax on the bed with Grandmother's diary, reading until I find the prayer Grandmother requested. Before I close my eyes, I ask the Great Spirit for protection around my loved ones, the People, and all the animals. Brayden and Nibs and the People of this village are now my family. I continue praying and thank the Great Spirit, my ancestors, and the Ghigau for watching over us. My spirit cries for Shasta and her family, and everything she endured at the hands of Michael.

"Why, did she have to die?"

Trust, Granddaughter, Grandmother says, and I can hear the tears in her words. *Nanye'Hi, tonight when the moon is out you must walk the medicine wheel.*

I know by now not to argue or try to talk Grandmother of out anything and just start putting things together. I call White Owl, and then ask Brayden and Nibs if they will be available.

"What about the deputy?" Nibs asks.

I shrug my shoulders. "He's welcome to join us if he chooses."

I don't know how all of this will evolve, but I'm certain the Great Spirit and Grandmother are right in the middle of everything. All I need to do is get the ball in play and be prepared.

I sit quietly in my room and enter the Dreamtime; I ask the Great Spirit to lead me in walking the medicine wheel. When I'm back, I hear a commotion outside. I look out the window and see Brayden and a couple of other young men moving things around. I join them.

"What's going on?" I ask.

"White Owl called and said to get everything ready for a circle, so that's what we're doing."

"Oh. Okay." I don't know what else to say. I know the term "circle" but never participated in one. This is not what I envisioned. I thought it would be a very private sort of thing with just us and White Owl. Brayden lights the fire in the firepit, and by its light I can see that they have made a huge medicine wheel around the fire outlined in rock and brick. There are chairs placed around the outside of the entire wheel. Deputy Gaston is standing on the deck, his eyes scanning the darkness for threats.

Nibs walks over to me, places a hand on my shoulder, and gives me the eye-sideways glance combo.

"Don't worry, it's time," she says.

"Right," I say, though I'm not sure what I'm agreeing to.

People from the village start arriving and quietly sit around the medicine wheel until nearly every chair is taken. Last to arrive is White Owl and Wind Song, the young man I'd met who plays the flute. Wind Song sees me and with bright eyes and a broad smile starts to come over. Before he can say anything, White Owl grabs the back of his collar and sets him firmly in the nearest chair.

"Ghigau," White Owl says with a tip of his head.

"I am not Ghigau yet."

"Close enough."

As Wind Song begins his beautiful flute music, the deputy waves me over. "Who is that old man with the gray hair?"

"That is our medicine man, White Owl."

The deputy stands with both hands on his hips, staring daggers at White Owl. I look back and forth, trying to figure out the reason for the animosity, but White Owl is oblivious to anything but the circle and the flute. Then he looks at me, nodding. That's my cue. I take a deep breath, trying to calm my nerves.

Granddaughter, we are with you.

Thank you, Grandmothers, I reply silently.

As I step into the center of the wheel, I become less aware of the present or the past; all I can see is the journey before me. I'm conscious of the flute music and the sound of White Owl's chanting and rattling as I ask the Great Spirit and my ancestors for permission to enter the Dreamtime. As I approach the East position, I meet Bat. At first I am startled, but when I open my heart I see what an amazing creature he is. Small delicate wings, intensely smart, and purposeful.

"I am honored that you have chosen to meet with me," I tell him. "I know of the powerful medicine of rebirth, but I have not experienced it before."

Bat quietly answers, "You have experienced the power of rebirth, many times. You were simply not aware. Now, in the East, you will experience it with complete awareness and purpose."

I thank Bat for his message and step into the position of the South.

Snake is slow and steady with his words. "You will shed the old beliefs that have limited you and empower yourself with knowledge in service to the People. Transformation and change are inevitable. Allow snake medicine to ease the process. Go forward, knowing that for all creatures and beings there is a season."

I step into the West, where I meet Deer. Her voice is soothing and nurturing, and she speaks to me like my mother on her good days.

"Deer medicine offers softness, kindness, and the power of the moon lodge. Deer is the nurturing feminine spirit that sustains and supports all. Allow deer medicine to uplift your mind, body, and spirit to assist in healing."

As I close my circle in the North, Wolf appears to me.

"Wolf brings the medicine of teaching and reminds you to share the information given from the ancestors and the Great Spirit. These spiritual teachings belong to all people, so that they may learn the ways of the ancestors and discern their voice from that of the Great Spirit. Call on wolf medicine to accept the teacher within."

When I step back into the center of the medicine wheel two of my totem animals, Bear and Horse, join me. They have been with me since birth and will be with me until I no longer walk the earth. Bear is at my right, and Horse at my left, and all who shared their medicine—Bat, Snake, Deer, and Wolf—surround me. A shimmer appears before me; it's Grandmother. Another shimmer next to her turns brighter yet; it is the Ghigau. My grandmother speaks.

My daughter's daughter, we are pleased. Soon, we will no longer be able to stay in this form. There can only be one Ghigau at a time. The second full moon is coming. It is time for you to go on your vision quest.

"Grandmother, what if I choose not to be Ghigau?"

You have already seen what can happen. The devastation and lives ruined. The People will be without a protector. There will be darkness and despair.

I leave the Dreamtime and find myself standing in the middle of the circle with Brayden holding one elbow and White Owl holding the other. The People are quietly moving, none of them saying a word to me. This feels appropriate. I nod with my hands in prayer position at my heart, thanking them for being here. As Brayden and White Owl remove their hands from my elbows, I realize they had been supporting me. I find the nearest chair and all but collapse in it. Brayden looks from me to White Owl and, seeming to sense our need for some privacy, begins helping everyone put things back in order.

"The first time can be a little unsettling, Young Nanye'Hi. You will get used to it."

"Why did we need to do that, White Owl?"

"Some things need to be experienced."

"Ah," I say, like I have a clue what he's talking about. "Grandmother says I have to go on a vision quest during the second full moon."

"Yes."

"You knew?"

"Yes."

"That's all I get?"

"Yes." He turns to the young flute-player, who has appeared by his side. "Let's go, Wind Song."

And just like that, they're out of there.

Later that night, I dream of the Sacred Place. My people are gathered around the medicine wheel as I stand in the center with my arms stretched to the sky in prayer. There's an owl on my right shoulder and in my left hand, an intricately carved talking stick.

14

It's A Daisy

The following day at sunset Brayden, Nibs, Deputy Gaston and I ride together to the village to attend Shasta's funeral. It is being held behind the Trading Post, where another amphitheater-type circle has been set up, complete with a fire surrounded by benches and logs to sit on. It seems the whole village is there, and people take turns telling stories about Shasta's life. When it's my turn to speak, I begin reciting the poem my grandmother asked me to say. I open my heart, lifting my hands to the sky, and see a brilliant light surrounding them, surrounding all of me. The love that fills me is so deep and intense that the words start to choke in my throat.

"Great Spirit, hear our prayer that the ancestors welcome and guide Shasta to them."

The voices of Grandmother and the other Ghigaus join mine as we recite the Old Indian Prayer:

"Do not stand at my grave and weep,
I am not there; I do not sleep.

I am a thousand winds that blow;
I am the diamond glints on snow.
I am the sunlight on ripened grain;
I am the gentle autumn's rain.
When you awaken in the morning's hush,
I am the swift uplifting rush
Of quiet birds, in circled flight.
I am the soft star that shines at night
Do not stand at my grave and cry.
I am not there: I did not die."

When I finish, I look over at Brayden and Nibs, who are staring at me with open mouths.

Shasta's parents walk over and thank me in Cherokee. I nod vaguely as I try to figure out what I'm feeling. I can see the rest of the people solemnly standing and leaving, but I am unable to move. I'm not too sure what happened, but I know *something* did. The power of prayer seemed to come from heaven and Mother Earth all at the same time. I thank the Great Spirit, my grandmother, and the Ghigaus for their assistance.

I see Nibs and Brayden approaching me and ask them, "Will one of you tell me what happened?"

Brayden speaks first. "I have only seen that one other time."

Nibs nods.

"When?"

"When we thought you were going to die, you started healing on your own. Just about the time Nibs and I thought you wouldn't make it, you lit up like a Christmas tree. The light pulsed around you, and you started healing."

"*What?*"

Nibs keeps nodding her head.

"Nibs, please say something."

Brayden grabs my hand. "It's just not that easy to talk about."

I'm annoyed at first, then I realize that I've been putting off telling them something as well. When we get back to Brayden's I decide it's as good a time as any.

"On, as Grandmother says, 'the second full moon,' I'm going on a vision quest."

Brayden's face turns red, and he starts pacing across the floor, clenching and unclenching his fists. He opens his mouth to say something, then closes it again and instead resumes the pacing and clenching.

After a stretch of awkward silence, Nibs finally says, "Are you out of your flipping mind?"

"That's a given, but I have to go."

Nibs takes her hand off her hip. Brayden, taking a deep breath, says, "Maybe this isn't an all or nothing thing." He continues like he's thinking out loud, "Maybe we can escort you to and from."

"Will, that work?" Nibs asks.

"I'll check with Grandmother."

Brayden takes another deep breath, this one ending in a sigh of frustration, then turns and marches out of the house without a word.

"Wow, what's wrong with him?"

"You have no idea, do you?" Nibs asks, with her hand back on her hip.

I shake my head no, puzzled by Brayden's behavior. It doesn't make sense why he would be so mad.

"My friend, you will see it when you're ready to. Let's make dinner. Are you hungry?"

Over the last couple of weeks, things have seemed relatively calm. I'm surprised at how well the four of us have managed to live together. Mornings around here are hectic, with all of us in and out of showers, eating breakfast, and taking care of the animals. Eagle arrives every morning, and I find myself looking for him. I swear he's on guard duty. I always send him a thank you when he arrives. I'm feeling so grateful for my newly found sense of belonging and purpose. If not for the overshadowing threat of Michael, it would be perfect.

One member of this foursome continues to baffle me. I have not been able to break the shell of Deputy Gaston, yet I sense a sadness about him that I have the urge to make better. I'm not sure how that would happen or even if it *could* happen, or if he'd be willing. It's just sort of this nudge that keeps him on my radar. He's pleasant enough, and works well in a group setting, but holds himself back at the same time. Maybe it's because he's the deputy? The jury's still out.

Our days are well planned. After dropping Nibs off at the clinic in the morning, I get to spend time with White Owl "unlearning," with Brayden keeping watch. The afternoons we spend at my place doing healing working with the horses. News travels fast around here–Nibs only had to recommend our work to a few patients and we find ourselves with a steady stream of clients. The truth is that the horses do all the hard work, and we're there mainly to guide and give carrots. I find myself becoming more sensitive during healing sessions, sensing and feeling what's happening between horse and human. That gift helps me know what to focus on during the healing session, and plan for what needs to be addressed next. I'm honored to be a part of this healing journey.

One of my greatest joys is watching Brayden with clients. He has an easy, genuine way about him that people and animals love. His whole demeanor changes from being all burly and manly to nurturing, soft, and compassionate. This is a side of him that others rarely see, including me. This is the real Brayden, the person I'm coming to know, trust, and respect.

Things are going so well that I try to ignore the knot that is starting to form in the pit of my stomach, telling me things are going to change again, and soon.

One morning as we're preparing breakfast I feel Grandmother's warm honey energy wrap around me.

Tell them.

This time I don't argue or question her.

"I don't know what's going on," I announce to the others, "but I feel something coming. I think Michael is planning something and getting ready to strike again."

Gaston surprises me by asking, "Do you get anything else, like when, who, where, or even how?" I hadn't thought he took stock in any of this stuff.

"No, it's just this feeling of impending bad mojo."

"Brayden and I will go out tonight after dinner and check things out. In the meantime, I'll make a call to the other deputies to have them beef up patrols."

He pulls out his cell phone and walks out of the room.

"You're right," Nibs says, "It feels exactly like impending bad mojo."

Brayden nods his head, agreeing.

My eyes flick from one to the other. "What do you mean *it feels*? Do you *feel* that? Do you *both* feel that?"

When they nod their heads again, I'm encouraged. "Is there anything else you're not telling me, or can't tell me?"

The cousins just shrug their shoulders. Nothing new there. But they have revealed something.

"So that explains all the looks you two are always giving each other. You have some sort of telepathic communication…?"

Brayden holds up both hands in mock surrender. "For the record, I'm pretty new at this. Just wanted you to know."

I get the strangest sort of fluttering feeling coming from Nibs as Gaston walks back into the room. I give her the eye-sideways glance combo, but she turns her back on me and pretends to be making toast.

After the morning chores are done Nibs is taken to the clinic, then Brayden and I head for the Trading Post for my lesson with White Owl, only to find a note on the door that reads, *Not today.* That's simple enough.

"We don't have any clients today," Brayden says, "What would you say about going on a ride?"

"I'd love to, but do you think it's safe?"

"I'm not sure. Why don't you check it out?"

I start to ask how, when it dawns on me. *Grandmother.*

Once Grandmother deems it safe, we head back to Brayden's to get things together. My body is crying out for fresh air, sunshine, and spending quality time with the animals. It doesn't hurt that I'd be looking at Brayden most of the time either. I wonder if he feels this spark between us. Sometimes it feels like the little sister vibe; other times, not so much. He doesn't treat me or interact with me as he does with Nibs. I refuse to spend the day worrying about it.

We gather food, blankets, and weather gear, storing everything in soft bags that we'll lay across the horses' backs. The horses are thoroughly groomed and checked from tooth to tail, especially their feet. Brayden and I prefer to ride bareback, and since we won't be going in rough terrain, we don't see the need to add the extra weight of saddles on them. As I'm finishing the preparations I get an odd nudge from Buddy. Apparently, the horses want to *speak* with me.

As I connect with Buddy, he shows me a picture of Brayden and me, holding hands as our horses trot side by side in the sunshine. Then I move to Daisy, who shows me an image of a beautiful buckskin paint, a foal. It's beautiful, and the joy I'm feeling from the proud parents is beaming through my body. They will not let me see if the foal is a filly or a colt.

Brayden looks to me with that frown and smile. "What is it? Is everything alright?"

"Well, Grandpa, from what I've seen, it's more than alright."

"Grandpa! Wait . . . really?" Brayden reaches around Daisy's neck and whispers things to her I wish I could hear. Then he steps across and gives Buddy the equivalent of a pat on the back. But I'm truly surprised when I get a brief hug and a swing around in honor of the new arrival.

It's lovely seeing him so happy.

"I did notice that she was gaining a little weight. I thought maybe she was getting too many snacks, Nan."

"Oh, don't blame that on me. Besides, in her condition, she can use a few extra carrots here and there."

The ride is quiet, peaceful, and calm. It's liberating and renewing just to be able to ride side by side in silence.

Reluctantly, I break the spell. "Brayden, the second full moon is coming up, and I'll need to leave soon."

"I know. But not today."

He grabs my hand, and just like Buddy showed me, we ride side by side. I don't pull away but allow myself to experience the feelings of receiving whatever it is that Brayden is sharing. We take nothing for granted, not the sun, the fresh air, our wonderful animal friends, or each other. We stop to dig into the mountain of food we brought, while the horses play in the field and munch on grass and clover, followed by a few treats we'd packed. I'm glad I remembered to bring some for Eagle, placing it on a rock nearby. We watch as he expertly swoops down to retrieve it. We talk about nothing important, just chatting about dreams, wishes, and Daisy's pregnancy.

"Would you ever want children?" he asks me.

The question shocks me, not only because it is coming from him but because it is one I have not allowed myself to consider for a very long time.

"I thought I did, but with everything that's happened, I just don't know…How about you, do you want children?"

"Hell yes, I'd have a baseball team if I could. And, food for thought: little Ghigaus come from somewhere, right?"

I throw an apple at him, which he catches in midair. The next thing I know we're chasing each other around the field like a couple of kids and throwing the apple back and forth like a baseball. The game is fun, until the apple got too close to Buddy, who devours it in two bites.

Suddenly, I feel a wave of melancholy fall over me. Brayden comes up behind me, putting his hands around my waist and his head on my shoulder.

"What it is, Nan?"

"I'm not even sure, sometimes the oddest emotions just seem to flood in."

"Maybe for today we can focus on just being together?" He turns me around and kisses me. Not on the cheek. Not a brotherly, concerned kiss on my forehead but one of those passionate, I-want-you-more-than-anything kisses. I return it, and then some. When we finally come up for air, I feel it, that knot in the pit of my stomach, and cold darkness coming from the edge of the woods. Instinctively, Brayden places me behind him, looking for the threat as the eagle screeches overhead and the horses surround us protectively.

"He's not going to attack now; he's waiting and gathering power," I whisper.

"That's all we need to know. Let's get home and warn everyone."

———※———

Well, isn't that adorable. The two of them all cuddled up together. They better enjoy it, because I have a few new tricks up my sleeve. I'll have to keep them apart; I see that now. They're too strong together.

There was a time when I could have reached down into this human soul and found the humanity that lived there, but no longer. No longer is there any trace of human inside this vessel of bone and flesh. It feels good to finally be free of that conflict of good versus evil. I don't know why they even try. It's such a waste of time, and yet many of them spend lifetimes doing it. Freedom, finally! Now I can do as I please with no struggles of consciousness to fight. It feels fantastic, and I know exactly who, and what, I'll do first.

———※———

15

The Second Full Moon

It starts with coffee and a glance at the calendar. The second full moon is only three days away.

"You're not going anywhere without me, Nan, that's all there is to it."

He is an ass, *that's* all there is to it. An unreasonable, stubborn ass with an attitude.

"You think because you kissed me, you think you get to tell me what to do? Well you don't. Not now, not ever."

"It was a pretty good kiss, though, right?" Brayden leans in, smiling.

"The best of my life," I say steadily, "but you're still not going to order me around."

"You're adorable when you're mad, irresistible, actually."

Brayden looks at me intently, the corners of his mouth twitching, while I try to breathe and get my blood pressure back to normal.

"Why do you have that goofy grin on your face?"

"You got mad—out loud—you got red-faced angry."

"You're kind of masochistic, you know, that right?" Then it dawns on me what he's saying. I trusted myself, and my feelings for him, enough to let my guard down. In fact, I let loose. Calling him a masochist may have been a bit on the tacky side, yet I get his point. I trust him, knowing that no matter what, he would not hurt me.

"Wow, you're right. Sorry I called you a jackass Neanderthal."

"You did?"

"Well, in my mind...?"

"You're forgiven," he says, and to prove it he holds me for a long, long time. Even wrapped in Brayden's arms, I can feel the darkness starting to creep around the property. *He's here.*

"I feel him too, Nan. It's okay. We'll take care of it."

———◆———

Brayden waits for me on the bench outside the Trading Post while I get my second full moon instructions from White Owl. It's not that White Owl's teaching is complicated, just the opposite, with a notable lack of information. Big surprise.

That evening at home with the cousins feels like home indeed. My best friend is giving me a hard time, and Brayden is... I'm not sure what it is, but it's lovely. I need to make decisions carefully and truthfully. The weight of it presses on my shoulders. Nibs feels the tension and reaches her arm around me, not saying a word. She doesn't need to.

"I'm leaving in the morning," I tell them and look at their faces.

Nibs's is full of concern and Brayden's is a blank slate. I get nothing from him except a quiet nod of his head. No arguing. Hmmm, something's up.

"At least let me teach you a few defensive moves?" he says.

"Not a bad idea."

He teaches me how to break a chokehold and a few other moves that I already learned in the military. I don't remind him of that, though. It gives me an excuse to be close to him.

Nibs excuses herself and goes to bed. Brayden throws a blanket on the floor in front of the fireplace, motioning for me to join him there. I don't hesitate. I feel what he doesn't express and wish that I could make it better for him. I don't have a clue how to do that, so I snuggle in tighter as the chill creeps across my body. Brayden takes his hand and places his fingers on the outside of my jaw, and with his thumb on my lips, his brown eyes staring into mine, he asks, "Nan, do you want this?"

"Yes . . . but," I whisper.

"There can be no buts, Nan, it's either yes or no."

"Then yes, absolutely yes." That is all it takes. Our passion is like a wild ride on a rollercoaster, rising and falling and rising and falling until neither of us can breathe.

I wake disoriented; the room doesn't look familiar. Then suddenly an arm comes around me, hugging me back in. With a smile, I remember Brayden picking me up off the living room floor as if I weighed nothing and then dropping me onto his bed saying, "Please stay."

"Hey, no fair, you're awake."

"After last night, I could be sound asleep and still smile."

When he opens his beautiful brown eyes, I catch my breath; they are still smoldering. Incredible. I would love to stay here forever, but I have somewhere to be. The Heritage Trail in Fayetteville.

"Are you sure you can't take Buddy at least? I get why no one else can go with you, but why not him?"

"White Owl was very clear. No horses and no companions. I need to make this vision quest like my ancestors made it. On foot."

"Yeah, but they didn't have a psycho after them, and you do."

"I'm taking Bernice."

"There's that at least." Resigned for the moment, he says, "I'll make a deal with you. If you make the coffee, I'll make breakfast when I get out of the shower."

"Deal."

When he joins me in the kitchen, I hand him his coffee. I sense he's about the bring up the vision quest again when Nibs appears behind him.

"Hey, lovebirds," she says. "You two forget who's living in this house with you. I'm just glad it finally happened. My empathic senses were going crazy with all that sexual tension."

Brayden shoots her an annoyed look then mutters, "I have to go." He stomps out the back.

"I don't know what to do," I say to Nibs, wringing my hands. "How can I make it better for him?"

"You can't, for either of us. Just come home safe and in one piece. The rest will sort itself out."

"Promise? I'm crazy about him."

"I know, White Girl, and the feeling is mutual."

I watch him quietly put my pack in the bed of my truck. My grandmother said he could drive me to the trailhead. It's roughly sixty-five miles from start to finish and will take me three and a half days to walk it. With any luck, and if I'm not dead, Brayden will meet me at the end of the trail on the morning of the fourth day. I hear Eagle cry overhead, letting me know that I will not be without an extra pair of eyes. I already feel stronger just knowing he's there. I open the back door to find Brayden standing in front of me with an armful of wildflowers and a cheesy grin.

I hurl myself into him, crushing the flowers and knocking him back a step. I throw my arms around his neck and place my face into the sweet spot between his shoulder and his neck.

"Me too," I say.

On the drive to Fayetteville, Brayden starts singing something in Cherokee. It has a beautiful melody, and I feel a sense of peace wash over me. In a moment, I recognize the Cherokee words.

For those above and as below,
Let the winds of change,
carry your name
to the four directions
we honor you
to the sky above
we honor you
and through Mother Earth
we honor you.

His mood shifts again as we arrive at the drop-off point. He helps me get my pack out of the truck.

"Nanye'Hi, I won't rest or sleep until you come home."

It's the first time he's called me by my full name. I hope it won't be the last.

"But I will come home."

"I'll be waiting." He places his lips gently to mine.

I feel his eyes on me as I head up the trail, a pack on my back and the hand-carved walking stick he made for me in one hand. I don't look back.

"Here we go, Grandmother."

I am here, my daughter's daughter.

Eagle cries overhead.

As I walk, I feel no sense of Michael or the darkness that accompanies him; I'm alone. It's eerily quiet, like I'm walking through a tomb with the expected reverence. Eagle isn't making any noise, and Grandmother is quiet, but I don't question it. I know they will communicate in the right time.

Over the next rise and to the right of the trail, I see what appears to be a ball of energy. As I get closer, I see inside the energy is a Cherokee woman in a buckskin dress and moccasins. She's kneeling beside an infant wrapped in a baby papoose. Tears are running down her cheeks and anguish is etched on her face. I *feel* everything she feels as she stands next to her dying child.

"Grandmother, I don't want to see this, and I certainly don't want to *feel* it."

Nanye'Hi, you must see the sorrow as well as the joy. You cannot make a decision without knowing why you are making it.

I keep walking and in silent prayer ask the Great Spirit and the ancestors to help me have the strength to face this initiation and see what I need to see. I grab the power at my core and center myself.

Nanye'Hi, trust. You are stronger and more powerful than you realize, Grandmother says.

Along the trail, I get periodic snapshots in my head of what the Trail of Tears must have been like for my ancestors.

They did not experience the Ozarks the way I am now, with the warm sunshine, beautiful trees, lush green meadows, and flowing streams. They endured the harshest weather conditions imaginable, with little or no protection. Most had no shoes or coats. Thousands died from starvation, disease, and exposure. This history was part of my unlearning lesson from White Owl. What he didn't tell me is what happened to the Ghigau during that time.

A shimmering light fills the space around me.

Catherine, my daughter, did not say yes.

"Ghigau?"

Yes, Great-Great-Great Granddaughter.

"Why, and why did you not do *something*?"

According to the covenant, I could not interfere. Catherine was of age and she made her choice. It was hers to make.

I feel the heartache and grief coming off her in waves. "Why did the Great Spirit allow this to happen, why did all these people have to die? It just doesn't make sense to me, and why have a Ghigau or covenant in place anyway if atrocities like the Trail of Tears can happen?"

She doesn't answer.

I try not to think about how tired I am; it just feels trivial compared to everything else. Below the crest of the hill I'm standing on, I see a small lean-to shelter and a firepit ring. The sun is starting to set, and this looks like a great place to stop for the night.

For the first time in many hours, I hear Eagle cry overhead and a wariness creeps over me. It is dark now, and the only light I see comes from my fire and the millions of stars glittering overhead.

"I will not be afraid," I tell myself, yet I can't shake the feeling of being watched.

Trust, my daughter's daughter. This land is protected by the blood of your ancestors. The darkness, his darkness cannot reach you here.

"You couldn't have just told me that?"

You must be willing to listen.

A bit of snark begins to creep up, but before I open my mouth, I remind myself of what my People endured on this very land.

"Okay, Grandmother."

I settle deeper into my sleeping bag and in that second between sleep and awake, hear the soothing sound of flute music.

My sleep was not restful but fitful, busy and full of dreams. I wake to a chill in the air and Eagle swooping overhead; my vision quest companion is on duty. In the bright, hot sun of midday, I crest the top of a hill that overlooks a beautiful green meadow. Eagle cries overhead, and I look around but see nothing at first. An awareness shifts in my mind's eye. I see images and a steady stream of old black and white photos playing like a slide show of what happened in this meadow. I watch a version of me standing beside my People, cold and shivering in the snow. I try to help those camped here, and try to aid the sick, and comfort the dying. There are so many of them. The soldiers stay on the outskirts of our camp, never offering help, food, or blankets. It's heartbreaking. So many children, so many people dead. I shake my head, trying to disconnect, but I can't.

Nanye'Hi, you must see it all.

I do. I see it all.

When I come back to myself, I feel a more profound sorrow than I have ever known.

"Why, Grandmother . . . why did they all have to die?"

Those scenes, those pictures, were horrifying, but though there was no Ghigau something guided them nonetheless. That much is very clear. Not all of them died. That alone was a miracle. *Something* or *someone* kept pushing them forward. There was hope, even then.

I grab the diary and start looking for the answer.

The Ghigau died in 1822. The Trail of Tears happened in 1830. That's how they survived.

"Ghigau, it was you, wasn't it? You spoke to them, and they heard your voice."

There were those that chose to see and hear; they prayed. The Great Spirit allowed me to help by giving hope. Those that had the gift heard my voice, and they were led to Galowhisdi. White Owl's people are part of that line.

"Thank you, Ghigau. I was having trouble believing that no one was helping."

There is always hope, Nanye'Hi. Everyone has a choice.

This is where I make camp. I gather my tools for a sage ceremony and bless the land, the People, my ancestors, and the animals. I dream of Bryant Ward and the original Ghigau. It is a wonderful dream full of love and wonder as the Ghigau found love for the second and final time in her life. He stayed with her and the Cherokee People long enough to father a daughter, Catherine. After a few short years, he returned to his white wife and family in Virginia. Ghigau would visit him often, taking Catherine with her so that he could get to know his daughter.

I woke with one thought. "How could you let him get away with that, Ghigau? What he did wasn't right."

Nanye'Hi, it was very different then, and not uncommon for Cherokee women to be married to white men who also had white wives and families.

"I suppose, but geez, are there any happy stories?"

The last day of my journey is quiet and peaceful. The land is so full of life. The trees are all decked out in their greenery, and the rolling hills are not too difficult to navigate. There is a soft breeze blowing, and every once in a while, I get a whiff of fresh pine or something blooming. The breeze keeps me cool and comfortable, though I know my body will definitely need to recover from this trip. I'm connected to the land here, and with the People. As I begin the last leg of my journey, an ominous feeling washes over me, and I check in with Eagle gliding overhead. He is quiet, and I get nothing from him as he continues to glide peacefully. There is nothing here, but the feeling persists. I check in with Grandmother.

"What is it, Grandmother?"

All is well, but it's time to go back.

I say a silent prayer for the People, Brayden, Nibs, and the animals as I continue. I don't know where I'm going. I haven't the entire trip, relying only on my map, Grandmother, and Eagle to guide me. I feel a sense of urgency to get home and pick up the pace. If nothing else, at least I can be honest with myself. I left a piece of my heart in Galowhisdi, and it belongs to Brayden.

I'm so deep in thought that when Grandmother pops in, I jump.

He is a good man, Nanye'Hi, trust him and trust your heart.

"I'm glad you approve, Grandmother, but how can I allow him to be connected to me when my life will be of service and protection for the People? I don't want him in any danger because of me."

My daughter's daughter, life is at the will of the Great Spirit. None of us knows, not me, you, or Ghigau how much time we have, and when we will be called. You must live now, not in the tomorrows that may never be. Live, love, and be.

The trail ends abruptly at the edge of yet another beautiful, lush, green meadow. This one I recognize. I'm at the Sacred Place. I am filled with a sense of knowing and find the water I know will be there. After drinking and washing, I sit outside the medicine wheel created by the Ghigaus that came before and renew my mind, body, and spirit with a sage ceremony. I prayerfully walk the medicine wheel, giving thanks to the Great Spirit, the four directions, above and below, the ancestors, the animals, and all the People. I pray for their protection. After closing the sage ceremony, the Ghigau greets me.

You have completed your vision quest, and we are pleased.

"Thank you, Ghigau. It was difficult seeing what happened to the People."

She does not respond, but a hush falls over me and I feel her warmth spread across my chest. Yes, she understands better than I do, I'm sure.

Granddaughter, trust. Even through pain and sadness, you must trust.

That ominous feeling returns briefly, and I sense this is a warning.

I step out from the Sacred Place onto the path that leads home, fully expecting to walk when I hear a familiar snort and Eagle cry overhead.

"Nan! Oh, thank the Great Spirit." Brayden rushes forward with a crushing bear hug.

"I can't breathe."

"Sorry, it's just that I was so worried." Buddy snorts. "Excuse me, *we* were worried."

For just a moment I allow nothing in, except the feel of Brayden's arms around me and his lips on mine.

"Time to go home," he says, as he helps me onto Buddy's back.

I feel a warmth flood through me from Buddy. I pat his neck and whisper in his ear.

"How much longer are you going to be able to ride Daisy? She's getting wide."

"Careful now, she's very sensitive about her weight."

Brayden grabs my hand, and we ride side by side until we're home. Everything should be perfect, but I feel more now than I did before my vision quest. Sort of like dialing into a radio station that used to be filled with static and now comes in clearer. I can't shake the darkness I feel creeping around the edges. I look at Brayden and tune into the horses. No one else seems to be feeling anything. Maybe I'm just tired, I tell myself, but I don't believe it.

Trust yourself, Granddaughter.

Thank you, Grandmother, I say silently, then I turn back to Brayden. "Hey, how did you know where I would be?"

He looks at me and smiles.

"Grandmother," we say at the same time.

16

It's Too Much

As I climb into bed next to Brayden, he pulls me in close, spooning. We're both exhausted—me from my journey and Brayden from worrying about my journey. I should feel safe, protected, and relaxed, but something is stirring again. Fear hits my chest, and the air becomes thick, making breathing feel like work. I hear Eagle screech a warning outside and jump from bed, throwing on whatever clothes are handy. I'm quickly putting on boots as Brayden starts doing the same.

"What is it, Nan?"

"I'm not sure; it's something."

Nibs meets us in the hallway, completely dressed, saying, "The deputy is out patrolling. I called him, he's on his way.

I have Bernice in hand while Brayden grabs the rifle from over the fireplace. Nibs aims a flashlight toward the sound of horses snorting and galloping toward the far end of the pasture. In the light, I see Buddy crash through the tree line thrashing around wildly and rearing up at something. Magic and Daisy are standing guard just this side of the current battle.

"It's Michael; I can feel him," I yell.

I start to run in their direction, but I'm stopped by something I can't see. No matter how hard I try, I cannot break through.

"Brayden, I can't move."

"Nibs, stay with her."

Brayden bolts to the horses, rifle up and ready.

"Nibs, I need to get to Buddy."

Nibs puts her hands on the invisible shield and tries to push her way in while I'm working to push my way out.

"It won't budge!"

"Grandmother, please let me through. I must get to them!"

Brayden yells, followed by two rifle shots. I am flooded with images from Buddy of our short time together. I feel his incredible love for me and his sense of duty to me. His bravery washes over me, as does the rage and darkness he battled on my behalf. I continue to try to break the shield and get to him, but nothing budges.

Everything stops, all of Buddy's emotions and the dark feeling of evil. My invisible shield drops. Nibs and I start running for Buddy and Brayden. I see the headlights of a vehicle on the roadway but don't stop. *I have to get to Buddy.*

"Brayden!" I cry out, then, "Ghigau, please help my friends!"

When I finally reach them, Brayden is kneeling next to Buddy with his hand on his chest. My breath catches, and I feel a sharp pain in my heart.

"Ghigau, Great Spirit, please, *please* help him."

I connect with Buddy as he takes his last breath. I lay across his body and put my arms around his neck. What a wonderful friend, and trusted totem he was. I will never forget him.

"Please, dear friend," I sob, "Go in peace."

My daughter's daughter, I have him. He is not alone.

The feeling of warm honey washes over me as it always does when Grandmother is near, but this time, I don't find it comforting. In fact, I'm incredibly angry. I don't understand why they would not let me pass to help Brayden and Buddy.

You are not ready, Granddaughter, and we cannot put you at risk. You are the only hope for the People.

I am still trying to digest this when I hear the crunch of footsteps behind us, then Deputy Gaston's voice. "I'm so sorry, Nan."

Some communication happens behind me as I continue to lay across Buddy, hugging his neck.

"Later," Brayden says.

Through my tears, I manage, "He was the best and bravest."

I feel Brayden's hand on my shoulder. "We need to get you home."

"Not yet, we need to cleanse this place," I say.

"That can wait."

"No, it can't, I feel it as well," Nibs says.

Brayden gathers my smudge bowl, then I say a prayer and do a ceremony for the land, Buddy, my friends, and myself. Taking the tobacco that has been blessed by White Owl, all of us walk the perimeter of the property, creating sacred space. Daisy and Magic follow us carefully, sorrowfully.

After thanking the Great Spirit, I walk over to Daisy, and Brayden to Magic; we put one hand on their withers and the other on their hearts, making connections. I ask the Great Spirit and the ancestors for healing for them, knowing they were traumatized by everything they just witnessed.

The cousins and the deputy don't speak as I take a few moments to honor the spirit of our lost friend. Suddenly, grief overcomes me like a wave, and before I even know I am falling. Brayden catches me, scoops me into his arms and carries me back to the house.

"Buddy . . ."

"I know sweetheart, I know."

When I awake the next day the sun is high and the pain in my chest has gone from sharp to an awful heavy throbbing. How could I have possibly slept?

Buddy.

I try to move, but my guilt, coupled with the anger at Grandmother for not letting me go to him, keeps me weighted to the bed.

My daughter's daughter, I'm sorry for your loss. We could not risk you. Your friend will be forever honored.

I am given a vision of the Ghigau in her white buckskin dress and moccasins, owl on her right shoulder, intricate carving stick in her left hand. Next to her stands Buddy, as proud and majestic as ever. My heart breaks a little more.

"Thank you, Ghigau. I love him dearly."

He is not alone, Nanye'Hi, and neither are you.

I appreciate the words, but it is the smell the coffee coming from the kitchen that gets me up. I find Nibs and Deputy Gaston silently sitting at the breakfast bar. There is something weird in the air, partly coming from Gaston's general awkwardness and a vibe between him and Nibs.

"How are you?" Gaston asks.

"I don't know. Sad, mostly, and mad."

Nibs gets up, giving me a side hug.

"Have some coffee, and when Brayden comes in we'll talk."

I use the downtime to corner Gaston. During the weeks at Brayden's he had avoided my subtler attempts to get to know him. Now I just fire away with direct questions.

"Where are you from—do you have a family—how long have you been here? You seem to be well-versed in all things weird–how did that come to be?"

Nibs suddenly appears fascinated with her coffee cup, but I can feel her cringe with every question. Yes, there's definitely something here.

"I grew up in the area," Gaston replies, his face and voice unreadable, "I'm single and have been in law enforcement for twelve years."

I wait a beat for him to elaborate on something, but he doesn't. Yup, I feel a mystery here and it has nothing to do with Nibs giving me the eye.

I open my mouth to say exactly that but before I can White Owl walks through the front door. He looks uncharacteristically sympathetic.

"Young Nanye'Hi, I'm sorry for your loss."

"Thank you, White Owl."

A moment later Brayden follows. I sigh as I feel his arms go around me.

"How are you?"

I shrug my shoulders.

We gather around the table.

"What's happening?" I ask.

"Given what happened last night," Gaston says, "I won't get any of the usual arguments about the lack of manpower and funding from my department. We need to tighten our security and expand the group we're protecting." He looks directly at White Owl. "That includes you."

"I'm just an old man."

"You're more than that," I say, "and yes, Deputy, I agree."

"You are not Ghigau yet," White Owl says.

"And you don't get to pull it out whenever it's convenient. You will have protection. End of discussion."

We go over everyone's daily routines, looking for gaps in security when Michael could make his move. Nibs has been at the greatest risk, logistically speaking, but no more. Gaston will make sure she gets to and from the clinic, and an officer will be posted outside while she's there. She will not go on home visits, or anywhere else, without an escort. Deputies will keep watch over Brayden's place day and night, and no one is to leave by themselves. This, along with Gaston now sleeping here at night, should keep us safe. During the day, he'll assist the local and federal investigators tracking Michael. As for White Owl, it is decided that he and Wind Song will be safety buddies; the Trading Post will also be surveilled round the clock.

The deputy asks, "What do the People know?"

"They know the Ghigau is going through initiations and that there is a lunatic on the loose," White Owl says simply.

"They feel evil and darkness around them," Nibs adds. "I've also been treating much more illness in the clinic this past week, and I sense that he's the reason for it."

I look at Gaston. "Why are you asking?"

"I think they need to be better informed. That means understanding that this lunatic is also a highly trained military officer who's clearly able to survive, and hide out, in the woods for extended periods of time. They need to know what we're dealing with, and what to keep an eye out for."

It makes sense.

"I'll take care of it," White Owl says.

"Good." He turns to me. "This has become a mind game to him. He's going after those you care about in order to make you vulnerable and hopefully break you down."

"Yes," Nibs says.

"We're not going to let that happen." Brayden takes two big strides and wraps me in his arms, but not before I see him give Nibs the eye.

"Okay, cowboy, what is it?"

Instead of answering, Brayden walks over to the window, opens it, and whistles.

"See for yourself."

Standing in the pasture is Magic, Daisy... and another animal, no more than half as tall as Daisy.

"That's either a really big dog or..." I look at Brayden then out the window again. "It's a miniature donkey!"

Without another word and without bothering to change out of my slippers, I run out the back door to meet him. He is compact but muscular, with the same lovely grayish-tan color you see on a full-size donkey and all the black edgings around his eyes, feet, tail, and nose. He's not a bit shy as he moves forward to greet me. I don't stand on ceremony either, just place one hand on his little withers and the other on his heart, connecting. The first thing I'm aware of is the presence of my grandmother. I feel her understanding of the great loss of my Buddy. I know that he is her gift to me, which makes him extra special.

"What is your name, gorgeous?" I say gently, and a beat later I have my answer. "Fabio, huh? Welcome."

In addition to his many wonderful qualities, Fabio also has the vocal cords and pitch of a full-size donkey, which is to say he sounds like the most obnoxious car alarm ever. In fact, that's what I think it is when I am awakened just before dawn the next morning.

"Oh. My. God," I groan, then jump up to go stop him. By the time I get downstairs everyone else is awake as well and headed to the coffee pot.

"I'll go check on your new friend," Brayden says.

"I don't recall ever saying he was mine." Silly thing to say. Everyone just stops and gives me a look. "Okay, he's mine." Looking out the window, I catch a flash of something over in the tree line close to where Fabio is standing. A chill goes up my spine.

"Deputy, there's something out there," I say, still staring out the window. "Nibs, better bring your bag."

It is a young woman, lying unconscious and barely breathing. Michael had carved his signature into her skin—a deep cut from her right shoulder to her left hip. There's a nasty bruise across her face and another large gash above her right eye that's bleeding profusely. From the marks on her neck, I see that he tried to strangle her. He must have been interrupted.

"This must have happened last night."

"Yeah," Nibs says, "no way she would have survived longer than that."

Fabio brays, and when I meet his eyes I realize he is trying to show me what he saw. I close my eyes and see Michael struggling with the girl. My heart goes out to her, and to the donkey, who'd witnessed such a horrible event his first night here.

"So that's why you started braying, my friend. You were warning us."

I turn to Nibs, who is at the girl's side, gently feeling for broken bones. A few feet away, Gaston is on his cell, calling for an ambulance.

"What can I do?" I ask.

"Go into the house," Nibs says, "and grab a blanket, some clean towels and peroxide. I want to try to clean these wounds."

I'm almost inside the front door when a shadow cast itself on the front porch. Another chill runs up the back of my neck; I feel him close by, but now is not the time.

"Grandmother?"

He is blocked, Nanye'Hi, for now.

I don't know what that means, but there is no time now to figure it out. I need to get back and help Nibs. As I rush around grabbing supplies, I vow that no more innocents will die or be harmed because of me, or my legacy. This stops now.

When I return, Nibs puts me to work cleaning the shoulder to hip laceration while she works on her head wound.

"Now let's wrap her in the blanket," Nibs says, "She's in shock and we need to keep her warm."

Brayden returns with a healing smudge and smudges everything and everyone. He has a faraway look in his eyes as he recites a Cherokee prayer asking the Great Spirit for protection and to aid in this young woman's healing. He also conveys our gratitude for the animals, and our new friend Fabio, who turns out to be the best home security system ever.

———※———

It's been a week since we found that girl in the tree line. I've had this constant feeling in the pit of my stomach that knots up and wants to climb out my chest. I know Michael's just waiting for one of us to make a mistake, to let our guard down for one moment and then he's going to pounce. He wants me but hurting someone I care about is almost as good.

I take a few deep breaths and head to the pasture to work with the horses. All of us, including Magic and Daisy, are still grieving over the loss of Buddy, and we are helping each other to heal. I'm trying to come to terms with the loss of friends and innocents, and my role in it. So far, I haven't been successful. Not over the deaths, the evilness, or even with my own choices that lay before me. Is it fair to be putting everything and everyone at risk? No, most definitely not. *Is* there a way that I can be the Ghigau, and not put everything and everyone at risk?

Nanye'Hi, would you stand behind and beside your friends if this were their choice to make?

"Yes, Grandmother, but -"

Trust, my daughter's daughter, that the light is stronger than any darkness.

With a sigh, I focus on the present and Fabio, who is earnestly trying to get my attention by walking back and forth in front of me. When I try to walk around him, he turns, faces me, and starts braying in my face.

"Shhh, alright, already, you have my full attention."

He shows me something puzzling and a little alarming. *"When?"*

Fabio shows me a picture of the sun rising and setting twice. I thank him and then go inside to join the cousins.

"Game night?" I ask. I just can't bring myself to tell Brayden we have another friend on the way.

"Sounds good."

It's just what everyone needed. A relaxing evening without thinking about evil, death, and all the horrible things that could happen at any given moment. After saying prayers, I fall asleep dreaming about a majestic, midnight-black Tennessee Walker named Storm.

The ever faithful, reliable, and annoying donkey alarm goes off before the sun is fully up. I jump out of bed, throwing open the window, and in a loud whisper tell Fabio, "Hush, be quiet, you're going to wake up everyone in the house."

I look left and see Nibs hanging out her window, and the deputy standing on the deck at the back door; Brayden is right beside me.

"Sorry."

"Hey, look at that," Nibs says, pointing toward the tree line.

Storm has arrived.

When Brayden sees him, he starts cussing and mumbling. He rummages around for his boots and stomps out the door to the pasture. About halfway to Storm, his body language changes, and becomes more relaxed, his stride slowing. I feel him get into that calm, centered place he goes to whenever he's working with animals. He reaches out and touches Storm, and his whole being lights up with joy. He turns and looks at me, giving me the thumbs up.

I grab two cups of coffee and head out the back door to meet him.

"Thanks, Nan."

"It's the least I can do," I say awkwardly, trying to identify this strange feeling that's suddenly gripped me. It is a feeling of guilt, of being beholden, almost, and I don't like it one bit.

"I promise that as soon as it's safe, I will go back to my cabin and take my animals with me."

He gives me a curious look. "What just happened?"

"What do you mean?"

"I thought we were doing fine here, all of us together. Then, out of the blue, you start talking about leaving. What's changed?"

"No, I mean, yes. I don't know. I just...I already feel like enough of a burden, and now with these animals... I don't feel like I'm pulling my weight and I don't want to put more pressure on you and now we have another mouth to feed and take care of and..."

I pause in my rant when I notice he has that adorable frown and smile thing going on.

"What?"

He laughs. "You worry about everything."

"Do not."

"Yes, you do. And you said we."

I walk away in what I hope looks like a dignified huff. Brayden's laughter follows me back to the house, telling me otherwise.

"I don't know which ass's braying is more annoying," I mutter, "Fabio's or Brayden's."

"What are you doing?" Brayden asks when he finds me putting a halter on Fabio. I glance at him, but don't meet his eyes. I'm still smarting from our exchange early this morning.

"I have things to do in the village. Now, before you get all excited, I'm taking Fabio with me. He's the great evil detector, and he can carry my packages."

I wait for him to start yelling or perhaps stalk off, but Brayden surprises me again.

"I think that's a great idea. When you get back, maybe you'll feel like going for a ride?"

I smile for the first time all day. "Okay."

17

Michael

She's lovely in her way, but not like my Nan. This one has dark hair and eyes and I prefer blondes, always have, but she'll do in a pinch. There's something very different about this one, too; when I watched her go into the clinic this morning it was almost as if she could feel me looking at her. She'd stopped a few times and looked over her shoulder before moving on, though she didn't pick me out among all the tourists milling about. Did the same thing when she went out for lunch. Yes, she definitely felt me.

The hunt is *almost* as delicious as the capture. Nothing will ever beat the satisfaction of putting my hands around some woman's throat and watching the life drain from her eyes. Getting my hands on that doctor will be almost as good as getting my hands on Nan. And when I do, there will be no one to stop me, and I will be one step closer to breaking her. No one gets away from me, ever. She was supposed to die; she *must* die, there is no other option. In the end, she'll beg for it, but I will take my time, enjoying the process. I won't let her die too quickly. No, not quickly at all.

⸻

The closer Fabio and I get to town, the more fidgety he gets— jumping at every sound in the trees, his eyes searching everywhere and finding nothing. Then I feel it, the unmistakable darkness that belongs to Michael. I stop and connect with Fabio, who shows me a picture of Nibs's clinic, and Main Street full of tourists. Fabio starts braying and pulling away from me. He's strong for a little guy, and I don't know how much longer I can hold him.

Trust him, Granddaughter.

Letting Grandmother's words guide me, I unclip Fabio's lead rope and let him go, following him the best I can.

He took off at a speed one would think impossible for a miniature donkey. I send Nibs and Brayden a quick nine-one-one text and then go after Fabio. Of course, I hear him before I see him. When I do catch up with him, I find him causing a huge commotion in the center of the village. All the shop owners and tourists move toward the noise, instead of away from it. The crowd parts and lets me through. Fabio is standing in front of the clinic, blocking the door. Nibs is on the other side of him with her hands on her hips, yelling at him and trying, unsuccessfully, to get him to move.

Everything fades away as I draw closer to the clinic. My legs feel like lead, as if I'm moving in slow motion. I feel myself shift and see what was, instead of what is. Then I see what Fabio sensed, and what Michael did. Abruptly, I'm thrust back into my body, and I bend over, putting my hands on my knees, to get my bearings. Nibs, sensing the change, looks in my direction.

I feel Brayden at my side before I even see him. How did he get here so fast?

Putting a hand on my shoulder, he leans in and whispers, "Is there anything I can do?"

"He, he was after Nibs."

Once Fabio is convinced it's safe, he lets me pass to Nibs. "Nibs, I –"

"Don't say it. I'm okay. We're okay."

Gaston arrives a moment later, along with several other deputies, and immediately begins barking orders to get the search underway. I'm amazed at his competence and his ability to lead. He is a warrior; a man of honor and one that can be trusted, dependable. That says a lot.

He walks over to us. "Are you two okay?"

Nibs nods her head, and I turn to see Fabio surrounded by a group of adoring fans.

"Thanks to Fabio, we're all safe, and I'd say we owe him more than a few treats."

While Fabio is being fawned over, I sit on the bench outside the clinic to catch my breath. After a few moments, Brayden approaches with two coffees. He hands one to me.

"Thank you, great idea."

"I'm going to get the truck; I'll be back."

When Brayden leaves, Fabio stands next to me. Out of the corner of my eye, I see that I had kicked over someone's old coffee cup they left on the sidewalk. I almost picked it up but see the lid pulled back and torn into a half-circle. There's only one person who ever turned a coffee lid like that, and it's Michael. I call Gaston over. He gives me an incredulous look when I tell him about the cup.

"You want to tell me how you found this?"

"I could, but I think you'd have a hard time believing me."

"Try me."

I do, and I leave nothing out. I tell the deputy how Fabio knew on our way into the village that something wasn't right, how he had run into town and stood in front of Nibs's door, because he knew that's where the danger was. As I speak, I can feel Grandmother's approval, though I realize this doesn't make me sound any less crazy. I look at the Gaston's face, trying to gauge his reaction, but his expression is unreadable as ever.

"Had a horse once," he says after a moment, "Saved my life." he then reaches into his pocket, pulls out a glove, and uses it to pick up the coffee cup. "I'll get this to the lab, and if I were you, I'd buy that donkey some carrots."

Just then, Fabio sends me a clear picture of a red apple.

"Okay, boy, an apple it is."

By the time Brayden returns, Fabio is happily crunching away on a McIntosh I bought at the farmer's market. I'm about to suggest another cup of coffee when I feel the warm honey flowing through my chest.

My daughter's daughter, Grandmother says, *go see White Owl.*

"You two keep an eye on each other," I say, then I tell them I'm heading to the Trading Post. Neither of them looks pleased, but they let me go. As wonderful as it is, it's impossible for all of us to be glued at the hip twenty-four hours a day, seven days a week.

White Owl is no longer the grumpy old man that shut and locked the door in my face only a few short weeks ago. This White Owl is warm, welcoming, and glad to see me.

"Nanye'Hi, what brings you here today, my friend?" We sit down, and but for a few nods of his head and a couple of "I sees," he listens without interruption as I fill him in on the day's events.

"Let's go to my secret workroom," he says when I'm finished. "It is a place for those with Owl Medicine to come and learn." He turns to me, his eyes searching mine. "Please reveal its location to no one."

"You have my oath as your new Ghigau."

"But you are not Ghigau yet."

"Cunning . . . okay, then you have my oath as your friend."

White Owl leads me through rooms and out a back door, then into another building and through more rooms. I don't know what he's worried about; I'll never find my way here again. It must be some sort of test his students need to pass. Inside, counters line the walls with baskets full of stones and crystals. Some I recognize from my unlearning sessions but most I have never seen before. It feels amazing in this space. There are grow lights and water misting systems everywhere with a mixture of different kinds of herbs and plants. It might have been tropical except for the medicine wheel carving in the wooden floor. A couple of his students are in the corner working on projects. They look surprised to see us but say nothing. I can tell by their demeanor that the students recognize this as a sacred space and treat it accordingly.

White Owl quietly says something to one of the students, who then puts dried leaves, stones, and crystals into four separate bags for me. Then there is a fifth, larger bag. White Owl hands everything to me, and we make our way back to the storefront.

White Owl gives me specific instructions on what to do and how to do it. Then I purchase everything else that I need. We are not going to go anywhere or do anything without added protection. I just can't risk it. Michael is getting bolder by the day, not caring if he is detected. I'm entirely aware that he is trying to draw me out.

You are not ready, Nanye'Hi.

As soon as the Ghigau speaks to me, White Owl starts looking around. He feels her energy.

"Yes, she's here," I tell him.

He nods.

As I come out of the Trading Post, I glance over to where I'd left Brayden and Fabio and see that they are still drawing a crowd. Satisfied that they're safe for the time being, I head over to the feed store, where I purchase apple chips, four horse blankets with straps, (one pony size), and another apple. When I return to them, Brayden greets me with that sexy smile and Fabio shares a loud get-me-out-of-here bray.

"Is Nibs done for the day?"

"Almost," he says, "She just texted me. How'd everything go?"

"Good. We have a project for the evening. I'm putting everyone to work."

Brayden raises an eyebrow at me. "Oh really..." He points over my shoulder. "See, there's Nibs now."

A few minutes later, the four of us walk to the end of the street where his truck is parked. My mouth falls open in surprise when I see he has built panels up the sides and a ramp for loading.

"When did you find time to do this?" I ask as Fabio walks up the ramp like a pro.

Brayden flashes me a grin. "Where's your car, Nibs?"

She points across the street. "Nan and I will follow you."

"Are you okay?" I ask as we slide into the front seat.

"Yes, I felt someone watching me a couple of times today, but couldn't pinpoint who or where. There were just too many people on the street."

"I found his coffee cup next to the bench across the street from the clinic. He had a perfect view of the entrance, and of you going in and out."

Nibs makes a small gasp. "It was so frustrating not being able to zero in on the energy. It was weird, like it was so dark it almost, I don't know, repelled my ability."

"I got some things in town today that White Owl recommended. We have some work to do tonight if you're up for it."

"I'm up for anything that keeps evil at bay," Nibs says.

As is our routine, I cook dinner, Nibs does the dishes, and Brayden takes care of the animals. Later, Brayden and Daniel will do a perimeter check around the property. I feel better knowing that we have a deputy in the house and several watching the property while we sleep.

I gather the bags of supplies White Owl gave me and put on some music.

"I was going to open a bottle of wine but I think while doing this kind of work tea might be a better choice."

Everyone settles, and I hand each of them a bag with their name on it.

"What's all this?" Brayden asks.

"This is everything to make your own Medicine Bags. White Owl personalized the ingredients for each of you. To be effective, wear them at all times around your necks and close to the heart."

No one says anything.

"It's physically impossible for all of us to be together twenty-four hours a day," I say.

Still nothing. I expected flak from the deputy, but not from these two. I try to stare them down, and after a few moments of uncomfortable silence, Nibs says, "Nan, there's a lot about our heritage that I believe, and there's some I don't. This falls under the category of 'don't.'"

"I have to agree with Nibs on this one," Brayden says. Gaston nods his head in agreement.

"Really? After everything you've seen and experienced, this is where you draw the line?"

My daughter's daughter, tell them that I wish it.

It's amazing. As soon as I tell them this is a request or, more likely, an order, from Grandmother, everyone starts moving right away. I don't know what Gaston was thinking at that moment, but he did it anyway, and that's the important part. I wish I'd known of this little piece of magic earlier.

I have no idea what's in their private stash. White Owl explained to me that there's power in making your own medicine bag, that the action and intent is just as powerful as the ingredients themselves.

When we're done, Brayden, Nibs and I put our medicine bags on leather straps and place them around our necks. When I do, I feel the power run through my body. Gaston sets his aside then walks from the room, mumbling something about beer and tea.

"Wow," Nibs says, placing a hand over her medicine bag.

Brayden smiles and nods. "What are you doing now?" he says, watching me open a larger bag and lay out the contents.

"I'm worried about the animals, even with Fabio on duty. Now that the weather is getting cooler at night, I'm going to sew their ingredients—also chosen by White Owl—into their blankets."

"Can I help?" he asked.

"Thought you'd never ask."

Brayden will work on the blankets for Daisy and Storm while I work on Fabio's and Magic's. As I lay Magic's blanket out before me, I shake my head, hoping it will fit him. He has the biggest butt I've ever seen on a horse.

"Nibs?"

"Hmmm?"

"How are you going to convince Gaston to wear his medicine bag?"

"I'm not. I'm going to *tell* him he's wearing it."

This should be interesting.

When the deputy returns, Nibs walks up to him slowly, places the medicine bag around his neck and slips it inside his shirt.

"Wear this at all times," she says.

Turning to face me, she winks and walks out of the room. The deputy stares after her, looking a little spellbound. Brayden and I slip outside, and as we place the blankets on Magic, Daisy, Storm, and Fabio, I ask the Great Spirit and the ancestors for safety and protection for all of my family, the two-legged and the four-legged.

18

The Spring

"You up for a little construction today?"

I look at Brayden blankly. How can anyone be so energetic *before* coffee?

"How about going for a ride instead?" I suggest. "I feel like I've neglected Storm. I know he wants to connect. He's been visiting in my dreams."

I still feel Buddy's loss so intensely that I may have unknowingly been avoiding the connection.

Brayden envelopes me in a hug, and I know he understands my unspoken feelings. He then places a hand under my chin and lifts it.

"You're right, so let's play hooky today. I want to take you somewhere."

"Oh?"

"It's a surprise."

We get everything ready to go, packing food, extra clothes, first aid kit, and weather gear. The sky is so blue you'd swear it was a spring day, but we know better. Late summer or early fall in Oklahoma's Green Country could mean a beautiful bright crisp day or a sudden downpour accompanied by heavy winds. This key is to be prepared. This reminds me of Bernice, and I retrieve her from her hiding place and place her on my hip. Brayden stows his rifle on his scabbard on the right side of his saddle. Between the two of us, we're ready for anything.

I send Nibs a quick text to let her know we're heading out, and as a reminder not to go gallivanting around by herself. After yesterday, I can't imagine she would do that, but better safe than sorry. We should be back before she closes the clinic, but either way Gaston will be there to meet her. He's an attractive guy, quiet but strong, dependable, and steady. He would be a good match for Nibs if she'd let him. I feel the energy between the two of them. I also still feel the mystery that surrounds him, though I don't have the slightest clue as to its nature.

As always, I'm struck by how well Brayden and I work together, each of us taking care of whatever needs to be done, together and separately, making it all work. No strain or tension. Until Brayden, I didn't think relationships like this existed–true partnership with the added bonus of passion. I can't allow myself to fall completely, though; not yet, not while Michael is on the loose and terrorizing the village. This is something I need to face head-on, and it will take everything I've "unlearned" since I've been here, my military training, and help from the Great Spirit and the ancestors to get this done. I must have a clear head as well.

Brayden gives me a leg up on Storm, that frown and smile I've come to adore playing on his lips. I see it in his eyes; he cares for me. And I'm beginning to believe that I have something to offer him in return. I pray I get the chance to share it with him.

"Thanks for that. Wow, it's like being in the cab of a tractor."

Brayden settles in on Magic. I know that Daisy and Fabio wanted to come along, but with the way she's expanding, we thought we might give her a day off and left Fabio to keep her company. Fabio was a bit miffed, but when I explained that we needed someone to keep an eye on Daisy, he was okay with staying behind. I take a big breath in and sigh it out. Such a great day to get some exercise and breathe the fresh air.

We settle into a comfortable silence, and I connect to Storm. Like Magic, he is a gentle giant, and one of the sweetest horses I've ever met. Stable, reliable, and dependable. I've watched him quietly become part of the herd, not with force but with gentleness. He is a dream to ride, with that back and forth gait that makes you feel like you're sitting in a rocking chair.

I lean over and whisper in his ear. "Thanks for coming, boy, I'm delighted you're here."

The farther from the village we get, the better I feel. With Brayden in the lead, I can just relax. I notice the changing color of the leaves and can taste the freshness in the air. For the first time in a long time, I feel relaxed enough to think about everything that's happened and how oddly quiet it has been lately. At least with regard to hearing and seeing dead people. It concerns me a little; maybe it's just the calm before the storm. I know it's coming but vow not to let it spoil today.

After riding for about two hours, we come to a little stream and let the horses drink and graze.

"We're here," Brayden says.

"Where is here?" I ask as Brayden helps me down from Storm's enormous back.

"It's just over there, behind those trees."

With the horses happily grazing by the stream, we walk through a stand of trees and come to a spring.

"Oh, it's a hot spring," I say, watching the steam is rising over it. "I didn't bring a suit."

"Everyone knows you don't wear a suit in a natural hot spring, it kind of defeats the purpose." He starts stripping. Not a bad view, not bad at all. I follow his lead.

We ease ourselves into the hot spring, and it's glorious. Muscles relax around bones and my spirit along with it. We stay in the water long enough for our skin to prune. It's almost as sweet as the lovemaking that follows.

After a long time of cuddling, my stomach grumbles. Chuckling, Brayden pulls on his pants and walks over to a little camp area. He builds a fire and sets up for our picnic.

Food always tastes better over and around a campfire. After lunch, we spend a long time talking about everything, well, everything but being Ghigau and all things magical and mystical. Instead, we share those things most couples who are getting to know each other talk about—our childhoods, families, what kind of music we like, and if we like snow, rain, football or baseball. Simple everyday stuff that I'll never take for granted again. My favorite part is when we fall into a comfortable silence around the fire. This day will go down in my diary as one of the best days of my life.

"As much as I hate to leave," I say finally, "we should get back to meet Nibs."

"Me too, and yes, we should."

The feeling of oneness stays with me as we clean up the site and pack up our things. I still feel it, enveloping me like a warm blanket, as we begin our ride home.

Suddenly, I see Eagle swooping overhead, his warning screech breaking the spell.

I hear Brayden shout, "Nan!" followed by a shot fired in our direction, then silence.

Brayden, are you alive?

I desperately try to reach out through our bond, but I get nothing. Blindfolded and bound, my only comfort is the feeling of Storm moving beneath me.

Thank you, Storm.

Although I've never spent any time with him, Storm never misses a beat. He gives me sight, allowing me to see through his eyes, and though I knew Michael was behind this my heart still begins to race when I see him leading the horse.

How stupid I was to underestimate Michael! Why didn't I argue with Brayden about going to such a desolate place? As if Bernice and a shotgun could stop a man with Michael's military training. No doubt he'd been following us all day, watching us at the spring and listening to all we said. He had set a trap for us, and now Brayden may be wounded–or worse–because of it.

Where is everyone, Grandmother, Ghigau?

Why had no one warned us, and why didn't we feel him coming? Even the animals hadn't reacted like they usually did. This doesn't make sense. I'm almost afraid to think right now, let alone move. I don't want to draw his attention.

Great Spirit, please help Brayden. Grandmother . . . Grandmother, are you there?

I stifle a gasp when Michael's voice breaks the silence.

"I can feel you, you know. I know you're awake, but it doesn't matter. You're not going anywhere, and I have a surprise for you."

He continues on as if this were just an ordinary day, humming and whistling that damn country western song he sang in the military on the rare occasion when he'd had a few too many. He'd also sung it when he was holding me captive and drunk on cheap whiskey. Today is different, I realize. Today he is not drunk; he is crazy, evil and very determined.

He's still humming as he brings Storm to a halt, then places something over my mouth and nose. I try to hang on to consciousness, but I'm losing the battle.

——————

It's almost dark when I come to, with Magic licking my face. I try to open my eyes and feel a white-hot pain across my right brow. I reach up to touch it, feel something wet, and wince. Blood, and a lot of it. That's when I remember the gunshot.

"Nan!"

I try to get up and immediately fall backward. I lay there for a moment, willing the world to stop its spinning. I *must* get to Nan. I rip off a piece of my shirt and press it to my brow, but it is bleeding too profusely. I try to stand again, but the ground shifts under me and I land on my backside. I do the only thing I know to do. I send a message to Nibs in the old way, praying she gets it.

"Please, Great Spirit, help Nan."

I hear a voice and turn my head, peering through my good eye. There, standing next to me, is a woman, dressed in white buckskin from head to toe. On her right shoulder sits an owl and her left hand clutches a walking stick.

You have a Warrior's heart, Brayden, just like my Nanye'Hi. Rest, help is coming.

I am about to close up the clinic when I feel it—dark and overwhelming. Michael has made his move. I run outside, where Gaston is waiting for me.

"I can't tell if it's coming from Brayden, Nan, or Grandmother, but it's bad."

Then I pull out my phone and call White Owl. He gathers the People, and by the time Gaston and I get to Brayden's they are already starting to arrive. As he had before, Gaston takes the lead, organizing the People and infusing them with confidence. They will be ready to start searching at first light.

"Fabio must come with us," I tell him. "He will lead us to them."

I look over at the donkey, who is staring at us expectantly like he is ready to start right now. I notice Magic and Storm aren't here and assume they're with Brayden and Nan.

I feel Gaston's hand on my arm.

"Mary, tell me everything you feel and sense. Anything and everything will be helpful. Try not to filter."

I am surprised by his willingness to believe, that he is doing all of this based on my feeling. It speaks to his character. He writes down everything I tell him, then he looks up at me and asks, "Anything else?"

"Yes, they're alive but not together."

"If I get some maps do you think you can feel where they are, or at least get us close?"

"I don't know, Deputy, but I'll try anything you think will help."

He nods. "Good, and for God's sake, Mary, please call me Daniel."

At dawn, with White Owl in the lead, the People arrive with their horses and packs. Many have weapons.

"Fire one shot if you find them," Daniel says, "and two if you need help."

Armed with the maps of where I feel Brayden and Nan are, Daniel splits up the groups and assigns search areas. The first order of business is to find Brayden. He's injured and frantic. I've been sending him all the information I have and pray he is getting it. Mostly, importantly, I hope he knows we're on the way.

Finally, we set out, with Fabio taking the lead. I see Daniel raise an eye at that one, but then he just looks at me and nods. I know Fabio will lead us right to Brayden; I just hope we can zero in on Nan before it's too late.

I hear a screech overhead and see Nan's eagle. The deputy gives me the eye, and it's my turn to nod. We now have our escorts. The sun is barely topping the trees as we set out. White Owl smudges and blesses each group as they leave. He will be back at the Trading Post, holding space for everyone.

Up ahead, Eagle screeches loudly, and I look up to see him circling over a spot off the trail. We follow it, and I recognize the place as the hot spring.

"We're here," I yell and jump down from my horse. Daniel does the same.

That's when I hear it, a weak, "Here . . . Nibs, I'm over here…"

"Brayden." I find him folded in on himself, lying in the grass next to a fire that never got made, shivering and bleeding.

"Where's Nan?"

"We'll get her back, Brayden, I promise."

Daniel fires one shot and the search party gathers. Using his radio, he calls in life flight. Brayden needs to get to a hospital and fast. He's suffering from blood loss, hypothermia, a nasty wound above his right eye, and probably a concussion. It's a good thing we still have some summer left, or he wouldn't have survived the cool night temperatures, not with these wounds.

I hear the whirl of helo blades, and Daniel asks me, "Ready, Doc?"

"Yes, I have to stay with my cousin . . . please find her." Then, knowing I don't have time to be sensitive or finesse my way around it, I blurt out, "Follow the eagle and listen to the donkey–he's got great instincts and a voice loud enough for the next county to hear."

The usually stoic deputy looks startled for just a moment, then nods his head in agreement.

"We'll find her."

In the chopper, I lay a hand on Brayden's chest, sending energy into his weakened body.

He opens his eyes. "Nan, where's my Nan?"

"She's alive, cousin . . . she's alive. Right now you must rest."

"No, I cannot rest," he says, trying to pull himself up, "not until we get Nan back…"

"I'm sorry, Brayden, but that was not a request," I say as I stick the sedative-filled syringe into his IV line.

———

I come awake slowly, painfully, yet I am careful not to move or change my breathing pattern. I don't want him to know I'm conscious. Whatever he drugged me with was powerful, leaving my mind groggy and my mouth bitter with its aftertaste. I am still bound and lying on Storm, the constant movement now making me nauseous. The temperature is dropping rapidly, and I realize that though my fingers are stiff with cold my body is warm. For some reason I cannot fathom, Michael has placed a blanket over me.

I telepathically reach out to Storm and am surprised to feel no fear from him, just a fierce protectiveness of me. Looking though his eyes, I can see that it's dark. I try to calculate how long it's been since Michael took me, since I heard the gunshot.

God, the gunshot. He shot Brayden. Please, Great Spirit, please let him be okay.

I can't live with the alternative.

Grandmother, please...

I get no answer, and the darkness pulls me under once again.

When I awake again I am lying on the cold ground. Through my closed eyes I can see a sliver of light, and I slowly crack them open. The blindfold has slipped just a little, but it's enough for me to see an arched opening. Is it the doorway to a cabin? But no; there is a musty earthen smell, and I hear water dripping, but not from a faucet. It's hitting something soft that muffles the sound. Could I be in a cave?

I had never realized there were caves around here, not until I heard Gaston and his deputies talking about them one day. They said Michael probably wouldn't use them because of the inconvenience and distance from the village. We must have been traveling for a lot longer than I realized. I try to focus in on Eagle, Storm, Magic, Daisy, Fabio, Nibs, and Brayden, hoping someone gets the message.

An odd noise over to my left grabs my attention. It's the heart-wrenching sound of a wounded animal, and just outside my line of sight. I desperately want to go to it, but I cannot risk Michael knowing I'm awake. All I can do is send healing energy in that direction and ask for help. In my mind, I hear my grandmother.

Connect with your Totems, Nanye 'Hi.

My mind races with fearful thoughts—is Brayden alive—will they find me—what is Michael's next move? I realize I haven't heard him since awakening and wonder where he has gone, who he might hurt next.

Suddenly it hits me. Michael, and the terror he inspires, has controlled me for far too long. Even before I came to Galowhisdi, I struggled with what he had done to my crew and my life. He'd made me a victim, and I let him.

Even now, there is a part of me that just wants to go back to sleep and dream my way out of here. But life isn't like that. I must choose differently. Not only for myself, but also for everyone around me. I know there's a showdown coming, and it will be him or me. I'll opt for the latter, but right now, at this moment, I allow myself to feel helpless, alone, scared, and very tiny. I feel and identify every crappy, negative emotion I can imagine, giving myself time in the dark to muster up visions of whatever diabolical plan Michael may have for me so that I can move past it. Sometimes anger is a great motivator. As I move through the fear, I find myself royally and righteously pissed.

I calm myself enough to move into mindful breathing, in through the nose and out through the nose, over and over. When I'm centered, I call Eagle first, knowing that he has the bird's eye view. I keep hearing the whimpering of a wounded animal off to my left. I desperately want to help, but first things first. I try to connect with Storm, but it doesn't work. I won't allow myself to think about what that might mean. Fabio is much easier to connect with. Being connected with him was like a little slice of home. He sends me pictures of where he is and what's happening. I try to communicate with him to see where Brayden is, but that is not successful. Fabio then shows me pictures of the deputy riding Magic; he is leading the large search party trying to rescue us. Any relief I feel is overshadowed by the fear that Brayden is beyond rescuing. As I lose consciousness once again, I am sure of two things: the rescue party will find me, and without Brayden, I don't want to go on.

I wake with my head in Michael's lap, his large hand stroking my hair. The blindfold has been removed, and I see a fire, then the figure of a woman. What I thought was a wounded animal is actually Stacy, Nibs's assistant from the clinic.

Oh, Great Spirit, please let her live.

Stacy, who is sitting in front of me, is also bound and gagged. Her clothes are ripped, she has bruises everywhere, and there is a mixture of blood and tears trickling down her face. Her eyes are wide and fixed and she continues to make that horrible wounded animal noise. She is in shock.

At that moment, my only desire is to rip off Michael's limbs one by one and throw them into the fire. Anger comes from the bottom of my feet, bubbling up like boiling water to the back of my neck, and the top of my head.

Just when I feel that energy begin to gather I hear my grandmother's voice.

Nanye'Hi, not yet, you are not ready. Steady yourself, find your center. Help is coming.

I have learned to trust her and the Ghigau, and I manage to find that rhythmic yoga breathing, which eases the nausea I feel at his touch. It is in the moment I am completely back in my body that I hear Fabio's braying. My whole body collapses in relief.

"I was so close to finally having what I wanted!" Michael snarls, then delivers his parting shot–a sharp kick to my ribs. Through the agonizing pain I can hear Gaston frantically calling to Fabio, whose braying keeps getting closer and closer.

Then I hear Gaston's voice. "What the hell? Where is everyone going?"

I yell in response, "Here, Deputy! We're in here!"

A moment later, I see Gaston enter the mouth of the cave, followed closely by Fabio.

"Oh, thank God you're here! Stacy needs help."

He runs over to us and crouches down beside Stacy, feeling for a pulse and examining her wounds. "I think she'll be okay, but she's in shock. We have to keep her warm until the others can get here." He stands up. "I'll be right back."

He steps outside the cave, and a minutes later I hear two shots. He is letting the others know we're here.

"Brayden, how is Brayden?" I ask when he returns.

"He's alive. Nibs went with him to the hospital."

My relief is so deep I feel it in my feet.

"Nan, do you know where Michael is?"

Michael. I can't believe I have forgotten him.

"I don't know; he was here and then he just disappeared..." "You mean he left you here?"

"Yes, I mean, he heard Fabio braying and..." I point to my rib and wince. Gaston looks at me with concern, but I wave him away. "She needs you more than I do."

He nods, and we turn our attention to keeping the fire going and taking care of Stacy. I take over because every time the deputy gets close to her she makes that godawful wounded animal sound. I never want to hear that noise again.

Gaston disappears again, returning a moment later with a blanket from Magic's pack. He places it around me.

"It might be a while before anyone can get in here. I've got soup, water and coffee. We'll take turns keeping the fire going and watching over Stacy."

He glances around the cave and I know he's also thinking that we need to be prepared in case Michael comes back. But I can't think about that right now. Brayden is safe, and that's all that matters.

"Did you say you have coffee, Deputy? I think I love you."

19

Healthy Anger

This isn't my first helo ride, but it is Stacy's. I try to settle her down during the flight to the hospital and keep myself calm in the process. We haven't been able to get any updates on Brayden, and my nerves have had it. At least I don't have to worry about the animals–Gaston is taking care of them. I know I can never repay Magic, Daisy, Storm and Fabio for all they've done for me, but I'm going to try like hell.

When we arrive at the hospital, I settle Stacy in, then run down the hallway to Brayden's room. I stop in the doorway to gather my breath and see him sitting up in bed with Nibs trying to feed him some soup.

"Want some help with that?" I ask.

Nibs darts across the room so fast I don't have time to react. "White Girl, are you hurt?" she says, wrapping me in a tight embrace. "Do you need food? How's Stacy, is she hurt?"

"I'm all right," I say, though my rib is killing me. "Stacy is . . . I'm not sure. How is your patient doing?"

"He's being difficult, stubborn, and refusing help. I'd say he's doing fine."

Seeing Brayden, I'm suddenly reminded how close I came to losing him. My knees want to buckle and I make my way to a chair. I tell them as much as I know about Stacy's condition. Brayden never says a word, but his eyes follow me as though he's never seen me before. Then I feel it, a small spark that starts in my chest, slowly building until it feels like a roaring fire.

Nibs leaves to check on Stacy, and I slowly make my way over to the bed.

"I'm really glad to see you," Brayden says, but he's not meeting my eyes. Maybe he's decided that I'm just too much damn trouble after all; can't say that I blame him.

He sounds so proper and aloof. It makes me uncomfortable and nervous, so I just start talking. "I'm glad to see you alive, awake, and talking. No one knew if..." I trail off as my voice begins to crack. From someplace inside of me I feel a dam break, and the tears flow. I don't try to stop them; it would be useless anyway.

Brayden pats the bed, and when I sit down, he puts his arms around me, guiding my head to the special place between his neck and shoulder. Brayden is the one in the hospital bed, yet he is the one comforting me.

"Brayden, I'm so sorry for all of this. For the trouble I've brought into your life, Nibs's life, and into this village. My heart breaks for the innocent lives taken in my name."

He hands me the box of tissues at his bedside. "I'm sorry I wasn't able to protect you. It's my fault we were out there anyway. What if you hadn't come back or if he'd hurt you? I wouldn't survive losing you."

"Michael doesn't fight fair and from now on, I won't either."

"*We*—we won't. By the way, when was the last time you took a shower?"

"Oh, now you're not fighting fair, and for that, I'm eating your soup."

At Nibs's insistence, I'm checked out by the ER docs and against my protestations kept overnight for observation. I sleep uninterrupted for sixteen hours and wake to find Brayden sitting next to my bed.

"Ready to go home?" he asks softly.

"Yes. I need to check on everyone. How is Stacy?"

"She won't talk to anyone. Hasn't since she got here, not even to Nibs."

Before we leave, I stop to see her. I walk over to her bedside, lean over, and whisper in her ear. She looks at me but doesn't say anything. I stare her down until I get a response.

Stacy finally says, "Okay."

Nibs is standing at the door with her hands on her hips and a puzzled expression. Suddenly, a look of understanding crosses her face and she nods at me.

———◦———

God, it feels good to be home. Deputy Gaston is owed at least one good home-cooked supper for taking such good care of the animals. They are all wearing their fortified blankets and happily chewing away. Fabio greets us as only he can, loudly and with vigor. Daisy is so pregnant she looks like a potato being supported by four toothpicks. Storm and Magic come to the fence, and Magic nuzzles my ear while Eagle screeches a hello. He squares off with me, trying to communicate. I feel what he's sensing.

"It's okay, boy, I'll deal with it."

There's no trying to pull the wool over the eyes of these animals. They pick up on everything. Of course, they're that way for a reason—to be healing partners for the people sent to us. Brayden and I are merely guides in this partnership. I reach up and scratch between Magic's ears.

"I'm so grateful, big boy. Thank you."

Everyone gets a thank you gift, including Eagle, whose raw hamburger is left on the fence post.

Now it's time to handle this yucky stuff I'm feeling; it's so awful I don't even want to subject the totems to it. The anger from this Michael thing is billowing inside me, almost making me sick. I need to do something, but what? Maybe Grandmother will know.

I go to my room at Brayden's and sit on the floor, where I smudge and enter the Dreamtime. Grandmother begins talking to me almost immediately.

My daughter's daughter, how are you?

"I have been better, Grandmother."

You must find a way to release the anger, Nanye'Hi, or it will consume you.

"I feel it already, this kind of sickness that hangs over everything."

Ask the Warrior; he will help you.

"Grandmother, how do you feel about killing?"

Granddaughter, there is a time and a place for everything. Taking a life cannot be undone no matter what you do. We all live with the choices we make; choose wisely by making the ones you can live with.

"Grandmother, why couldn't I hear you in the cave?"

It was the drug the evil one gave you, Nanye'Hi. It blocks everything.

No surprise there. I had witnessed and lived with the effects of drugs and alcohol my entire childhood. It was the reason my mother hadn't heard the elders.

I find Brayden in the tack room, cussing like a sailor and throwing things around.

"Hey, let me ask you a question."

He whirls around and the mad is oozing out of him. "Sorry, Nan, I'm not in the mood."

"Yeah, I hear that, and neither am I. Got any suggestions on how to get rid of it?"

"Why in the hell would you ask me that?"

I throw my hands up in mock self-defense, knowing he's not mad at me.

"Let me think about this for a minute." He has his hand on his chin. I see when he gets the answer because a smile starts at his eyes and spreads outward toward the rest of his face.

"I think I've got it." He starts filling up the back of the pickup with tools, lumber, and God knows what else. When I try to help, he tells me, "I got this." I stay out of the way.

"Demo," he says, ushering me inside the cab of the pickup. The next thing I know we're back at my cabin pulling bloodstained boards off the deck.

"There is nothing like getting sweaty to release a proper mad," Brayden says.

We work in silence, settling into that unspoken rhythm of our partnership. We both wrestle with our individual emotions, and I'm feeling that Brayden is kicking things around in his head, as I am. By the time we finish putting the new boards in place, I am cleansed on every level.

"How did you know?" he asks.

"Grandmother."

"Ah."

"I have another project I'd like you to help me with, if you don't mind."

"Let me guess—you want me to build you another cabin?"

"No, just a corral and a few stalls."

The smile on his face disappears into something I wish I hadn't put there.

"Does this mean you're leaving?"

"I've imposed on your hospitality long enough."

"I was hoping you'd stay."

"Maybe when we both have some time post-crazy-psycho killer to find our bearings. I don't want to be away from you, Brayden, but I'd like not to rush anything, more than we already have."

I stand there, bracing for the argument I'm sure is coming, but he just cocks his head to one side, looks at me oddly and says, "Okay."

If he had fought me, I would have told him it's better this way. If I'm at Brayden's and under guard twenty-four seven, Michael won't try again, and he *must* try. His ego demands it. I know this as sure as I'm standing here. Drawing him out is the only way I can end this once and for all without anyone else getting hurt or dying.

I also would have told Brayden that I'm not trying to run him off; I'm just trying to get a little distance and perspective.

"We can start on the corral tomorrow," he says, but there's a glint in his eye. He's up to something.

"What do you have up your sleeve, Mr. Dove?"

"Hmmm?"

"Okay, if that's how you want to play it…"

For the next couple of weeks, we focus on building. Brayden and I do a lot of the work ourselves, and when we need more hands and strong backs, he calls a few of the guys he uses on construction jobs to help with the heavy lifting. When our project is complete, we have a beautiful and expanded version of a deck and a large corral with four individual stalls and built-in feeding boxes. Brayden will not allow me out by the stalls anymore because he and his team are planning some surprise. No complaints here; this is the kind of surprise I enjoy.

To thank everyone and to celebrate, I invite all the workers, Nibs, White Owl, Gaston, and a few others from the village over for an old-fashioned barbeque and deck christening. White Owl very graciously blesses the cabin, the grounds, corral, and stalls. As the sun begins to set, Brayden builds a fire in the firepit, and everyone gathers around it. It takes me by surprise when the drumming starts. One of Brayden's workers starts singing a Cherokee honor song, and though I don't remember ever hearing it before I find myself singing right along with him.

When the drumming stops, I tell them, "My friends and family, the Great Spirit and the ancestors have truly blessed me with your presence in my home and in my life, thank you." I think I'm finished, but somehow the words keep flowing through me. They are the words of my people. They are the words of Grandmother and the Ghigau.

20

Standing My Ground

Today is the day; I have butterflies in the pit of my stomach just to prove it. But it must be done; there is no other way. The smell of freshly brewed coffee stirs me from my bed.

Brayden and Nibs are waiting for me in the kitchen. *Ambush.*

Brayden hands me a cup of coffee. "I'll have the horses ready to go."

I see the set of his jaw and think, *Here it comes.*

"Are you sure about this, White Girl?" Nibs asks.

"There's no other way, Nibs. If I'm ever going to be rid of Michael I have to reclaim my space. And yes, it has to happen now. The third full moon is right around the corner."

Armed with another cup of coffee and feeling like I haven't heard the last of this, I focus on getting all my stuff packed. It's amazing how much stuff I've collected in the short time I've been in Galowhisdi, though aside from a few items from White Owl most of it is horse supplies. Not like

I've had a lot of time for clothes shopping, what with discovering a family legacy, meeting Brayden and connecting with my totem animals, not to mention being stalked and kidnapped by my psycho former commanding officer.

When I'm ready, Brayden helps me put everything in the back of my truck; he has also gotten the horses and Fabio ready to go. Even though Daisy is technically his, we don't want to separate them. The totems have all become so close, and Daisy is due soon.

"You look beautiful," I tell the horse when she waddles her way over.

Brayden says nothing as he slips into the driver's seat; he will drive the truck while I lead the herd back to my place on foot and Eagle flies overhead. Though I'll miss Brayden it feels right for me to be going home, and I know I've made the right decision. It will also feel good to get the animals home, and into their new accommodations. Soon I'll have to face the inevitable, but not today. Today I'm grateful for the sun shining through the trees and the freshness in the air that hints of fall. As we're walking, I allow myself to let my mind wander and feel my connection to Mother Earth. By the time we arrive home, I feel more grounded and present.

Brayden is waiting on us with a carefully neutral expression. "Are you ready?"

I nod and follow him around the corner of the house, my face splitting into a grin when I see the individual stalls. The fence will be the last thing built, but for now, the horses aren't going anywhere, the fence is more for keeping someone out than them in. The gate is a nice complement to the cabin and stalls we've already built, and it's not lost on me that he has gone above and beyond to beautify my home even though he prefers that I stay with him. I can only hope he still feels the same way when the time is right.

"Is something wrong?" I hear Brayden say, and I realize I have stopped walking.

"No, just the opposite. This all feels very right. Thank you."

As we draw closer, I see that there is more to my surprise—Brayden has added to the stalls the artsy, distinctive personal touches I recognize and love about all his work. I run my hands over the wood on the outside of the stall and see the expert craftsmanship of his work, no detail overlooked. He has even engraved each animal's name on the outside of their stall. I come to the last one and run my hands along the carved *Daisy*.

"Oh, Brayden, this couldn't be more perfect."

We had built this stall extra-large so when Daisy foals there will be plenty of room for both. For a time, mom and baby will need some privacy from the others. They even have their own outside area for exercise and grazing.

Just then Daisy waddles over and nuzzles his shoulder with her head as if to confirm a job well done.

As the horses and Fabio settle into their stalls, Brayden and I head inside.

"Come on, you wonderful, thoughtful, and talented man. Let's go make some coffee."

He's grinning from ear to ear, looking very much like a proud father.

"Nan, I know you have to do this your way. But for the record, I don't like it one bit."

I knew it! I also know how hard all this must be for him, especially after he'd been beating himself up for not protecting me from Michael last time.

"I appreciate that you care about me, more than you know, but this needs to end. Michael is not going to stop and I will not risk anyone else."

I see the look in his eye and brace for battle, but again Brayden surprises me by shaking his head.

"I know you have to do this, but I don't have to like it. Just don't forget your check-ins."

Our agreed upon safety plan includes me texting Brayden, Nibs, and White Owl every two hours and right before bedtime, no matter what. Gaston will send someone out on frequent but unscheduled times and they will always be in unmarked vehicles. Plus, I have Fabio, and he's better than any home security system on the market. What more can a girl need?

I offer him a ride home, but he declines, saying he "needs the walk"–Brayden-speak for sulking. After he leaves I spend an hour or so getting reacquainted with my cabin and realize how much I've missed home. It's special to me now, knowing what my ancestors had to go through to get here, and in a way it reminds me of my decision to serve as Ghigau. It wasn't that long ago when it felt like a curse; now I realize that is both a blessing and the result of the struggles and sacrifices of my Grandmother and the women before her.

I soon find myself back in my old routine: coffee, yoga on the deck, and healing work with the horses. Every day I connect with Grandmother in Dreamtime as she guides me in the ways of all things Ghigau. When I reach out to Grandmother today, she is not alone.

My daughter's daughter, Mrs. Dove is here to ask you something.

Then I hear another, rather melodious voice. Nibs' mother.

Honorable Ghigau, may I ask something of you?

I feel the pain emanating off her like a torrential rainstorm.

"Mrs. Dove, I am only your daughter's best friend, and am in service to the People. How I can help you?"

Please give my daughter a message for me. Tell her that I am sorry to have left her alone so soon and that my disease got the better of me. I am so proud of her. She will find love, but first, she must heal. You, Ghigau, can help her. You will know how.

"I will be honored to give her your message."

Thank you, Ghigau.

When Mrs. Dove fades away, and I'm alone with Grandmother, I ask her, "What happened to Nibs?"

I already knew her answer, and we say it together: "It's not my story to tell."

There are times when I'm totally uncomfortable with the whole Ghigau thing; this is one of those times.

My daughter's daughter, you must remember that the ancestors come from a different time. They are more traditional than the people of your generation. They pay respect to those that hold the position of Ghigau. Beginning with the original Nanye'Hi and all the sacrifices made over the years. They honor you and you, in turn, honor them. I am very proud of you, my granddaughter.

I send Nibs a text asking her to come over Saturday and join the horses and me for a ride. I get a response right away: *Yes, coffee first.*

I haven't seen or heard from Brayden in a few days and other than his responding to my texts we've had no contact. I'm the one who decided to leave, yet here I am feeling left out and forgotten. You'd think he'd check in on me, or something.

"Geez, girlfriend, get a grip," I tell myself.

Maybe he's glad to have his house back.

Saturday arrives, and I'm up early getting everything ready to go. Our favorite coffee that has just a hint of cinnamon is brewing and I set out a couple of cheese Danish to go along with it. The horses are fed, watered, and eager for adventure.

"Hey, White Girl, that coffee smells amazing." Nibs bounces into the kitchen looking like she'd had a week's vacation instead of a busy week at the clinic.

"It's just not fair how you can look this good after all the hours you put in at work."

"What's up?" she asks.

"What do you mean?"

"Why do you always try to do that when you know I know when something's up."

"Okay, but let's get on the trail first, and then I'll tell you all about it."

We'll take it easy today; Daisy's getting close and way too big to be wandering too far from home. I check the animals and make sure they're wearing their protection, then Nibs climbs on top on Magic and I on Storm. We opt for blankets instead of saddles since we're not hardcore trail riding. The sun is full and bright, and there's a crispness to the air. It feels like a little slice of heaven, and I turn my face toward the sun to feel it fully. We ride side by side, along the unmarked trail that leads through the sparse trees and will end up at yet another beautiful meadow. A perfect place for the horses to graze and water. Daisy and Fabio are trailing behind with Eagle screeching above as we ride.

"Okay, I've been as patient as I can, White Girl. Spill."

I tell Nibs about meeting her mother and the message Mrs. Dove had asked me to convey. I leave nothing out because it wouldn't be right to filter that kind of information. The ancestors and the Great Spirit know more than I can ever dream of knowing. I take a deep breath when I get to the tricky part. Nibs says nothing when I relay what her mother had said about finding love and the necessity of healing from the past, but her slumped shoulders and downcast eyes speak volumes.

"Nibs, please, whatever it is, you must know that you can tell me anything."

My best friend shakes her head, unable to speak. We continue to ride until we reach a clearing in the woods where the lush green meadow and clear running stream greet us.

"Whoa." I stop the horses, and slide off Storm, walking over to where Nibs and Magic are waiting. Nibs is still not speaking, but she dismounts. I place her right hand on Magic's withers and the other on his heart space.

"Just breathe, my friend. You don't have to say anything, not to me and not to him. Just allow your heart to open, and he will do the rest."

As Magic begins to work his extraordinary healing, I step away and pretend to be busy fussing with Daisy. In fact, I am doing my own magic by holding sacred space for them.

Whenever healing is taking place, the horses connect in a way accessible only to them. My heart swells as I see that faraway look in Daisy's eyes. I feel the energy shift as all of the horses and Fabio connect, creating an energetic link that completes a circle around Nibs.

When I hear Nibs sob, something I've never known her to do–*ever*–I'm a little taken aback. Do I go to her, or do I give her room? Privacy be dammed, I think, she needs me. I step forward and place a hand on her shoulder.

After shedding many tears, Nibs says, "Now I understand what you mean about the horses. For the first time in years my heart feels whole, full, and open."

I give Nibs a hug, then go to each animal and embrace them as well. I send Eagle my love and a "thank you." The air around us is different on the ride home. We talk like two teenagers about the latest gossip and who the most handsome men in town are. Nibs doesn't tell me what happened, and I don't push her. The Great Spirit and the horses healed her. That's what important.

When we get home, we brush down the horses and feed them, giving Daisy a little extra pampering. As I tuck myself into bed and reach over to turn out the light, Grandmother speaks to me.

It's your turn to heal, Nanye'Hi. You must face what you do not want to see.

"Great, there's more?"

21

Medicine

I am worn out from the day, yet sleep eludes me. After hours of tossing and turning in frustration I finally get up and go to the living room. This night is going to be a long one, and I'll need a book to get me through it. I scan the shelves and come across one I haven't seen before. I don't know how that's possible since I've scoured these shelves more than once. This book has no title, the cover is faded and brittle. As usual, I create a ritual around it, first building a fire in the fireplace and making some chamomile tea before retrieving the book.

It takes a moment for me to realize that what I am looking at is the original Ghigau's personal diary.

By now, my eyes and brain adjust quickly to the words. I don't stop to think about them being English or Cherokee; they're just words, and they come alive under my hand as I run it across the page. I begin to hear them in my ear, like she's telling me a story.

I read through the night, spellbound. It is not just a diary, but the Ghigau's healing journal. It makes me feel connected to her in a way that I haven't before. We share many of the same gifts, and her words will help me to help others. I'm particularly drawn to an entry about calling the energy of the ancestors and how to access it in ceremony to cleanse the healer after a session. I've always worried about the horses and how they deal with the aftermath of a healing session, and now, as I read this, I feel guilty for not finding a way to help them.

Set your guilt down, Nanye'Hi. Everything has happened in the right time.

"Thank you, Ghigau."

As the sun comes up I head outside and find all of them standing at the fence, waiting for me.

"Well, it seems I'm the last one to know, as usual."

Fabio brays his agreement as I step into the corral.

I spend time with each one, thanking them for the work they do and just loving and brushing them.

After everyone settles down, I take Fabio into the adjacent corral. I offer a smudge ceremony for healing and a prayer for protection to the Great Spirit. I visualize a brilliant golden light coming from the heavens to filter through me into my hands and flowing into Fabio. I feel an overlay of warmth surround us with the energy thick, comforting, calm, and peaceful. I allow myself to be guided by the ancestors and the angels as they enfold us.

I follow this same pattern with Magic, Daisy, and Storm. They have the same reaction as Fabio, and I feel the immediate renewal of their spirits as they become lighter and happier. I apologize profusely to all of them for not doing this sooner, but they convey to me that no apologies are necessary. They are happy, healthy, and extremely relaxed. I'm excited to share this with Brayden, providing he still wants to do this work. Now that I know, we will do routine healings on all of them. I pick up a pitchfork and start mucking stalls. There is nothing like cleaning up horse manure to get some clarity.

There are eight days left until the next full moon—my last initiation. Daisy can have that foal at any time, and Michael is still out there, targeting everyone I love—not just Nibs, Brayden, White Owl, and Gaston, but the People of Galowhisdi. Do I have what it takes to protect them? The answer is almost irrelevant, for there is no one else who can do it.

"A moment of self-doubt is all that's allowed here; the stakes are too high."

But of course it is much more than a moment; the thoughts of Brayden and everything else play on a loop in my mind until I feel the beginnings of a headache. Instead of pushing them away, I allow myself time to ruminate on them. At this rate, the stalls will be spotless by the time I'm done. I let it all out in sweat as I sift through all the worrisome thoughts, irrational fears, and just plain crankiness. When I'm done, I take a deep breath and release them, along with all the mental gymnastics.

Will it always be so difficult if, or when, Brayden and I get together? There's so much to consider. Becoming Ghigau is kind of like being a single parent. The People of Galowhisdi are my children, and they come first. I place my hand on my heart, marveling that the inhabitants of a village I never wanted to visit have, in a very short time, come to mean everything to me.

Now you see, Nanye'Hi.

"Yes, Grandmother, I do. "

My daughter's daughter, there is always room for love.

I arrive at the Trading Post to find the door locked with a note that says, "Coffee." I find White Owl sitting at an outside table waiting for me.

"Are we playing hooky?" I ask.

"No, Nanye'Hi, we are done."

"What do you mean, *done*?"

"You have unlearned everything very well. Everything that you still need to learn, you will learn over your lifetime. There is no reason to rush or force it. The information you need will be there for you when you're ready."

"What now?"

"Quit hiding from your friends."

"What do you mean? I'm not hiding from anyone."

As soon as I say it, I hear the truth behind his words. Crap.

"You're right, White Owl, I apologize. I have more than a few things to make up for."

"Young Nanye'Hi, people love and care about you, they only want to be a part of your life."

I suddenly have the oddest and very powerful feeling that I need to get home.

White Owl, seeing the look on my face, says, "What is it?"

"Excuse me, White Owl, but I need to go."

At first glance, I don't see anything off, but when I go out back to the horses, I see Daisy, restless, breathing odd, and walking up and down the fence line. Daisy reaches around and nudges her belly with her muzzle. I text "baby" to the cousins and start stroking and talking to her, trying to reassure her.

Brayden is first to arrive, saying, "Good call. She's definitely in labor."

Poor thing can't keep still; she just keeps walking up and down the fence line and in and out of her stall. All we can do is watch and encourage her. Magic, Storm, and Fabio are in the same boat.

"I'll go make some coffee," I say.

"And sandwiches, please; it's going to be awhile."

"Great idea."

From the kitchen window, I watch Brayden as he takes care of his girl, mixing her a special batch of sweet oats topped with molasses. He puts fresh hay in her stall and fills up her water tank, quietly singing to her. My heart just about bursts open from all the love.

"Hey, White Girl!" Nibs announces as she bounds in the front door.

"In here."

"How's our girl doing?"

"Look," I say moving away from the window so she can watch Brayden with Daisy.

"Pretty sweet, huh?" Nibs says, "He has a way with the ladies."

"Yes, yes he does."

Nibs put her arm around my shoulder, giving me a half hug. "Just tell him, that's all."

"I've been a horrible friend, Nibs, I'm sorry."

"I don't have a clue what you're talking about. Did you think we wouldn't understand that you needed to take a minute to yourself? You've been through a lot and have had some pretty important decisions to make." She makes a big circle with her finger. "We... are all good."

"Thank you, Nibs, for understanding and for being the best friend anyone could hope to have."

"Don't you know it," she jokes. "Let's grab our coffees and head out to Daisy; it won't be long now."

"How do you know –" I begin, then I remember Nib's empathetic gift, which sometimes seems like anything but. "Oh my God, how horrible does that feel?"

Nibs shrugs. "It only lasts long enough for me to know what's going on, and then it leaves. It's not like I get the full experience of the pain. It's more like an impression of the pain."

Brayden sort of grunts as I hand him a sandwich and a cup of coffee. Nibs and I sit on the deck and watch as Brayden expertly makes his way around Daisy, helping when required, and then staying out of the way. Nibs times—and feels—when the contractions are coming, and Brayden continues to encourage and support Daisy, which I look on in awe.

Daisy is sweating and becoming even more restless. She lays on the ground, moving from side to side, then she gets up and walks some more. This cycle continues for a while. Finally, the time comes and she goes down for the final push with Brayden at her head and me directly at eye level. An overwhelming feeling of love envelops all of us as I place a hand on Daisy's forehead, sending her energy and love; it courses through all of us.

She arrives. A beautiful palomino and brown paint foal with a white star in the middle of her forehead, just like Buddy. Sniffling is heard all around, along with a lot of snorting and grunting from Daisy, which I understand as, "Love you, now go."

It's time to leave and let mom and baby get acquainted.

We don't even make it to the deck before I fling myself at Brayden. He doesn't ask any questions, he just holds me in his arms, saturating my face with kisses.

"Finally," he says.

Nibs disappears into the house, making noises about making more coffee. We sit shoulder to shoulder, hands entwined, as we watch Daisy.

"Hey, she needs a name," Brayden says.

"Cowgirl, her name is Cowgirl."

After we make sure that Daisy successfully delivers an intact placenta, Brayden puts down more fresh hay and we head indoors. Nibs has a fire going, and it bathes the room in a rosy glow as we talk and prepare a simple supper.

"The next full moon is less than one week away," Nibs says.

"Yes."

"Well?" Brayden asks.

"Well, what?"

"What have you decided?" Brayden asks, and I can tell by Nibs's smile that she already knows.

"If the Great Spirit will have me, I am going to make myself available to be Ghigau."

Brayden smiles. "I knew it from the very beginning."

I don't know what I expected him to say, but it wasn't that.

"What do you mean, you knew it? How could you know when I didn't even know?"

"Because I knew you would do what is right and for the best and highest good of everyone. I just knew."

Nibs nods her head in agreement. "Yep, me too."

I look from one cousin to the other and start shaking my head. "I don't know what I'd do without you two. You're absolutely nuts, both of you, but I love you."

Nibs give us a sly look. "You know, suddenly I'm not all that hungry. I'm going to head out, give you two a chance to catch up."

"You're going back to my place, right?" Brayden asks.

"Yes, cousin, and Gaston is there. No need to worry." She turns to me. "Girls day tomorrow?"

"If I can get Brayden to watch over my girls, then yes."

After Nibs leaves, the quiet becomes a little uncomfortable, at least for me. Brayden has that unreadable frown and smile thing going on.

"Are you checking out my bicep again, lady?" he asks when he sees me watching him.

"Of course."

Brayden's arms are around me in an instant. It's like we have always been together. Being smothered in kisses is nothing to complain about, but shouldn't we at least have a conversation first?

"Brayden...Brayden? We need to talk."

"Yes, go ahead. I'm listening," he says.

"Okay, but it's tough for me to talk with you seriously when you're doing all of this."

"Doing all of what?"

"You know exactly what."

I force myself from Brayden's arms and sit on the ottoman to face him directly. Grabbing both hands, I looked him straight in the eye.

"I'm worried."

"About?"

"I'm worried about becoming Ghigau and what that means for us. I'm worried about Michael still being out there. I'm worried about what he could do to the people I love. I'm worried about Nibs, the horses, and the People. I'm worried about *everything.*"

Brayden grabs me, bringing my rambling to a halt, and leads me back to the sofa. He puts his arms around me and swings my legs onto his lap; my head rests on his chest. The last thing I remember before falling asleep is the feel of his protective embrace, a light kiss on my forehead, and a whispered, "I love you."

The smell of freshly brewed coffee and the sound of male humming coming from the bathroom wakes me. The sun is shining brightly, and I'm still on the sofa. I can't believe that we slept together on the sofa, completely clothed like teenagers. What could be better? That question is answered when Brayden comes out of the bathroom still dewy from the shower, wearing only his pants slung low on his hips. Yes, that is definitely better.

"Sleep well?" He encircles me in a hug.

"Yes, as a matter of fact, I did, better than I have in a very long time."

"You know we didn't get very far in that talk last night," he says, his tone serious, "Maybe we should try again?" He puts his hands on either side of my face and tilts my chin up so that we're looking eye to eye.

"Yes, of course."

"Quit worrying so much. Everything's fine, and I love you."

"I love you too," I say, then I quickly push past him and head into the bathroom, lock the door, and turn on the shower. I am not having this conversation with bedhead and morning breath. That is not happening. I refuse.

"Hey, that's not fair," Brayden calls, but I'm already standing under the warm water.

When I come out of the bathroom, Brayden hands me a steaming mug. Definitely nothing sexier than a shirtless man bearing a freshly brewed cup of coffee.

"What was that all about?" he asks.

I shrug, not wanting to explain the whole bad breath thing. Now that I'm somewhat presentable, I want to ask a whole bunch of questions like "What now?"" and "What does this mean?" Questions I know he can't answer. Still, I want to ask them. But I don't. Instead, I decide to let him take the lead, relax, and enjoy where we are at this perfect place in our relationship. My heart does a little fluttering at the thought of *relationship*. I say it to myself a few more times until my heart stops skipping a beat.

"Oh, look," I say and point out the window so that Brayden can see this glorious sight. Cowgirl is running up and down the fence line with Fabio on the other side running along with her. Daisy looks unamused as she munches on her hay. I can feel the protective energy flowing off Magic and Storm as they stand, tails to the wind, holding space for the herd. They even seem different this morning. It makes sense that having a baby around would do that to someone, whether that someone was two-legged or four-legged.

Brayden and I stand there for a long time, arms linked, watching the horses. The moment of complete peace is interrupted by a knock on the door, and we look at each other, eyebrows furrowed. No one we know would knock.

"Wait here," he tells me.

I'm right behind him.

Brayden carefully opens the door. It's Nibs.

"What are you doing, you never knock?"

"Well, I didn't want to interrupt anything."

Brayden looks to me and then to Nibs. "I love her, she loves me, end of story." He turns to me and adds, "We'll talk tonight" before going outside to feed the horses.

"He's a man of few words," I say.

"Yes, but they are powerful words."

"Is this too weird for you, Nibs? Do you approve, disapprove?"

Nibs laughs. "You ask now? Really, White Girl? It's not like you two have been fooling anyone. Of course, I'm very happy for you. Just don't ever ask me to take sides when you're in a fight."

22

A Mystery Revealed

While Brayden is keeping watch at home, Nibs and I head to Tahlequah for a girl's day, something we haven't had time for since I arrived at Galowhisdi. At the top of our to-do list is shopping, having lunch, and most importantly, making a visit to the Northeastern University Campus. I'm hoping to visit the Center for Tribal Studies to get a better understanding of my family tree and shed some light on some of the many unanswered questions still running around in my head. Some of the information is available online, but the text and manuscripts I need most are only available in hardcopy. I tell myself that whatever we find is better than we have now.

Nibs uses her alumni card to get in, and we hunker down for a cram session. At first, nothing stands out as particularly important. Most of the information we find is in folklore form, more story than fact. This is the way of my People, handing down oral history through generations. Finally, I come across something I've not read in the Ghigau's healing journey or the Ghigau diary.

"Nibs, look at this."

"What'd you find?"

She moves behind me and looks over my shoulder as we read an account by the original Ghigau. We are both glued to the words.

I made my way to the stream through the forest and sat down on the bank, putting my bare feet into the cool water. I watch as the clear mountain stream flows over the rocks, enjoying the chill that runs up my body. The heat has been unrelenting for days, and I've been struggling to do the simplest of tasks. Maybe I shouldn't be trying to do anything in this heat. Instead, I should be resting and staying cool.

Being alone is not so bad. My bare feet are dangling in a fresh mountain stream, and I'm listening to the birds and just enjoying being outside. I can relax and let everything be quiet and peaceful. I stay like this for a long time, listening to the water as it runs over the rocks to its destination. It's an amazing experience every time I remember to come out here and be at peace with what the Great Spirit created. The cold water feels so good and is rejuvenating in this heat. I can't help myself and strip off my clothes, plunging into the cold mountain stream. No sooner do I get comfortable, when I begin hearing the soft hypnotic sound of a flute. As quickly as I can, I try to scramble to the riverbank. I'm not fast enough.

"Huntress, I see you've been waiting for me." The Kokopelli laughs.

He does not look like the Kokopelli, but I know from the sound of his flute and the laughter in his voice who and what he is.

"Stay where you are, Kokopelli, you can't fool me, I see through your disguises. We have met before. Those of us that have met you can't be fooled by your nonsense, so you'll have to make do with the naïve and those who choose not to see."

Ever the prankster, he talks to my bruised and broken heart, "Huntress, I know that you've felt me in your Dreamtime. I have spoken to you. Have you not felt me?"

I almost come out of the water, my heart so full of longing and loneliness after the loss of my husband. In my weakest moment, the Great Spirit calls to me, "Call your totems."

First, I call on Bear for his courage and protection. When I don't feel that I have the strength to resist, I ask Horse for the power to carry me above the sound of his flute and handsome disguise. It's here that I see him for what he is, a hunchback Casanova running around the country, without a home, without love, and without any real family.

When I feel my power and strength return I tell him, "Kokopelli, take your flute and your seed somewhere else. You are not the one foretold in my Dreamtime. The Great Spirit does not make mistakes, nor waste sweetness on an imposter. I am done with you."

As I turn my back on him, Kokopelli walks away with a sad and soulful flute. I go back to the water's edge and sit on the bank. Looking into the water, I slide into Dreamtime. My reflection in the water blurs slightly, and I slip into another time. Many women are sitting on the other side of the riverbank. It startles me to hear their voices and the music of the Kokopelli's flute. The sun sets and rises, finding in this morning that many of the women are with child, their lives ruined from disgrace. Throughout time, Kokopelli has done this, fills his insatiable desires at the ruin of so many.

Suddenly the room seems way too small and sweat is running down my back. I need to get out of here and quickly make my way through the dusty shelves and archives, finding the closest exit. Fresh air hits my face, and I find a step to sit on. Nibs follows me, handing me a bottle of water.

"Is this what Michael is doing?" I ask.

"It seems very familiar to me, and it does *feel* that way."

"Sometimes it just gets to be too much."

"Yes, it does," Nibs says.

On the drive home, Nibs asks, "Have you seen him—Kokopelli—in his true form?"

"No—maybe—I'm not sure. Things get confusing sometimes between what is my memory and what belongs to the grandmothers."

"I guess it would be like me trying to decipher if a feeling I'm having belongs to me or someone else. Sometimes it seems so clear and yet, even after a lifetime of doing it, it still gets confusing."

That's the end of serious discussion as I feel the energy shift around me.

"So, what happened last night?" I ask.

"Oh my God, you did not just go there."

It makes me laugh; rarely do I get the chance to surprise my friend.

Nibs had left my house early and returned to Brayden's… and Deputy Gaston.

"What do you mean?"

"What I mean is, why are you blushing? Nibs, you can't keep secrets; it's not fair when you know all of mine."

Nibs's laugh is one of my favorite things to hear. I don't let it distract me from my mission.

"He is very handsome, capable, strong, and yet there is some mystery, right?"

"I agree, let's find out what it is."

"Yes."

Only Nibs and I can switch from saving the world to girlfriend stuff so quickly.

"If it weren't for the mystery?"

"I'd be all in."

"Okay, then sleuthing it is." I put my head back, smiling at the thought of solving a fun puzzle for once. Then I remember what Brayden had said to me earlier.

"Crap!"

"What's wrong?" Nibs asks.

"Brayden wants to talk tonight."

"Oh?" Nibs asks, "And you don't want to?"

"No, yes, I don't know. I actually brought it up last night, but then we fell asleep and this morning he said the whole I love you thing and now… I don't know if I'm ready."

Nibs raises an eyebrow at me. "Do you believe that it will matter to him?"

When we arrive at my cabin Brayden has dinner waiting. Nibs makes a swift exit, excusing herself and requesting a doggie bag so that she can go back to Brayden's and take a hot bath. I shoot her a look to say, "Not cool," but she just winks at me and heads out the door.

Once we're alone, I start feeling very fidgety and nervous. I don't know what could be making me feel this way.

Right.

"This is a wonderful dinner, and you are a wonderful man."

"I'm sensing a *but* coming."

"I care for you very deeply, and yes, I love you. Which is the main reason I need to put this on hold for now."

"What's going on? I thought we passed that stage?"

I can see the hurt on his beautiful face. I feel his disappointment and frustration.

"Nan, I don't know how much more of this merry-go-round I can handle. Yes or no. Figure it out."

The next thing I hear is the door slamming shut behind him. I'd hurt him deeply, again. For that alone, I will forever regret the last few minutes of my life. He is gone, and that's on me. I can't make it right, at least not now.

The stakes are high, both in the present and the past. The research at the library has confirmed my worst fears. From the moment I'd been born, *he* had been destined to stop me. Michael's predisposure to evilness made him susceptible. Now, Michael doesn't even realize what he has become. The entire reason for his existence is targeting anything and everyone I love and care about to keep me from becoming the next Ghigau. And he will not stop until that mission is accomplished. He has already proven that. I must face him alone to keep them safe.

Not alone, Nanye'Hi, never alone. You cannot protect them.

"I am sure as hell going to try."

Remember what it means to be Ghigau.

Grandmother sends me a picture of Magic, Storm, and Fabio holding space for Daisy as she gave birth to Cowgirl.

All we can do is hold space for each other. The rest is all about choices, destiny, and the plan the Great Spirit has for all of us.

After checking on the horses, I climb into bed and cry for Brayden. I cry because I know I've hurt him. I miss him and having his arms around me. I even miss the way he smells.

Three days, Nanye'Hi... Grandmother says, her voice drifting away as I fall asleep.

The sun filters in through the trees, making shadows on my bed. Slowly I stretch and listen to Fabio voice his desire for breakfast when I hear a familiar humming.

Brayden, what is he doing here?

After looking in the mirror at my swollen eyes, I am determined not to let Brayden know how devastated I am at my own decision. Quickly, I dress, brush my hair, and try to disguise my swollen eyes the best I can. I stop at the coffee pot, fix Brayden his liquid candy bar and head outside.

"Good Morning."

"Morning," he answers. As he turns to face me, I brace myself for his sadness.

What the hell? He doesn't even look fazed. Not in the least.

"Thanks for the coffee."

"You're welcome."

"I think it's about time for a little halter training for Cowgirl. Do you want to help?"

"Of course, love to." Wow, so adult and very polite.

"What would you like me to do?" I ask.

"Let Daisy know what I'm going to do so she doesn't get upset. That would help tremendously."

I send Daisy the images of what Brayden will be doing, and she watches. He talks to Cowgirl gently, rubbing her all over with the halter so that it smells like her. It's a beautifully handcrafted halter, and I know without asking that he made it.

He clips it around her neck with a lead rope and just leaves it there to gauge her reaction. He doesn't try to force her. Cowgirl is unaffected by any of it. The halter not only smells like her now, but it also smells like him. She and her mother are his world. Everyone else is okay too, but I know that these two are his sun and moon. When Brayden reaches up to put the halter over her ears, head, and nose, she doesn't even flinch, standing very still. I'm in awe of Brayden's gift with the horses.

"That went better than expected."

"I expected nothing less."

He thanks me for the coffee and leaves, saying, "I'll come back to feed them at dinner."

I'm puzzled by his behavior, and if I'm honest, maybe even a little hurt that he's not devastated.

I have three days until the third full moon. The time of choosing for me, and acceptance for the Great Spirit. Have I prepared enough? Am I enough? After doing yoga on the deck, and smudging, I enter the Dreamtime and ask the Great Spirit.

"If it is your will, I wish to see what is most important for me to know."

I am gifted with the appearance of Owl. This totem is unlike any other I have seen before. The sheer power of his being makes me want to run and leave the Dreamtime. Ghigau's voice calms me.

Nanye'Hi, you must see what you do not want to see. Light and dark are only opposites, just like day and night. It is the intention of the one wielding the request for power that makes it either of the light or of the dark.

I close out Dreamtime by sending blessings to the spirit of Owl, Ghigau, and the Great Spirit.

I try to remember what I know about Owl medicine. I know of White Owl's medicine, but this is not the same. When I first arrived at Galowhisdi, I would sleep with the windows open and hear the owls, their voices of "hoo, hoo" putting me to sleep. This is something different. This is more of a foretelling or warning. I know from my lessons with White Owl that Owl medicine, when used for the light, can illuminate the truth in all things. Owl medicine allows the gift of being able to discern truth when major deception is at hand.

The real question is, who is trying to deceive me and using Owl medicine to do it?

I know it isn't Michael. He is too single-minded to be using this kind of deception. No, it must be someone with some degree of skill. This is the work of someone extremely good at hiding the truth about who and what they are. It's someone with the ability to disguise themselves from everyone, including an empath, a medicine woman, and an energy worker. Who could it be?

This is way beyond my skill level and bigger than me. I need the cousins to weigh in on this and get proactive, before the third moon. I'll need to let go of anything personal right now and tackle the problem at hand. Becoming Ghigau is the most important thing for the People, and now it has become *everything* to me. For so many years, I ran from my heritage, even as far as Afghanistan, but if I've learned anything since coming here it's that there is no escaping one's destiny. I must be worthy and fight for it. But I don't have to do it alone. In my soul, I suppose I've always known. This is my job, my life purpose, destiny, and honor–to hold space for the People so they can live, love, and grow in the light.

As Ghigau, I must be able to see evil for what it is and respond accordingly, rather than cowering in fear. I feel the empowerment growing within me as well as the awareness that all I have to do is accept it. No more doubts, halfway ins or halfway outs. In order to become Ghigau, I must surrender fully.

23

The Third Full Moon

It's the morning of the third full moon. As the coffee pot does its thing I gather everything I need and wait for Brayden and Nibs to arrive. The cousins, along with the horses and totems, will hold space for me and witness the ceremony. If I want to save myself and the People, nothing, absolutely nothing, can interrupt it.

The enormity of what is about to take place presses in. This is not only my destiny but the destiny of my grandmother and so many who came before her. It is also a partnership of the People and their decision to continue to live in the light. If they had not made that decision, I would not be here.

"Thank you, Ghigau, for guiding me and for holding the space for so long. I am deeply grateful, and I will miss you."

Thank you, Nanye'Hi, for hearing and answering the call of your spirit.

"Hey, White Girl," Nibs calls as she walks in, but her voice and her tone are very serious. Brayden is right behind her. Quiet.

"Thanks for coming."

Brayden meets my eyes. "We're in this together, right?"

I pour the coffees and we sip them as we work out the details, then Brayden slips out back to feed and ready the horses. Thirty minutes later, he has Magic and Storm saddled. Fabio, who will follow with Daisy and Cowgirl, will carry our supplies in his packs.

I glance around at the horses, then back at Brayden. "Hey, aren't we missing some transportation?"

Just then, Deputy Gaston comes riding up on a sorrel mare leading a gelding.

"Thanks for coming, Deputy." I throw a quick look at Nibs, who is suddenly fascinated with something on the ground. Although the deputy is here to help in any way he can, my gut tells me that in his heart he's doing it for my best friend. I like it, and him.

"Meet Jack and Jill," he says.

"Really, Deputy, you couldn't come up with anything more original than that?" It makes me laugh.

"Don't judge until you get to know them."

It doesn't take me long at all to size it up. Jack and Jill are extremely bonded; their names are perfect.

We get in line, Jack and the deputy side by side with Nibs and Jill. I'm in the center on Storm, followed by Brayden on Magic. This is one time I will not fuss about being protected. The stakes are too high.

I offer a smudge ceremony before we begin, asking for protection for the two-legged and four-legged alike. As we begin, Eagle screeches his cry from above. We are complete. I should feel safe, protected, and surrounded by love. I do feel that, but something else as well; an encroaching energy held at bay by the thinnest of shields. Invisible to the eye but significantly felt. Nibs confirms it by turning around and nodding to me. The horses become jittery and spooked.

"What is it, Nan?" Brayden asks.

"I'll try to find out."

After connecting with Storm, I see the picture of what he can smell rather than see. In the tree line are several totems scattered along the trail. I connect with the horses and calm them down quickly.

"To the right, Wolf. On the left, Bobcat. Ahead on the rock above is Bear," I tell them.

The deputy starts to remove his rifle from his saddle scabbard.

"No need for that, they are paying tribute," Nibs says.

I close my eyes and send them my gratitude.

Up ahead on the left is the little clearing in the tree line that marks the opening to the Sacred Place. My heart wrenches a little as I remember being here the last time with my beloved Buddy.

Brayden feels it. "Nan?"

"Yeah?"

"I'm sorry."

The relief of being at the Sacred Place fills me, but I'm not satisfied until everyone is inside.

We all get busy unsaddling horses, unpacking gear, and setting up camp.

The deputy turns and looks at me, eyebrows furrowed. "How could I not know this was here?"

"Because you weren't supposed to know yet," I say simply.

"Okay, you three try to take it easy on me. This stuff is pretty new to me."

I give him a wry smile. "You're not the only one."

Brayden gets busy finding firewood to distract him. I know it's Brayden's way. When he doesn't know what else to do, he gets busy with something.

"Let's go by the river," I say to Nibs.

She nods her head.

It's such a beautiful place, especially this time of year; the leaves are beginning to turn color, and the water is almost too cold. The grass is green and soft, inviting.

"At sundown, the People will come," I say.

"Are you nervous?" Nibs asks.

"Nervous and afraid." I kick my feet in the cold river water. "I'm scared of what this means for you and Brayden. Neither of you asked for this."

"Okay, White Girl, let's clear this up right now. You didn't ask for it either, yet here you are."

"You're right, I didn't, but now I wouldn't change any of it except that you and Brayden are in danger."

"We've always known that we're different. Now we can make that difference mean something. Something to be celebrated and to be of service with our gifts. What could be better?" Nibs takes a breath and continues. "It isn't your decision to make, or your responsibility. Each one of us, at some point, said yes."

"Is that it?"

"Yes, that's it, so quit pushing us away."

"Am I doing that?"

Nibs looks at me for a moment, her hand on her hip, then she goes to join the deputy.

I take a few moments to observe my friends. I watch Nibs explaining to Gaston the significance of the ceremony and what they should expect. I watch Brayden as he does his busy work. He has been polite and friendly but withdrawn. Did it even bother him in the least that I had stepped away? Am I so easily forgotten? I can't think about this now. There's too much to do.

When the sun starts to set, I go to the river to get ready for the ceremony. The water is freezing now, so I bathe as quickly as I can then rush, shivering, to the large folded towel I'd placed at the riverbank. When I'm reasonably dry I brush my hair until it shines, then slip on the dress handed down from Ghigau to Ghigau. My jewelry, also passed down, is a mixture of silver and turquoise. The beaded headband was made by my grandmother. Everything that I put on has a special significance, and I have never felt so loved, or so *adorned*, in my entire life.

I step to the edge of the river again and glance down, startled by what I see. There, looking back at me, is not only my reflection, but that of Grandmother and all the Ghigaus who came before her.

"Thank you for being here; I am honored."

Remember, Nanye'Hi, that you are never alone, my great-great-great-grandmother says.

I hear the drumbeats and start to step from the tree line into the circle. I quickly look around me, knowing Michael's out there. I feel him. Taking a deep breath, I remind myself that there's no immediate danger; he cannot come into the Sacred Place and I will not let him taint this evening by dwelling on him.

When I step from the tree line, I'm shocked; the whole village is here! Some I know by name, others only by sight.

Some have come to Brayden and me for healing. My eyes search for him, and when they land on his I feel him beaming a love so strong it almost physically knocks me over. Next to him, Nibs stands tall, sending strength through our shared bond. The deputy finds my eyes and slowly lowers his head in acknowledgment. This is the kind of love that withstands time, is supportive, kind, truthful, and resilient; it is one of service and community. I am grateful for all of it.

I step into the circle and scan the crowd, silently acknowledging each person as well as my four-legged totems. It is only when my gaze returns to my friends that I realize someone is missing. Where is White Owl?

Before I can ask anyone, I begin to feel a strange sensation, like a pressure building inside me. The air around me becomes electric, the way it sometimes does before a summer storm. I open my mouth to speak and though it sounds like my voice I know it is the power of all the Ghigaus flooding through me.

"Great Spirit," I say in Cherokee, "please hear me. I dedicate my life, and all that I am, to serving the People as Ghigau, for as long as my life lasts, and beyond."

The very second I finish saying the words, power and strength wash through me. I feel different–renewed, somehow–and something else I cannot immediately identify. A moment later it comes to me: for the first time in my life, I feel *complete*.

For a beat there is only silence, then everyone erupts in whooping yells and applause. They begin to move as one toward me, and for the next ten minutes I allow myself to be embraced, squeezed and enveloped. Somewhere in the melee I feel Brayden's quick, rather stiff hug; it stays with me long after he has stepped away. And that's not the only thing bothering me. Where is White Owl? Where are Grandmother and my great-great-great grandmother? Were they no longer able to come to me, now that I had officially accepted the role of Ghigau?

At daybreak, we leave the Sacred Place to return home. Everyone, including the deputy, feels the heaviness in the air. A storm is getting ready to dump on us, but there isn't a cloud in the sky; nor is it like the power surge I'd felt in the air during the ceremony. No, this is a different kind of storm. The horses are restless, and the People quiet and on alert. We ride home the same way we rode in. Nibs and the deputy in front, me in the middle, and Brayden along with Cowgirl and Fabio bringing up the rear.

Suddenly, Brayden starts singing in Cherokee. His voice is like an angel's, lifting the air around us as well as our spirits. For just a few short minutes I forget that someone is trying to kill me and the people I love.

The large group stops when we reach the fork in trail, as most will break off here to head back to the village and Brayden, Nibs and Gaston will accompany me the rest of the way to my cabin. I thank the People again for coming and say goodbye, then our little group continues on in silence. When we get to my place I realize that I don't want to be alone just yet and invite everyone in for lunch. Nibs declines, saying she needs to check in at the clinic; then, after giving me another hug she heads out. I can't keep the smirk from my lips as I watch a smitten Gaston trailing behind her.

"Does she know?" Brayden asks, which tells me he approves; if he didn't he would have already had this conversation with Nibs, or Gaston, for that matter.

I shrug. Sure, Nibs suspects the deputy is interested in her, but I'm thinking she doesn't know the extent of that interest. Either way, it's not for me to say.

An uncomfortable but not surprising silence falls on the kitchen. Other than good mornings, thank yous, you're welcomes, and now this three-word question, he has not spoken to me in two days. Just when I think he's going to head out, he pulls out a chair at the kitchen table and settles into it.

Who the hell does he think he is, anyway? I think as I clean out the coffee pot, *Well, he's got some nerve, acting like a..."*

While I continue to tell him off in my head, he just sits there doing whatever he's doing and ignoring me. I refuse to give him the satisfaction of letting him know he's getting to me.

"I'm going to take a nap, make yourself comfortable," I say.

"K."

I had planned to walk away, but that "K" shredded my last nerve. I whip around, and when Brayden sees my face he stands and backs up a little.

"I don't know who you think you are, but you don't get to treat me like this. I can't stand the silent treatment, and I don't deserve it."

"Is—is that what you think," he says, red in the face and stumbling over his words, "that I'm giving you the silent treatment?

I open my mouth to say something but he cuts me off. "Do you have any idea what it's like to . . . to be in love with someone you *know* loves you back, and for them to say they don't want it; don't want you?" He runs a hand through his jet-black hair. "I've waited my whole life to feel this way and take none of it for granted, but you blew it off so quickly. Why, Nan?"

Suddenly I feel uncomfortably warm. "How could you think for one second that I blew it off? There is nothing cavalier or easy about my decision, period. It's the hardest decision I've ever had to make, and I did it to protect you."

I know from the hiccupping that I'm getting into the ugly girl cry, but it won't stop. He starts to say something, but I stop him by putting my hand up. "You make it sound like I just put you up on a shelf. I made myself sick over that decision."

Brayden hands me a box of tissues on his way out the door, which only makes me hiccup more. *He's leaving?* A second later I hear him pacing back and forth and realize he's only gone as far as the deck.

I step out on the deck and watch several rounds of pacing, accompanied by the clenching and unclenching of fists. The horses are standing at the fence, watching the drama unfold as they munch their hay.

"Do you have any idea what it's like to feel everything that I feel from you but not be able to act on it? To wonder why you're feeling that way and if those feelings are about me? I may not say much, Nan, but I feel *everything,* do you understand?"

"Then why so distant?" I ask as I dab my eye with a tissue.

"Because my feelings for you are so strong. I knew the minute we started talking that all of *this* would come out and I didn't want you to feel pressured. You have enough going on. I want you to come to me when you were ready and not because I pushed you into it."

"I just wanted to protect you," I say.

"That's not your decision to make."

"That's what Nibs said."

"My cousin's a smart girl, listen to her."

"Now what?"

He crosses the deck in three steps and then I'm in his arms.

"We have to get better at communicating than this," I murmur in his ear.

"Yes, I agree. You do," Brayden says, laughing.

I punch him in the shoulder. "I have a suggestion. If you feel something and want to know what's going on, ask."

"And if *you're* feeling nervous about anything, or uncomfortable about something I'm doing or not doing, or saying or not saying, then ask."

We seal it with a kiss and then more kisses, and then I hear myself say, "Be back in a minute." I slip into the bathroom and turn on the faucet to the tub. His eyes widen when I return wearing nothing but my bathrobe.

"It's a big tub," I say, "Join me?"

"See," he says hoarsely as he takes my hand and we walk toward the bathroom, "we're communicating better already."

He doesn't take his eyes off me for one second as he helps me out of my robe and into the tub. I'm equally entranced as I watch him take his clothes off, piece by piece. I want him so badly it actually hurts.

"Nice, Cowboy."

He climbs into the tub looking as intense as a lion ready to claim its prey. No ambiguity or mixed messages here. I feel his arms encircle my waist and I lean in toward him. We hold onto one another as if our next breath depends on it.

The next morning we're having our coffee when Nibs comes bounding in the house, the deputy right on her heels.

"Hey, White Girl-" She stops short when she sees Brayden sitting shirtless across from me, then her lips curl into a smile. "Oh. I was just coming to check on you but it looks like you're doing fine."

I blush. Brayden smiles and winks at me from across the table.

Gaston glances around at us, clearly nonplussed. "What?"

24

Empath 101

"So, Deputy, any news about Michael?" I ask as I pour coffees for him and Nibs.

"Call me Daniel," he says. It's not the first time but for some reason it doesn't seem to stick.

"Sorry, Daniel. Any news?"

"No. That son of a bitch is smart and cunning. We're always one step behind–finding the places he's been, and not where he is."

As Daniel says the words, I can feel Brayden's energy change, going into warrior mode. I look at him, a chill going up my spine. Of course, I had *felt* Brayden before–I had felt his love for me the night of the Ghigau ceremony, and his joy when working with horses, but this is different. This feels like the empathic stuff the cousins do, at least the way Nibs has described it to me. It has never happened to me before, so why now?

Brayden nudges my leg under the table and I come back to the present.

"Well, as you can imagine I have plenty of work to do," Gaston is saying, "so I'm going to leave Nibs in your capable hands. I'll keep you posted."

He turns puppy dog eyes to Nibs but if she notices she gives no indication.

"See you later, Daniel," she says with a cheerful wave.

"Okay," I say after he's walked out, "how are we going to do this? I need to go into town and see why White Owl wasn't at the ceremony."

"I need to go to the clinic," Nibs replies.

Brayden stands up. "Perfect, I'll take you."

"Better put a shirt on first," Nibs chuckles.

He gives her a warning look then heads into the bedroom.

As Brayden drives into town, I tell them how I had felt the shift in his energy when Gaston was talking about Michael.

"What do you think it means?" I ask, "I mean, I could *physically* feel it, almost like it was my energy, but not…"

Nibs nods. "Interesting."

"Welcome to my world," Brayden says, wrapping his free arm around me. "Oh man, this is going to suck, at least for a while."

Just then he pulls up in front of the clinic, where a small line of patients has already formed.

"Empath 101 will have to wait," Nibs says, "Right now it's work time."

After making sure she's safely inside, Brayden and I park the truck and go our separate ways—me to the Trading Post and Brayden to the feed store. The plan is to meet up later for lunch then pick up Nibs at the clinic before going home.

After a quick stop at the bookstore, I arrive at the Trading Post to find Wind Song standing behind the counter. I get a chill when he tells me that White Owl isn't there and hasn't been since the day of the ceremony.

"Why didn't anyone call me?" I ask, hearing the panic in my voice. "Has anyone checked on him?"

Startled, Wind Song takes a step back, then shakes his head.

I feel terrible. I should have known that White Owl would not have missed that ceremony.

I pull out my phone and call White Owl, but it goes straight to voicemail. I then call Gaston. He answers on the first ring.

"It might be nothing," he says, but he doesn't sound convinced. "Get Brayden and Nibs and we'll all meet back at your place."

An hour later my living room and kitchen have been turned into Search and Rescue Mission Headquarters. Maps, courtesy of Gaston's fellow deputies, are hanging on the walls, and Wind Song and several other people from the village arrive to offer their help. Again, the deputy amazes me with how quickly and expertly he gets things organized and in motion. It is small comfort, though. How could I not have checked on him sooner? I should have known White Owl would not miss the ceremony. I push the feelings of guilt down, knowing that won't help the situation. Right now I need to focus all my energies on finding White Owl. I just pray it's not too late.

"Grandmother," I whisper, "please help us find him."

She doesn't answer, and once again I wonder if the ceremony marked the end of my communication with her and Ghigau. I really hope not, because I desperately need them now.

I feel Brayden's hand on my arm. "We'll find him," he says, but I can hear the worry in his voice. He peers at me. "Is something else going on?"

"I'm not sure. I haven't heard from Grandmother since the ceremony, and that's the same time that White Owl went missing. It's not a coincidence, is it?"

He opens his mouth to say something when Nibs and Gaston walk over. "What's going on, Nan?" she asks.

I repeat what I'd just told Brayden, and not surprisingly, they don't have any answers either. We're just standing there staring at each other when a thought comes to me.

"Come with me," I say.

I gather all of them in a circle in the pasture, and as usual the horses and Fabio stand tails to the wind to hold space for us. I offer a smudge ceremony to ask the Great Spirit to hear us and answer our prayers. Where is Grandmother? Where is White Owl? Why is no one communicating?

I get dizzy and feel nauseated, a sign that a vision is coming, and sit down cross-legged in the grass. The cousins do not stir, nor does Gaston, though he does have a puzzled look on his face. I close my eyes and see an image of my grandmother and the Ghigau; both have cloth bindings around their eyes, mouth, and hands. They are unable to see or speak to me. My heart starts to race, and I wonder what monster could do this to two such honorable women. I send them my love and my thoughts.

Grandmothers, know that I am working on this side to free you. I will find the answer.

I try to get information about White Owl but see nothing.

When I come back to the present, Brayden puts his hand out to help me stand, steadying me. I send him a grateful look and tell them about my vision. The deputy doesn't flinch.

"I don't think it's Michael," I say. "It would take someone, or something, exceptionally powerful to best these women. Michael is evil, sick, and twisted, but he just doesn't have the skillset."

Suddenly, I feel a rush of rage, starting at the bottoms of my feet and travel up my body like a geyser. *What the -?* I turn to Brayden and see that his face is red, his fists are clenching and unclenching.

"It isn't bad enough that Michael is out there running around killing people," he shouts, "and is after the woman I love, now we have another evil-doer to battle!"

As he paces back and forth, I feel his anger and fear coursing through me, can feel my own fists clenching and unclenching as his are. After a moment I feel the storm start to dissipate and I step toward him, place my arms around his neck, and kiss him lightly.

"It's going to be okay," I say. "Are *you* okay?"

"Yep."

I know he means it when he looks at me and his face softens. His whole demeanor changes.

"You okay, Cousin?" Nibs said.

"Sorry about that. I just get so worried about everyone. I get tired of the bullshit, wondering when we're going to have a chance at a normal life."

Nibs and I erupt into laughter.

He looks like he's going to storm up again, but instead holds up both hands in surrender. "I see what you mean."

"This has been very…interesting…" Gaston says, "but I really have to get back inside."

We return to the cabin, where Gaston's fellow deputies have divided everyone into teams to look for White Owl. I can only hope they find him and that when they do Michael is not there as well. The horses are skittish, jumping at everything, and I know they are picking up on the nervous energy. I vow to do some healing work with them this evening.

Brayden helps me onto Magic's back, then walks over to Daisy, puts his foot in the stirrup and swings his other leg over.

We've done this search party thing so often, I tell myself, *we should be able to do it blindfolded.* This reminds me of Grandmother and the Ghigau, and I get a shot of concern right in my midsection. That feeling always tells me when there's something off, and I realize it's been happening more in the past few days, since White Owl and the grandmothers have been absent. I should have paid more attention. It's probably been them all along. I take a deep breath. Guilt is a useless emotion, and I just don't have time for it. Instead, I need to refocus and work the problem at hand. Find Michael, find White Owl, release the Grandmothers, not necessarily in that order.

I take time to connect with Magic and tune into his feelings, letting his intuition be my guide. As soon as I do, I feel his unease. I can't identify it, though, and it's not even registering on my radar. All I know is that it's elusive and powerful.

Sensing my distress, Brayden and Nibs turn to look at me, but I just shrug, unable to give them anything. I continue to try and pinpoint what I'm feeling, and at the same moment I figure it out Gaston stops the group and jumps off his horse. Again, I feel Brayden and Nibs's eyes on me.

"I feel death," I say with a shiver. "I can't tell where or how recent, but I know it was not a natural one."

I look around, my eyes landing on the entrance to a cave. Though it was dark the last time I was here, I know without a doubt it is the same cave Michael held me captive.

"Deputy, can we check in there?" I ask.

He doesn't answer me but heads the group in that direction. This is the last place I want to go, but I cannot deny that this is where my instincts are leading me.

We ride in silence, each of us dreading what we might find. Flashes of the night Michael had held me there flood my mind. Though he had fled, I have no doubt I could have died that night, and Stacy certainly would have, had Gaston not found us in time.

Brayden looks back at me, frowning. I know he is feeling everything I am, and after my own recent empathetic experiences I am beginning to understand how difficult this is for him. It makes me appreciate and love him all the more for sticking this out with me. I had unconsciously slowed my pace, and now Brayden circles Daisy around so that we are once again riding side by side. He reaches over and gently he takes my hand, rubbing the inside of my wrist with his thumb. We're here.

"Brayden, you're with me," Gaston says.

Nibs and I dismount and wait outside the cave. We wait and then wait some more.

"They get one more minute then I'm going in," I say.

"I agree," Nibs replies, but the words are no sooner out of her mouth when the men return.

"Anything?" I ask.

"Nothing, absolutely nothing," Gaston says.

I look at him, eye wide. "But how can that be?"

If I was the only one who had sensed something, I might have doubted it, but the animals had clearly felt it too.

Gaston shrugs. "It's so clean in there it looks like some-one power washed it."

"Can I go in?"

Brayden slips his arm around me. "Are you sure you want to, you know, after everything?"

"I'm sure I *don't* want to," I reply, "but have to. I need to see if I can feel anything."

"All together then," Nibs says.

Gaston goes in first, followed by Nibs and then Brayden and me. I stifle a gasp as I walk through the entrance of the cave, so powerful is the emotional imprint of pain and fear left by Stacy.

"Stay here, please," I tell the group, then I go out to Magic and remove my smudging tools from the saddlebag. I perform a healing smudge on the place for the earth, the cave and the four-legged, winged and crawly creatures that live in it. When I'm done, the space is completely cleansed, as am I.

I look at the others, feeling both revived and completely confused.

There is no Michael.

No White Owl.

No answers.

We head home as darkness starts to fall and the air chills. When we reach the cabin, Brayden and I immediately tend to the animals, doing a healing and cleansing on them even before we give them their food. By the time we head into the house we're exhausted, but there is no rest for the weary. The search parties are beginning to trudge in, and they're even colder, more tired, and hungrier than we are. After cleaning up and changing clothes, Brayden and I stand side by side in the kitchen, making them a huge pot of chili and cornbread.

Gaston makes a fire in the fireplace and Nibs tends to any cuts and bruises the searchers sustained over the course of the day. It's such a small way of thanking them for the enormous service they're providing. There is nothing I can do, though, about the disappointed looks on their faces, or the concern for White Owl flowing through them. I am overwhelmed with love for this great, caring group of people. *My* People.

"Before anyone leaves," I say, "let's gather in a circle." Quietly, they join me outside. I offer a smudge ceremony for the search parties and to the Great Spirit for keeping everyone safe. I ask the Great Spirit for the continued safety of the grandmothers and White Owl, and that their knowledge and wisdom not be lost.

After bringing the ceremony to a close, I thank them once again for everything they have done. The search party then disbands for the night, with Gaston and Nibs following shortly after. When they're gone Brayden and I look at each other, and we don't have to be empathetic to know what the other is feeling: we're thrilled to finally be alone. He draws us a bath and we sink into it, taking turns massaging each other's sore spots until the water turns cold. By then we're almost too tired to pull ourselves out, but a warm bed is a great motivator. A few minutes later we're lying, arms and legs tangled together between the flannel sheets. Brayden is asleep almost before his head hits the pillow, but not me. As I lay there, a wave of dizziness and nauseas overtakes me, then *whoosh,* I'm out of my body, right through the top of my head.

In Dreamtime, an enormous white stygian owl greets me. The owl does not speak to me, but morphs into a very dark, almost black owl with scary red eyes. The evil radiates off him like nothing I've experienced before, including time spent with Michael. I feel my body start to shake uncontrollably as the cold and fear grip me.

"Nan, wake up," Brayden says gently, but though I can hear l him I can't seem to nudge myself back into my body and wake.

"Nan, please wake up, you're having a nightmare." It sounds like he's coming to me from far away. Then I hear myself whimpering like a scared puppy.

The phone starts ringing off the hook. I hear everything, but I can't make any voluntary movement.

"Please, Nan, wake up!"

This time I connect with my body, and my eyes fly open just in time to see Brayden reaching for the phone.

"Yes, she's okay–nightmare–thanks, Cuz. Talk to you tomorrow." He never takes his eyes off me.

"It was horrible, Brayden," I whisper, "Black and dark. It felt like it was trying to devour me."

"Do you know what it means?" he asks.

"No. I bet I know who does."

"Grandmother," we say in unison, then I slip out of bed and run to get Grandmother's diary. When I return, Brayden slips his arms around me and just listens as I read aloud.

Owl medicine is the most powerful of Magic and has been used from the beginning of time by medicine women and men to aid those in dire need of healing, to heal, cleanse land or dwellings as well as assist others in transitioning to the Great Mystery. Owl medicine, more than any other, can be corrupted for use in dark magic and is often called the "deceiver feathers" for that very reason. Utilized in the light, Owl medicine is one of the greatest gifts healers can use. Used for dark practices, its power yields harmful and evil results for the object or person targeted. This use will also turn the practitioner from light to dark.

Just as there was a "Wolf Clan" and the birthplace of the original Nanye'Hi, there was an "Owl Clan." Their job was to heal the land and all its creatures. The Owl Clan is traditionally a light practice, but many have been seduced by false claims of power and have turned to the dark practice. If you have received a message from Owl, deception may be at hand. Open your eyes, ears, and heart to see the truth. You must be able to look into the dark and recognize it for what it is. Only then can you reclaim your power from it.

25

Nibs, the Deputy, and Feathers

I'm exhausted, praying for sleep, but my mind refuses to stop. It doesn't help that the couch and the pillows, hell even the blanket, smell like her. With each breath, I'm reminded of this woman who has plagued my thoughts and baffled my mind since the day I met her. Nibs has been forthcoming, shielding, and hiding nothing from me since I arrived. In fact, she's gone out of her way to make sure I'm included in everything, no matter how magical and mystical it appears. Still, there's something about her, something I can't figure out.

I turn over to my other side, hoping this will be the position that allows me to drop off, but all I can think about is Nibs, lying in the next room. It's like this every time I'm around her. I feel this magnetic pull, a need to protect and take care of her, which makes no sense to me at all. I've never been that way around anyone before, so why her? And why do I feel the need to protect Nan? The pull is not as strong as with Nibs, but it's there all the same. Is it because

Nan is so important to Nibs? And why is Nibs so important to me? I tell myself that it's because she's tall, leggy and gorgeous, but I know it's more than that. If only I could shake this feeling that she's not telling me everything.

Of course, I'm no one to talk. No one, including the one person I came to Galowhisdi to see, knows who I am. I want to keep it that way, at least until we find Michael and White Owl. It's been hard keeping it strictly professional when the long-lost father you want desperately to meet has gone missing. I wanted to approach him before but, I admit it, I was afraid he would reject me. I was willing to risk it, though, and overlook my own resentments, because he's my only living relative and I wanted to learn about him and his side of my family. Now it may be too late.

What will Nibs and the others think of me if and when they discover my secret?

I have to find White Owl.

It wasn't until I ended up at Sequoyah that I even knew I had a father. I will be forever grateful to them for taking me in when Mom died–I could have ended up on the street like so many other kids–but at first I didn't believe them when they told me. My father, a Medicine Man? Then, once I started to believe it, I got angry, because why was he helping others when he had a son out there, thinking he was an orphan? Eventually curiosity set in, and I decided I wanted to learn about this supposed Medicine Man. That curiosity has only grown since coming here. I am a man of reasoning and science, but after everything I've witnessed I've definitely expanded my ideas of what's possible. Perhaps it's even possible for me and my deadbeat dad to find some middle ground.

Maybe that's why I feel such a connection with Nibs. Like me, she is a person of science, has studied a lot and has tons of training, yet she also believes in whatever this *stuff* is. Why can't everyone fit into a nice little box and just stay there? Life would be simpler.

This crap going on in my head is not helping my sleep. *She* is not helping my sleep. I get up from the couch, and in my bare feet, pad softly toward her room. She's left the door open, and I can see her, lying on her side, breathing deeply, even and slow. Even now, there is something mysterious about her, and I wouldn't be surprised to hear that she had left her body and was orbiting the solar system.

———◉———

What is he doing? Is he just standing there, staring at me?

I try to tune in, but I don't feel anything from him, which in and of itself is a mystery. Typically, I feel *too* much. I'm usually very good at being able to identify who I feel what from, and why. I've always had this ability. Why it isn't working with him, I haven't a clue, I don't feel unsafe, though, just uneasy and more than a little intrigued.

I continue to pretend to sleep until I decide that discussing this with Nan, preferably over coffee, is a good option. We need some serious girl time anyway. He's still standing there, watching me play possum when I finally drift off.

The next morning I feel awkward and quiet around Daniel as he busies himself with his laptop, phone, and maps. He's still diligently sending crews out looking for Michael and White Owl. As I get ready to go I steal glances at him. He has that hard look of someone who has seen his share of adversity, maybe more than his share. I can only imagine what he has seen in his job and what a tremendous burden that is to carry. Yet I've also seen him be warm, sensitive, and even caring. He'd be a perfect candidate for Nan's healing work, if only he was open to it.

We are both silent on the ride to Nan's, and though the air between us is thick with energy, I cannot get a handle on it. The thought occurs to me that maybe my "feeler" is broken, which scares me more than I care to admit. That fear is put to rest, though, as soon as we walk in the cabin and I feel a wave of love and lust coming from her and Brayden. *Ewww.* Too much information. Well, at least my "feeler" is working fine; it just doesn't work on Gaston.

"Morning, Cousin...Ghigau," Nibs says while giving me a mock bow.

I roll my eyes at her. "You know where the coffee pot is. Hey, Daniel."

Daniel gives me a curt wave, and I can tell by the set of his jaw that he's ready to get another day of searching underway.

"Nibs, do you have time for a field trip?" I ask her.

"Yes. Where are we going?"

"Tahlequah. I need to go to the library."

I see Daniel flinch. It's slight, but I see it. So does Nibs, but she just gives me a slight shrug of her shoulders.

"You're not going anywhere without me," Brayden says.

We just look at him, and rather than face a battle he knows he can't win he offers to stay and help Daniel with the search.

"Yes," Daniel says, "I can use someone who knows the area as well as you do."

I reach over and squeeze Brayden's hand. "I'll feel better, knowing you're out there looking for White Owl."

He smiles at me, but I can see the concern in his eyes as they follow me out the door.

"Did you see Gaston's face when I asked you to go to Tahlequah?" I say as Nibs and I turn onto the highway. "What's up with that?"

She gives me an odd look. "I'm the last one to ask about Gaston…"

"Okay, Nibs, spill. What does that mean?"

I listen as Nibs recounts the strange story from last night, how Daniel stood in her doorway, watching her, and how she was—is—unable to feel anything from him. Her frustration about this is evident, and not surprising, considering how attuned to others she usually is. Then I remember feeling there was something off about Daniel, something I couldn't figure out. I had just been too caught up in everything lately to think about it.

"This doesn't make any sense," Nibs is saying, "I've always been able to size someone up empathically."

I give her a vague nod, still thinking. "Yeah…"

"Yeah, what, White Girl?"

I shrug. "I don't know. But I've come to understand that there are times when for whatever reason, we're not supposed to know stuff. This is one of those times."

"I suppose you're right. It's just that, well, you know…"

Nibs is quiet the rest of the way, and I know she is still trying to figure out why her spidey senses are on the fritz.

"Okay," I say lightly as we pull into the library parking lot, "You ready to do some research the old-fashioned way?"

As we're climbing the steps to the front door, sitting in the sun and looking very relaxed is an older Cherokee gentleman.

"Osiyo," he greets us in the Indian way.

"Hello . . . Osiyo," I say.

"Who are you talking to?" Nibs says.

I laugh. "Very funny, Nibs."

She looks at me, dead serious.

"Are you telling me you don't see the Cherokee man sitting on the step to my right?"

"Uhhh, no."

"Great."

"What does he want?"

I ask him, and what he says makes no sense.

"He's telling me to check the death certificates."

"Great, another effing mystery to solve," Nibs says.

I laugh; I can't help it. It sounds ridiculous hearing anything close to a cuss word coming from Nibs. It's like seeing polka dots on a zebra. The two don't equate.

"Come on, Nibs. We'll worry about the *effing* death certificates later. Right now I need to learn more information about Owl medicine."

I'm about to say goodbye to the Indian when he says, "The boy. You will find the boy in the archives."

When I relay the message, Nibs's brow wrinkles in confusion.

"What a minute," she says, "Could he be talking about Daniel?"

I turn back to the man and he solemnly nods.

"Let's go, Nibs."

We settle into the stacks of dusty census records and start plowing through all the Gs until we find it. A brief snippet of information about Daniel Gaston, age ten, the only surviving family of his mother, Elizabeth. Her maiden name, Gaston.

"Why would Daniel go by his mother's maiden name?" I ask.

Nibs shrugs, then keeps reading. "On the census Elizabeth's race was listed as white and Daniel's was Indian."

That was the last yearly entry census records for Elizabeth, or Daniel, for that matter. Suddenly, a thought comes to me. That's what friendly gentleman on the steps was trying to say.

"Nibs, we need to check the death records."

A few minutes later, we're looking at Elizabeth Gaston's death certificate. She had died of natural causes, and according to the obituary accompanying the certificate, she had one surviving son–Daniel Gaston, age ten.

I look at Nibs. "What would have happened to a half-Indian kid back then?"

"Sequoyah," she says. "Hey, remember you said you felt like you had met him before…?"

I shake my head. "No, I'm sure I didn't know him at school. I do think he's maybe four or five years older than us. Maybe he went there, but that's not why I had the feeling. Still, definitely worth checking out. Do you think we can get into the records?"

"I'm not sure."

"What about Daniel's father? Maybe we can find something out about him."

"Let's see if we can find Daniel's birth record."

"Okay, that sounds easier than making up some story to the school."

"You know, you've never once talked about your father," Nibs says.

"That's because I don't know who he is, and there's no one to ask."

"Did you ask Grandmother?"

I shake my head. I knew that sooner or later this would come up for me, but I've done a pretty good job of avoiding it all these years and now is not the time. One, two or three mysteries later, when we have things under control, I'll deal with it then.

We dig and find Daniel's birth certificate, which only confirms what we've already discovered. Daniel Gaston was raised by a single mother and went by her maiden name of Gaston. The father is listed as unknown. We've hit a wall.

"Tell your Indian thanks for nothing," Nibs says, disgusted.

I laugh. "Will do. Right now, I need to find everything I can about Owl People and Owl Medicine."

We move to another section of the library and are soon pouring through books about the Cherokee's original seven clans. But though we find many references to the Owl People, there is no direct information on them. We ask the person at the resource counter, who tells us that Owl People were not among the original seven clans. Furthermore, those practicing Owl Medicine were not considered part of the Cherokee teachings because many considered it to be "dark" magic.

"Do you know where I can get information on Owl Medicine and its people?" I ask.

"Yes," she says, peering at me over her glasses, "but you'll have to take a drive."

I punch the address into the GPS, and we head north toward Fayetteville, Arkansas. Sixty-five miles and an hour later, Nibs and I are driving through a part of town that resembles an old village when the GPS indicates that we've arrived at our destination.

"There it is," Nibs says, pointing to a blue awning with the word "Feathers" in cursive.

I pull into a spot right in front, and as we walk into the store we are greeted by a slightly built, bookish, and beautiful woman with long chestnut brown hair.

"Welcome to Feathers. I'm April," she says, then suddenly her eyes widen. "You are the Ghigau," she gushes, "I'd know you anywhere. You look just like her, even with your blond hair."

Finally, she takes a breath. Nibs has her hand over her mouth to keep from laughing out loud at my discomfort. I didn't know what to say; the only person to ever gush over me was Wind Song. It's just as awful now. I look around the store and see several other people staring and listening very intently. Oh geez, I think, bracing myself for an onslaught, but thankfully, they go about their business, content to steal glances at us every so often.

"Hi, April, this is my friend, Nibs Dove. We are looking for information about Owl Medicine, specifically how someone would be able to bind a spirit?"

"What do you mean, *bind*?" April whispers as she moves closer.

"Bind as in, hold a spirit so that it can't communicate," I whisper back.

"Oh, dear."

"Well, that doesn't sound good," Nibs says.

"Give me five minutes to lock up, then I'll give you all the answers I can. It just won't be helpful for any of this to get out." April makes a sweeping motion with her arm. "In the meantime, feel free to check out the store."

Feathers is very much like every other New Age shop I've ever visited–crammed with self-help books, crystals and talismans of all sorts. There is one corner of the store that keeps *pulling* at me. I follow that pull, and when I get there, I see it's filled with magical items. Books on spells and incantations, recipes for old healing remedies, and tarot cards. There is nothing here that feels dark in any way. In fact, to me, it feels the very opposite of that, very light and healing. Maybe I'm just getting used to all things magical.

"Nibs, how do you feel in here, anything dark or icky?"

Nibs shakes her head. "Just the opposite."

We watch as April goes around, quietly informing each customer that the shop is closing and to bring their purchases to the front. After the last one has left, each throwing me a final curious glance, she closes and locks the doors. We then follow her into the back room, which consists of a nice little kitchen and sitting area. April makes tea for us and joins us at the table.

"What would you like to know?" she asks.

"Everything," I say.

"The original seven clans of the Cherokee were Deer, Long Hair, Bird, Wild Potato, Blue, Paint, and Wolf, each of which had a specific purpose. The fiercest of all was the Wolf Clan, from which you and your ancestors originated."

April gets up and returns with a book entitled *Owl Medicine, White Witch* by April Reed.

"That's you!" Nibs exclaims.

"Yes, when they were alive, both my parents were Owl People and believed in and worked with Owl Medicine as healers. What you described, binding spirits and such, is a twisted version of this practice. Any time 'medicine' or 'magic' is not used for healing, but to try to bend the will of another, it becomes dark and perverted. Authentic Owl People don't do it."

"Why does anyone do it?" I ask, but as soon as the words are out of my mouth I know the answer.

"There are people, medicine men and women, who instead of serving through a healing practice seek power. This search for power turns the medicine on the user, and he or she becomes an entirely different person. The People saw the corruption and the darkness that can happen. As a result, Owl Medicine people were pushed to the boundaries of the tribes and kept separate; in fact, most have been in hiding ever since. The few who decided to stay practice their craft in secret, knowing that if discovered they would be made to leave all their relations and the tribe.

I take a sip of tea. "What can you tell us about someone who can bind a spirit?"

"To be able to do that a person would have to be very, very powerful," April says, "I would not want to be on their bad side."

"Is there any way to reverse or interrupt the binding?"

"May I ask...who is bound, what spirit?"

"It is my grandmother and the original Ghigau," I say, my voice catching a little.

"I see. This is an attack on you, a way to keep you from getting information."

"Yes, and anything you can tell us about how to reverse it would be–"

"I'll do better than that," April says, "I will help you."

"Oh, that would be wonderful!" Nibs exclaims.

"It is my pleasure. I can come on Saturday if that works for you."

"Of course it does." I rise and grab April's book. "And I'd like to purchase your book."

"No, please," April says warmly, "accept it as a gift to my Ghigau. I still consider myself part of the Cherokee Nation."

"With pleasure and gratitude," I say. "One more question?"

"Of course."

"What can you tell me about White Owl and his teachings?"

"Well, I cannot reveal anything sacred." Suddenly a look of alarm crosses her face. "You don't think he's involved in the binding?"

"No, nothing like that. He went missing around the same time the grandmothers were bound. We're quite concerned about him."

April pauses, her eyes heavenward as she considers my words. "Ghigau, you are correct. The two are connected. I'll do a little research myself before coming to you." She plucks a business card from her pocket and hands it to me. "Write your address on the back of this so I know how to find you."

I grab her in a tight hug. "Thank you, April. We'll see you then."

As Nibs and I leave the store, I feel the first glimmer of hope.

Hang on just a few more days, I silently say to White Owl and the grandmothers, *Help is on the way.*

26

An Addition to the Family

It's almost dark by the time we arrive at the cabin. When we walk in the door, Daniel is sitting at the table writing notes on a map while Brayden paces back and forth across the living room. He stops short when he sees us, his face lighting up, his brown eyes searching mine. I smile, and he reaches me in two steps. I am embraced and thoroughly kissed.

"Nice."

"Nice doesn't even come close to what I have planned for you later," he whispers in my ear.

His words send an immediate flash of heat through my body. I know he feels it because when he pulls away he is smiling like the Cheshire Cat.

"Enough, Cowboy," I say, making him laugh. It's a beautiful sound and one I haven't heard nearly enough of lately. Granted, someone is trying to kill me and there is dark, evil magic happening.

"I'm glad you're both back safe and sound," Daniel says, but his eyes are glued to Nibs.

"Yes, we're fine," I say, "and we have plenty to report. What do you say Nibs and I fill you in, then we all take the night off and just have dinner and drink some wine?"

Everyone, including the solemn and very serious deputy, agrees. Brayden pours everyone some red as Nibs and I recount the day's events; we leave nothing out, except of course for the snooping Nibs and I had done on Daniel himself. The deputy's eyes widen when I mention seeing the ghostly Cherokee man on the steps of the library, but he really begins to squirm when we get to the part about going to Fayetteville, and Feathers. And it is more than just crossing his arms or draining his wineglass; I can feel his emotional discomfort.

Finally, I ask him, "What is it?"

Daniel looks genuinely confused. "What do you mean?"

"Okay," I say.

"That's it," Brayden says, "Will someone please tell me what's going on?"

I shake my head. "It's nothing. C'mon, let's cook; I'm hungry."

Clearly Daniel's not ready to talk about anything yet, and I'm not going to pressure him, for now.

A look of annoyance flashes across Brayden's face, but he shrugs it off and heads outside to light the grill. I smile in anticipation. Brayden can grill cardboard and make it taste good.

After a couple of bottles of wine and perfectly cooked New York strips, we're all feeling pretty good. Even Daniel loosens up as we listen to music and talk about everything except magic and our seemingly never-ending battle with evil. This evening will go down in my diary as one of my favorites. Yet as I watch Nibs and Daniel chatting, I can't help but wonder, does she have any inkling that he is the love of her life? Somehow, I feel she doesn't, and I can only pray that he will do *everything* he can to deserve her, including coming clean with his secrets.

It's after midnight when Nibs pleads exhaustion and she and Daniel head to her place. Brayden and I stumble into bed, too tired for anything but quick kisses on the lips. I take a minute to thank the Great Spirit that Nibs is in the reliable and capable protection of her deputy, and that I am in the arms of my own wonderful man. My last thought before falling asleep, though, is a prayer: *Great Spirit, please keep my grandmothers and White Owl safe. Please let them know help is coming.*

"April will be here any minute," I announce after receiving her text. It's eight a.m. and the four of us are sitting at my kitchen table, nursing cups of strong coffee.

Immediately, I feel a shift in Daniel's energy, see the slight clenching of his jaw. For a minute I think it's my imagination, but then I feel the cousins' eyes on me. I shrug. I don't know what's going on with him but I have a sneaking suspicion we're going to find out soon enough.

Daniel has been updating us on the search parties, which is to say they've looked everywhere they can think of and have found no trace of Michael or White Owl. They've even returned to a few places several times, where Michael has been spotted before. I try to listen to what he is saying, but I'm finding it difficult to focus.

"This needs to be over." Everyone looks at me, and I say, "Sorry didn't mean to say that out loud."

Brayden comes around the table and puts his arm around my shoulder. "Do you need a break?"

"I'm sorry, I don't know what's wrong with me today. I just feel off."

"Describe *off*," Nibs says.

"I feel frustrated and a little angry, and there's a weird feeling in the pit of my stomach that doesn't even feel like me. It feels very *intrusive*."

"That's because it doesn't belong to you," she says matter-of-factly.

"Huh?"

"Feelers 101, White Girl. If it doesn't feel like it belongs to you, then it probably doesn't."

"I'm confused. Explain, please."

"Well, that intrusive feeling could be part of your new empathic abilities, and you're picking up someone else's energy."

I think about that for a moment. Can it be that I am picking up on Daniel's nervousness?

"Makes sense. Go on, Nibs."

"Another explanation for the feeling is *clairsentience,* which is similar to empathy in that you are feeling the feelings or sensing the feelings of someone, either living or in the spirit world. Doesn't it make sense that if you can see and hear spirits, you'd be able to feel them as well?"

"Yes, I suppose it does. How do I make it stop?"

"Are you sure you want to? Maybe this is the grand-mothers' way of communicating with you right now, assuming they can after being bound. Wouldn't you rather be able to discern what is important for you to know and what you can release?"

"How do I do that?"

"You learn to protect yourself emotionally and repel those emotions that don't belong to you or serve a purpose. Eventually, it will just happen naturally. First, you need to learn protection. What are you doing now?"

"Uh, nothing," I say sheepishly. "Most of my communicating until now has been with the grandmothers and I didn't think I needed to protect myself from them."

"Haven't you been doing a daily smudge ceremony?" Nibs asks.

"I was, but . . . crap, with everything going on I guess that kind of went to the wayside..."

"Okay, well, that's the first problem. You need to do some kind of cleansing practice, every day, without fail. I feel like you need something more specific than smudging."

"You know, I'll bet that April will have some ideas."

At the mention of April, Daniel grips his mug just a little bit tighter. I want to yell at him, tell him to come out with it already, that I don't have the time or the patience for one more mystery.

As if sensing my frustration, Daniel finishes the last of his coffee and stands up.

"Well, I need to go to headquarters and check on some things. I'll be available by phone if you need me. I'll be gone all day."

So, making your escape, huh? I think as he heads toward the front door. Clearly he does not want to be around when April gets here.

I hear the creek of the door as Daniel pulls it open, then the sound of a woman's voice.

"*Daniel?*" April says, "My goodness, it must be fifteen years!"

Daniel doesn't say anything as she embraces him, just stands there like a deer caught in the headlights.

"April," I call out, ignoring the curious stares of Brayden and Nibs, "Come on in."

"You know each other?" Nibs asks as April steps inside.

I take in Daniel's shell-shocked expression and find myself feeling sorry for him.

"Why don't I just put on some coffee and tea so we can all catch up."

"That would be lovely, Nan," April says, seemingly oblivious to the tension in the room.

Nibs continues to stand with her hand on hip, her eyes silently daring Daniel to explain himself.

I feel when he makes the decision, his demeanor shifting from flight to resolution.

So how do you two know each other?" I ask as I turn on the coffee pot.

"Sequoyah," he says finally.

"As in Sequoyah Boarding School in Tahlequah?"

April smiles. "You've heard of it? Daniel and I were lucky. If it weren't for the school, we'd have been living on the streets, right, Daniel?"

When he doesn't answer her, April reaches over and places her hand on his. "It was hard, but at least we had each other."

I feel it when Nibs's walls slam back into place. She mutters something about tending to the horses, then she quickly walks out the back door, with Daniel watching her every move.

"Good to see you again, April. Can we catch up later?" He doesn't wait for an answer before following Nibs outside.

April watches them leave. "I'm sorry, did I say something I shouldn't have? It was just so nice to see Daniel again, he was like a brother to me. Should I go explain?"

"You have nothing to apologize for or explain. Let's just say Daniel could have been a little more forthcoming about his past."

"Wonder why he wasn't," Brayden muses.

My thoughts exactly.

"He had it pretty rough growing up," April say, "I hope Nibs won't be too hard on him."

"Nothing will set you free faster than the truth."

April smiles brightly. "You're right. Let's get to work then."

"In a minute," I say, "But first, coffee."

I've barely set three mugs on the table when Nibs and Daniel walk back in.

"Uh, welcome back," I say, taking in Nibs's stern expression.

"I asked Nibs to come back inside," Daniel says, "This is not something I want to tell more than once."

"Two more coffees coming up," I say, turning back to the pot.

The kitchen is entirely too quiet as Nibs and Daniel take their seats

Daniel thanks me for the steaming mug I set before him, then takes a breath. "As April said, we grew up together at the Sequoyah Boarding School. I was ten years old when my mother died and I was sent there. We dated–briefly– our senior year but soon realized were better friends than sweethearts. None of this is a secret. I just don't like to talk about it–don't even like to think about it–because it was such a painful time for me."

As he speaks, I can feel the waves of long-held loneliness and abandonment coming off him. No wonder he keeps it to himself.

"Anyway, I went on to college and then to the Deputy's Academy. It wasn't until then that I decided to find out who my father was. You see, my mother had always said he was dead, but then the staff at Sequoyah told me he was alive and that he was a medicine man, but they didn't know his name. It wasn't until I graduated and started working that I could afford a private detective. He's the one who finally found out who my father is, which is what brought me here.

"Who . . . who is it?" I ask, but I already know the answer. It is why Daniel has seemed familiar to me all along.

"White Owl."

Nibs, Brayden and April look at him, stunned. I feel Nibs's resentment melt when she recognizes the truth in his words. She says nothing, just stands up, walks over to Daniel and puts her arms around him.

"What you must have gone through," she says, and I know she's thinking of her own childhood, and how she'd ended up at Sequoyah.

"Let me guess," I say, "You never felt like you fit in anywhere, and when you tried, it failed miserably, right?"

Daniel nods, a quick jerk of his head. "I grew up with a white mother who never spoke about any family, her background, or mine." His voice becomes deep with sorrow. "When she died, I thought I had no one."

"Does he know?" Nibs asks, "White Owl?"

"No. I wanted to give myself a chance to try and connect here first, plus I hadn't decided whether to tell him or not."

"Why didn't you just tell us?" Nibs asks, "Or me, at least?"

"I didn't know what to say. When we first met it was because of Michael's attack and then as I got to know all of you...well, it just never seemed like the right time. Then White Owl went missing and—"

He trails off, and when he looks into my eyes I can see the fear that he will never get to speak to his father again. I know the feeling, because it's the same fear I have about the grandmothers.

"And that's why we're here today," I say, taking a deep breath. "We're going to try to get White Owl back."

27

Finding White Owl

Owl Medicine is way more involved than I ever would have imagined. One could spend years studying it and barely scratch the surface. Nibs and I listen as April combs through the enormous volume on the medicine she brought from Feathers, searching for ways in which we can free the grandmothers from the binding and, hopefully, find White Owl. No wonder he has such a lengthy training program, I think as I flash on the special training rooms behind the Trading Post, filled with jar after jar of mysterious stuff. I know in my heart that he has nothing to do with the binding of my grandmothers, that he only practiced the pure form of Owl Medicine.

April is in a world of her own, mixing things and chanting a prayer. She seems to start and stop several times. "Nothing, I'm getting nothing, something's missing."

I continue trying to send him and my grandmothers mental pictures of what we're doing and our searching.

White Owl and Grandmothers, we are looking for answers, any help you can give us would be awesome. Don't give up.

I immediately get a response that feels like warm honey spreading across my chest. At the same time, a picture of White Owl flashes through my mind. Exuberant that I have gotten through to them, I look up to see everyone staring at me.

"What?" I ask.

"You were glowing," Brayden says.

"As in glowing like a light?"

Nibs nods. "Yes. What were you doing just then?"

"I was communicating with my grandmothers and White Owl. At least I was trying to communicate and hoping they could hear me."

"What were you feeling?"

Interesting question; she always knows what I'm feeling.

"I want you to be able to match what you *feel* with the response," she explains, "so that you know what's causing it, as a frame of reference. In this case, you were communicating with Spirit or from spirit to spirit, soul to soul, and you glowed."

April nods. "I think Nibs is right. It isn't telepathic, as in mind to mind, but spirit to spirit. To make that connection, you have to *feel* your way through it rather than think it through. Does that make sense?"

"Perfect sense. I was feeling gratitude and love toward my grandmother and White Owl, and then I felt the connection and his response. He is alive, but I still don't know where he is or what kind of condition he's in. So, what now?"

April closes the book. "That's it, I'll do what I do and you do what you do best?" she suggests.

We stare at her for a moment, and then I get it. "Oh, Great Spirit, you're brilliant."

"I am? What did I say?"

Nibs laughs, putting a hand on April's shoulder. "This happens all the time. She had an 'ah ha' moment and will catch us up eventually. Wait for it."

Suddenly, we hear Fabio braying with all his might.

Crap, not now, I think, afraid he is alerting us to danger.

We run to the deck and are relieved to find Fabio calmly waiting for us. No threats seem to be present.

"What's going on?" April asks.

"Okay, my friend," I say to him, "I'm here, and I get the message."

I try to step around him, but he moves and blocks my path. I try again and again, each time he stops my movement. I place one hand on Fabio's withers and another on his heart space and allow his message to come. Once I do, Fabio stands to the side, allowing me to pass. I open all the stalls and let the horses go where they want, then offer a smudge ceremony to all the creatures present—four-legged, two-legged, winged and crawlers and, finally, myself. I hear Eagle cry overhead and watch as the horses create a circle around us, their tails to the wind, facing in, holding space. Fabio, ever my spiritual warrior, stands with me.

I envision myself drawing a medicine wheel, walking the outline, which is gleaming and sparkling like diamonds. Each position is marked, N, E, S and W. I gather my smudge bowl and feather, standing in the center. So many things are going through my mind that at first, it's almost impossible to connect with Spirit. I feel it when I make the connection; it flows over me in that sensation of warm honey. It's a feeling of unconditional love so deep and overwhelming that for a moment I find it difficult to breathe. I hear April chanting and the smoke of sacred herbs fills my nostrils; instantly adding her power to mine.

I begin by thanking the Great Spirit for the Animal Totems, for the ancestors, and for the experiences and people who have been a part of my journey. I also thank the Great Spirit for the opportunity to serve my People as their Ghigau. Suddenly, *whoosh,* I am out of my body and am shocked to see, standing before me, the spirit of my mother.

My daughter, I am here as a gift of the Great Spirit. You are the Ghigau. If you were not worthy, you would not be here. Do not be afraid of your power, trust in the spirit animals that surround you as well as the two-legged that have become your family. Most importantly, trust your heart. You are the Ghigau and destined to be exactly as you are.

Mother, I say, *thank you for coming, and thank you for delivering that message.*

I have so many questions for her, but before I can ask them she says, *There is no pain here, my child. Only unconditional love and forgiveness.*

Until that moment I hadn't realized how much space those thoughts were taking up inside me. Now, as they are released, I put my hand to my heart, marveling at the feeling of lightness there.

I replay my mother's words and remember the feeling of being connected spirit to spirit. I trust myself and allow my inner power to increase. My vibration rises, and I feel the warmth of that energy coursing through me. When I look up again my mother is gone and the grandmothers are now seated before me.

In the name of the Great Spirit, you, Grandmother, and you, Ghigau, are now unbound, I say. I visualize myself removing their ties and coverings from their eyes and mouths.

Thank you, my daughter's daughter, Grandmother says.

I close the Dreamtime and the medicine wheel, thanking and blessing all who came to assist. I recognize this as a pivotal moment, after which I will never be the same. I open my eyes and watch as the horses and Fabio calmly walk back to their stalls.

"How do you feel?" I hear Brayden ask as he comes up behind me and wraps me in a bear hug.

"Amazing, grateful, loved, and empowered."

I put my head on Brayden's chest, staying there a moment to let it all sink in.

"The grandmothers are safe and unbound. Thank you, April."

"We saw it when it happened," April says in amazement.

"What do you mean?"

"You glowed," Nibs says.

"Glowed golden light, it was all through you and around you," Brayden adds.

At a loss for words, I just shrug my shoulders. I guess I'll have to take their word for it.

I ask April to stay for dinner, but she begs off, saying she is drained from the day and has an hour's drive back to Fayetteville. After promising we'll get together soon, she heads out. Nibs and Daniel leave shortly after for what I hope will be a long overdue talk.

"Finally, I have you all to myself," Brayden says once everyone has gone. "Dinner or bath?"

"Bath first, then dinner," I say.

"You got it." He heads off to the bathroom and a second later I hear the water running.

As we soak in the tub, I tell Brayden about seeing and talking with my mother.

"How did that feel?"

"I was amazing, actually. To know that she's no longer in pain, it's as if I've been set free as well. I never realized how much her story was weighing on my spirit."

He pulls me to him and gently places my head on his shoulder. Dinner forgotten, I allow the man in my life to love me and be my soft place to fall.

I wake to a familiar pressure across my chest and with one eye open say, "Good morning, Grandmother."

My daughter's daughter, there is not much time. You need to find White Owl.

"Is it Michael? Where is he?"

It is not Michael.

I am shown in my mind's eye a picture of a young man. He is far away but there is something familiar about his posture. The figure draws closer and then I see his face. *Wind Song*!

I sit up straight in bed. "What could Wind Song possibly want with White Owl?"

Grandmother doesn't answer.

I shake Brayden awake. "Let's go, duty calls."

Brayden rolls over and groans. "I knew it wouldn't last."

"Sorry," I say, already running to the kitchen to make phone calls and coffee.

This is my fault. I have been doing this for so long I got complacent, stopped keeping a close eye on things. I should've seen the boy starting to succumb to the lure of false power. He might be dark and evil now, but he's not dumb. Had enough sense to bind my hands and gag me, knowing that I would use every tool to save myself, and more importantly, the community I swore to protect. Our only hope now lies in the strength of our new Ghigau. I felt that strength when she said the words. I just hope she and her friends find me in time. I don't know how much longer I can hold on. If Wind Song had gotten further along in his training, I would certainly be dead by now.

Here he comes again, and he has that vile liquid with him. I try to fight him off, but the poison has made me weak.

Please hurry, Ghigau.

———◈———

Nibs and Daniel arrive just as I finish brushing my teeth. I rinse and spit and am walking into the kitchen to greet them when suddenly I feel as if a fist has landed squarely in my stomach.

"Nan!" Brayden yells when I double over.

I feel another punch and my coffee cup falls to the floor. "Oh!"

Breathe, Granddaughter, focus, and follow what you're feeling.

I do and realize it does not belong to me. At the same time, White Owl flashes through my mind. I know where he is.

"I'm okay; it's not me."

Brayden is there to support me as I sit on the floor and cross my legs beneath me.

"Okay, I've got you," he says.

"I feel like shit, but it's not me. It's White Owl and he's sick, very sick. I think he may have poisoned him."

"Who's got him?" Daniel asks, "Michael? Is it Michael?"

"No, not Michael; it's Wind Song, and he's got him locked in one of the rooms of the Hot House."

"Wind Song?" Nibs says incredulously.

I nod. "We have to go."

"You're not going anywhere," Brayden says.

"I have to…I know which room White Owl is being held in. Besides, he needs me to be there."

"She's right, Cuz," Nibs says, "The Ghigau needs to be there."

On the way to the village we hurriedly formulate a plan, one that hopefully involves the least amount of risk to both us and White Owl. It all hinges on the assumption that Wind Song doesn't know we're on to him.

Brayden parks down the block from the Trading Post, then I get out and walk up to the door, praying White Owl has received the information I've been sending him, that he knows he has to hang on just a little white longer. I beat on the door until Wind Song cracks it open. There's no gushing over the Ghigau today.

"Hey, Wind Song, can you let me in? I need supplies." I pause for a beat. "White Owl won't mind."

"Sure," he says and pulls the door open wider, but he doesn't meet my eyes.

"Have you heard from him, Wind Song? We're worried about him…"

Wind Song shakes his head. "No, I haven't."

"Oh, I just thought that maybe since you two are so close that you might..."

He shakes his head again. "No. It's crazy, right, the way he just took off?"

"What about any of the others in the back. Do you think anyone else would know?"

"There's no one else here."

"Really, where did they go?"

Suddenly, I feel the emergence of a strange, dark energy, one that until now has been carefully disguised beneath that of a nerdy kid. Wind Song's eyes lock on mine and they're nearly glowing with malevolence.

"You mean you don't know?" he says with a humorless laugh. "I thought the precious Ghigau was supposed to know everything..."

"It's over, Wind Song," I say quietly.

For a brief second the room falls silent, then with a snarl Wind Song lunges for me. Would have gotten me, too if Daniel and Brayden didn't come crashing through the door and tackle him to the ground. Nibs follows a beat behind them, clutching her medical bag. As Daniel cuffs Wind Song, I lead her and Brayden through the labyrinth of hallways toward the door of the Hot House. It's locked, and I can't help but look on admiringly as Brayden kicks it open. We rush into the rooms beyond and find White Owl in the last one, barely alive. He has a slow pulse, shallow breathing, skin dry, no sweat.

"Quickly, let's get him to the clinic," Nibs says, then stoops to pick up an empty container on the concrete next to White Owl. "We'll need to have this tested."

Brayden scoops White Owl into his arms and carries him out front, where we find Daniel handing Wind Song off to a fellow deputy. The young man who had once been so enamored of me now seems to have nothing but hatred in his heart. If looks could kill, I know I would surely be a goner.

Brayden gently eases White Owl into the backseat of his truck, then he and Nibs climb into the front. As I slide in beside him, the medicine man opens his eyes, then reaches over and pats my hand.

"Ghigau . . . You are Ghigau."

"White Owl, please live," I say, my heart breaking.

We arrive at the clinic at the same time as Daniel, and he and Brayden carry White Owl to the exam table. They have no sooner laid him out when Nibs places an I.V. in White Owl's arm. If we reached him in time, the fluids will take care of the dehydration. But what's in the vial? Nibs smells it and hands it over to Daniel.

"Anything you recognize?" she asks.

"No, it'll have to be sent to the lab. In the meantime, I'll do my own search." He glances at White Owl, his eyes sad.

"I'm going to do my best for him," Nibs says as she squeezes Daniel's hand. "Come on, I'll show you where the computer is."

"Maybe he should call April," I suggest. "She may know what Wind Song used."

"Good idea, Nan. I'll give him her number."

"This is not your fault," Brayden tells me as Nibs leads the deputy from the room.

"I know it's not, but I still feel responsible. It's my job as Ghigau to keep everyone safe."

"Nan, there is no way that you can keep an entire tribe safe. It just isn't possible."

He's right, Granddaughter; you have no power over someone else's choices. You can hold space for them, to heal, along with the Spirit Animals, and to lead. That is your job.

I know what they're saying is true. How I feel, though, is a very different story.

A few minutes later, Daniel appears in the doorway.

"Well, if it's what we think it is, he'll be fine," he says.

"I sent a picture of it to April–it's Golden Poppy Seed," Nibs says, "It has a sedating effect and there's no antidote. We'll just have to keep an eye on him."

Daniel walks over and puts his arm around me. "Thank you. Thank you for saving my father."

"Whose father?" says a faint voice.

All heads whip toward White Owl, but he's already out again. At least this time he looks quite peaceful, rather than in pain.

Suddenly, Daniel crosses the room again, this time to plant a kiss on Nibs's cheek. "Thank you for saving his life."

My eyes widen at this uncharacteristic display of emotion from the deputy. I glance from him to White Owl, thinking this is going to be one family reunion I don't want to miss. But that's for later. Right now I need a bath and my bed, not necessarily in that order.

"I think they've got this covered," I say to Brayden "Let's go home."

"How lucky are we?" I ask Brayden as he pulls out of the parking spot.

"Damn lucky, I'd say, almost as lucky as White Owl."
Brayden looks at me, a smile playing on his lips. "Now, wouldn't
you like to be a fly on the wall when White Owl wakes up?"

We laugh all the way to the cabin.

28

Gone

I wake with a smile on my face and my head burrowed into
the shoulder of a very handsome man. My man, Brayden
Dove.

"I love you too," he says, rolling over and kissing me
exactly the way I like it. He never disappoints. Our kisses
start out innocently enough until our passion builds and we
are a tangle of arms and legs. We're starting to get this "feeling" thing down, and as uncomfortable as it is at times it's
proving to be invaluable in communicating when words are
difficult or not enough.

"Let's get up, Cowboy. We can't stay in bed all the time."

"Are you sure, because that's what I'd love to do today."

"Okay, we'll discuss it over coffee."

"Is that your way of asking me to make some?" he laughs, but he's already getting out of bed and heading toward the kitchen.

"What are you thinking about?" he asks when I follow him a few minutes later.

"Nothing, just boring old Ghigau stuff."

"From the way I'm feeling, I doubt that very much."

He embraces me and gives me more passionate kisses. When we come up for air, he hands me a steaming cup. Brayden and coffee; I can't get enough of either.

"Be back in a few minutes," I say, heading outside to the deck.

Holding space for my tribe. It's one of my favorite daily duties as Ghigau, and one of the most important jobs I'll do every day for the rest of my life. I greet the day by offering a smudge ceremony for the People, the land, and the animals. I honor my ancestors and enter the Dreamtime.

My daughter's daughter. Soon you will face Michael. Remember who you are. You are ready.

"Thank you, Grandmother; I will do my best."

Walk the wheel on the next full moon.

That's tomorrow; we have a lot of work to do before then.

Brayden does a double take when I walk back into the cabin.

"Wow, you look amazing. What happened out there?"

I shrug, because there's some things I still don't know how to answer. "We need to call everyone and get ready for a circle."

"Okay, I'll make some phone calls."

I watch as he scrolls through his contact list, in awe of him and the way he approaches life. He never questions me or complains but helps me anyway he can. A true partner in all ways.

While he's talking on the phone, I replay Grandmother's words in my mind. I have known for some time that Michael and I will be facing off at some point. And I can't tell Brayden.

Brayden looks over at me, his mouth doing that smiling and frowning thing. Adorable as it is, I know he's sensing my feelings and is concerned about me. I come up behind him and put my arms around his chest, nuzzling in for just a second, sending him as much love as humanly possible. As soon as there's a break in the conversation, he politely tells the person he has to go, then he turns and grabs my chin, lifting my gaze to meet his.

"The circle's not starting yet, is it?" he says slyly, then leads me back to the bedroom.

An hour later, Brayden pulls up to the clinic. He has a few errands to run in town and then he'll come back to meet me.

When I walk in I'm greeted by a happy sight: White Owl is sitting up, eating soup, and talking a mile a minute to Nibs as she fiddles with his I.V.

"Young Nanye'Hi, you found me," he says, giving me a toothy grin. "Or should I say Ghigau."

"You did a great job staying alive long enough for us to find you. Where is Daniel?"

Nibs rolls her eyes. "He had 'business' to attend to—that's Daniel-speak for 'I don't want to have an uncomfortable conversation right now.'" She gestures to White Owl.

"Two peas in a pod; so stubborn you'd think they were born of the Mule Clan."

White Owl pretends to be offended but he can't keep the proud grin from his face. "I have a son–a son. Can you believe it?"

"Daniel told you already?" I ask, eyes wide. "I'm impressed."

"Don't be," Nibs says, "White Owl overhead us talking yesterday and the minute he woke up he started grilling Daniel. Eventually the good deputy cracked under the pressure. He admitted they're father and son, then he took off."

"Don't be too hard on him, Nibs. He just needs some time to get used to all of this."

"Well, I hope he doesn't take too long," White Owl says, "I have a lot to make up for." He narrows his eyes at me. "Ghigau, you have that look. What are you up to?"

"I agree with you, White Owl," Nibs says, turning to look at me. "Don't think for a minute that I'm going to let you go anywhere by yourself."

Brayden walks in and gets just enough information.

"Brayden, it's okay, just listen."

"No, it's not okay!" he shouts, clenching his fists, "You cannot go running off by yourself *anywhere* while Michael's still here. We can't take that kind of chance!"

"I would not be pushing this if it weren't important. If it wasn't necessary."

"Do you feel so little for me that you would go off and risk yourself?"

My heart breaks a little with his words, but I know if the situation was reversed, I would feel the same.

"Brayden, wait," I say, but he is already out the door.

"Crap, this is not how I wanted this to go."

"Better give him a few minutes," Nibs advises.

I ignore her and follow Brayden outside the clinic. Suddenly, I feel *him.* Michael's energy is everywhere. It creeps slowly at first, low to the ground, almost like a fog, hovering and sticking to everything.

"Brayden!" I shriek, oblivious to the passersby who turn to stare at me.

"Nan, it's okay," Brayden says, walking toward me. "I'm right here. I just had to get some air."

"Oh, thank God. I'm so sorry, Brayden. I didn't mean to upset you or worry you."

"I know you didn't. It's hard when I can't do anything, and I feel like you're taking unnecessary chances."

"The grandmothers told me I have to do it alone."

"You know as well as I do that not everything is always so cut and dry when it comes to the grandmothers. Can we at least talk about it, like family, you know, with everyone?"

I pause for a minute. "You may be on to something."

"Dinner meeting at our place?"

"Okay, good. Oh, and I like the sound of that."

"Sound of what?"

"Our place."

A look of surprise crosses his face, and I know he had said it automatically, without even thinking about it, which makes it even better. Still, I can't suppress a shiver as he wraps his arms around me. I can feel the evil and darkness starting to flow through the village–Michael's sick calling card that he's coming for me.

We return to the clinic to tell Nibs about the dinner meeting and have another visit with White Owl, then we head back to the cabin. We spend most of the afternoon in bed, then Brayden heads out to feed the horses before it's time to put his chef's hat on. I'm in the kitchen basking in afterglow and peeling potatoes when I hear Fabio's alarm.

I run outside, screaming, "Brayden!"

He doesn't answer.

I race to the stalls then the edge of the woods, still screaming his name.

He's gone.

I feel the inky energy that I recognize as Michael and with a shaking hand pull out my phone to call Daniel and Nibs.

They arrive fifteen minutes later, with tires screeching.

"The search teams are already out looking, Nan," Daniel says.

"It will be too late. I need to go find him; Michael wants me."

"Now is not the time to go off unprepared, Nan. Think of Brayden."

"I am thinking of Brayden. I'm thinking that I won't be able to live with myself if something happens to him."

"I get it, but we have to be smart about this. I want you to think about what you know about Michael. Then try to do that... uh... connection thing with Brayden. That will help us find him."

"Okay," I say, trying to calm myself. All I can feel is fear. The fear of losing Brayden and what Michael might be doing to him. "I need a minute."

Daniel turns to Nibs. "Can you help her?"

"Yes. Nan, breathe slowly and get grounded, see your energy going down into Mother Earth. Connect there. Keep breathing deeply, that's it, just a few more times."

I close my eyes, listening to her words and taking slow, deep breaths. I feel the fear begin to dissipate as my energy expands.

"Okay, it's working. Thank you."

Our bond is right where it always is. At least for the moment, Brayden is alive. I share that news.

"As for Michael," I say, "you know everything I do–he's skilled, sick, twisted, and evil, and he wants me dead."

"Is it that simple?"

"You know the story, Daniel. It started back in the military, when I rejected his advances. He tried to kill me then and it didn't take."

"Right," Daniel says, "You're the one that got away. That's what he can't handle. He's obsessed. It's a failure and a character defect for him that you're still alive. He won't stop, Nan."

Suddenly the faces of my dead crew flash before my eyes, then Michael's superiors as they tell me they don't believe my story. All the things Michael has done to torture me since then. I feel my breath starting to quicken and sweat forming on my palms and face. I will not go there, not–ever–again.

Grandmothers, help.

Outside, Nanye'Hi. Let the totems help you.

I open my eyes to see Nibs staring at me intently. "What is it, Nan?"

"I need to connect with Magic."

"We'll stand watch," Daniel says, and he isn't kidding. He hands Nibs a firearm and they stand not ten feet away, scanning the land as I place my hand on Magic's heart.

The other horses and the Fabio take their places, holding space. Magic shows me where and how Michael got to Brayden, and then he shows me the cave. I thank Magic and the totems for their help.

"He won't kill him unless I'm there to watch," I say.

Daniel's jaw clenches. "We leave at first light."

"I'll be ready," Nibs says.

"I wish you wouldn't go," Daniel says to her.

"You're not telling me what to do."

Oh, boy. I know this argument well.

"Dr. Nibs might come in handy tomorrow, Daniel."

"I just don't want her to become another target."

"Neither do I."

"Hey, right here, you two," Nibs says, waving her hands at us. "And despite what you may think I'm perfectly capable of taking care of myself."

At daylight, we set out for the cave–Daniel on Jack, Nibs on Jill, and me on Magic–all of us armed to the teeth. We had discussed getting a larger group together as backup but dismissed the idea, not wanting to alert Michael or put anyone else at risk. Instead, Storm, Daisy, Cowgirl, and Fabio bring up the rear of our small caravan. We aren't on the trail very long when Eagle makes his appearance, crying and swooping overhead. I keep sending loving, comforting thoughts to Brayden, trying to connect with him.

Please stay alive. We're coming. I love you.

For the longest time there's no response; then, as we get closer to the cave, I feel a tingle from him.

Thank the Great Spirit.

"He's alive."

"I feel him too," Nibs whispers. It is the first thing she has said in hours. I tried to draw her out a couple of times, but she is so worried about her cousin she can barely breathe, let alone speak.

Magic neighs, and I let him take the lead. He knows this area better than anyone. Every so often he lifts his head as if he's trying to feel his way toward Brayden too.

"We're close," I tell them a few minutes later.

Daniel nods. "Okay, dismount, let's walk in quietly."

29

The Cave

It makes sense that Michael would bring Brayden back to this wretched cave, back to the place where he almost did me in. In Michael's mind, there is a symmetry to it, a perfect place to complete his mission. My mind flashes through a lifetime worth of experiences that have happened in only a few short months. Three months and three full moons, to be exact.

My daughter's daughter, he is yours to do with what you will. Just remember that you will have to live with your decision for the rest of your life.

I will remember, Grandmother, I reply silently.

A voice, both familiar and distorted by rage, reaches us from the dark opening of the cave.

"Stay right there, or he gets it."

"Bring him out and I'll do whatever you want," I tell him.

Nibs and Daniel both move towards me, saying, "No."

"That's not the way this works," Michael says, "You'll do whatever I want anyway. Otherwise, your *friend* here is going to get cut from ear to ear."

I motion them to stay back. He means what he says.

"Stay where you are, Deputy," Michael says as if reading my thoughts, "or they both die. You know I'll do it. It makes no difference to me who goes first, though I'd rather leave the best for last."

He is trying to throw everyone off. Fear is the tactic in play. I give Nibs the eye, and she puts an arm on Daniel to steady him. It works because I hear him take a deep breath. He nods at me, and I know he gets it. I silently ask the Great Spirit, my grandmothers, and the ancestors for their help. Then I shield myself from the evil, the way April taught me. He will not win this time.

"No, they aren't coming anywhere near the cave. It's me you want, right?"

Michael pauses for a beat. "Get over here now, or he dies."

I take slow steps toward the cave. I have no weapon and no plan. Hopefully, someone else will. I have to trust. The last thing I hear is Eagle crying overhead. When I get close enough, Michael roughly grabs my arm, pulling me into the dark cave. As I step into it, I hear muffled angry sounds coming from the back of the cave.

Brayden.

I send him my love and as much confidence and strength as I can muster, along with courage, love, trust, and faith. As I do, the same emotions and power fill me, so much so that it might as well have been just me and Brayden in that cave.

Michael is now a mere annoyance. Certainty and calmness wash over me in waves.

I keep an eye on Michael but move closer to Brayden.

"Get over here, or I'll gut him," Michael says.

I hold up my hands. "Fine, just take it easy."

I move toward Michael, moving so that I put myself between him and Brayden. In a matter of half a second he lunges for me, but it's too late. The shield I created is holding, wrapping Brayden and me in its protective barrier. It shines as brightly as the sun and as strong as a steel cage.

Michael cringes, moving away from the light and shielding his eyes.

"NO!" I say, and though the words are coming out of my mouth it doesn't feel like my voice. "You *will not* harm one more person. You. Are. Done."

In the glow of the shield, I get my first look at Brayden, who is bleeding somewhere and staring at me as though I'm an alien. Michael is now cowering in a corner, rocking back and forth and mumbling.

There is nothing I can do to him that will ever make up for the lives he took or the pain he caused. I lower my shield and cry out for Daniel and Nibs.

"Daniel, Nibs, come help us, please."

In a flash, Daniel rushes into the cave and has Michael's hands cuffed behind his back. As he hauls him outside, Nibs rushes over to Brayden and kneels beside him.

Brayden is oddly quiet, continuing to stare at me with his eyes wide.

"How is he, Doc?"

"He has significant concussion, and a moderate head wound that I can stitch right here."

"Can we move him outside first? I'd like to get the hell out of here."

"Damn straight." Brayden says, his eyes softening to me, and in that moment I know he will be okay.

As soon as we get Brayden to his feet, he bends over and vomits.

"That's attractive," he rasps.

"What's attractive is that you're alive," I say.

Suddenly, everything hits me at once—Brayden's life at risk, the relief of Michael finally being caught, and the end of his reign of death and destruction. Tears that seem to come from some unnamable place deep inside me start to flow. When they do, I can't make them stop. Not as we carry Brayden from the cave, or when we help him get astride Magic, and not as I slip behind him, holding onto to him for dear life all the way home.

When we reach the cabin, Brayden is taken directly to bed. While Nibs is setting up triage in his room, I take care of my four-legged partners and safely tuck them in.

Something indefinable had happened today. The power of spirit so magnified that it lit up all the dark spaces. I have learned it is impossible for the light and darkness to exist in the same place, and, more importantly, that the light will snuff out darkness every time. It had rendered Michael, who had been such a powerful force of despair in my life, utterly and completely powerless. I know in my heart and mind that he is nothing more than a shell now and will never again be a threat to anyone.

I offer a smudge ceremony and enter the Dreamtime in gratitude to the Great Spirit for everything in my life. I celebrate my family here on earth, the ancestors, my grandmothers, and my totems. I linger for several minutes in the quiet before sending them all love and gratitude, and to the four directions, above and below.

Ghigau, you did well today, Grandmother says.

"What happened?"

My daughter's daughter, there will be many mysterious and magical things that will happen in your lifetime.

"Michael?" I ask.

He will never see freedom again in this lifetime. You could have done more to him, but you did not. You chose wisely.

"There was no need, Grandmother, you saw him."

Yes, and so did you. That is one of the reasons you will make such a good Ghigau.

"Thank you, Grandmother, for being there; I love you."

With a heart as big as the sky, Nanye'Hi.

When I go inside, I feel grounded and back to myself.

"Okay, White Girl, dish!" Nibs says.

Brayden would have nodded his head, but I know sudden movements are excruciating.

"Oh, I see the *cousins* are ganging up on me," I say, earning me one of Brayden's brilliant smiles.

"What do you mean?" Nibs asks, innocently batting her eyelashes.

"How about large flashes of light with a shimmering gold medicine shield that appeared out of nowhere and a booming voice that came from heaven?" Brayden says.

"Is that why you were looking at me so funny?"

"I was trying to figure out if the bump on my head was making me hallucinate." He laughs, but it quickly turns into a groan.

I turn to Nibs. "Is that what you saw too?"

She shakes her head. "I only saw flashes of light coming from the dark cave. I didn't see or hear anything else."

"Umm . . ." I pause, not quite sure how to put it into words.

Brayden pats the edge of the bed and motions for me to sit next to him.

"I'm going to make some tea," Nibs announces, then slips from the room.

I tentatively sit on the bed, wondering why I suddenly feel shy and a little vulnerable. As I look into his eyes, the real questions rise to the forefront of my mind.

Does he still love me? Does he still want me?

He looked at me the way he always looks at me. With love and tenderness mixed with a healthy dose of passion and need. I feel what he feels. My worry evaporates.

"Can you please open the drawer?" he asks, gesturing vaguely to the bedside table. "I'd do it myself, but if I bend over, I'll puke again, and that is not how I want to remember this."

"Remember what?" I say as I slowly open the drawer. I glanced down and see the little black velvet box. *"Oh."*

"Would you hand it to me please?" he asks.

Inside is a beautiful ring in the shape of a horse's head, and in the center are three stones–a very nice-sized diamond nestled between a moon-shaped coral and a lovely piece of turquoise. It couldn't be any more perfect if I'd created it myself. Just like Brayden.

"It is the most beautiful ring I've ever seen. Did you design this?" I ask, knowing full well he did.

"Yes, for you. I love you, Nan, with all my heart, and I want to be your partner in all ways." He takes the ring out of the box and holds it in between his fingers. "Will you, Nanye'Hi Ghigau Ward, the Beloved Woman of the Cherokee, be my wife?"

Every emotion floods through me as pieces of my life flash in my mind. It seems like an eternity before I can speak.

"Yes, but…" I say.

I don't get to finish that sentence because he interrupts me by placing the ring on the appropriate finger.

"We can talk about the *buts* later. I love you, sweetheart." He takes his hands from mine and places them on his head before yelling, "Hey, cousin, she said yes!"

Nibs runs into the room with tears in her eyes and her mouth stretched from ear to ear. "Can I see it?"

"Of course," I say, rolling my wrist dramatically before holding my hand out to her.

You have chosen well, Granddaughter, we are pleased.

"Thank you, Grandmother, I am too."

Nibs and Brayden are staring at me.

"What?" I ask them. "Oh. The Grandmothers said they are pleased."

"That makes me twice as happy," Brayden says.

"That's the first time you've done that *out loud* since all this started," Nibs says, "I could always tell when there was a conversation going on; this way is better."

"Really?"

"Yes, now we won't feel left out of the conversation or at least won't have to play catch up if you just include us, you know?"

"And besides, we loved Grandmother," Brayden adds.

"I know, and that makes this just that much sweeter."

"You know what I really want to know, though?" Brayden asks.

"What?"

"What really happened in that cave."

There's a quick knock on the door, and Deputy Daniel lets himself in.

"How are you, Bray?" he asks, crossing the room to give Brayden a fist bump.

"Bray?" Nibs and I say together, taken aback at the deputy's uncharacteristically informal demeanor.

"Aside from the whole pounding head and nausea," Brayden says grinning, "I'm fabulous."

Which is my cue to show off the ring, again.

After offering his congratulations, Daniel turns to Nibs. "And how are you doing today?"

"I'm fine," Nibs says, her tone curt. "Thank you for asking."

Uh oh.

Daniel turns away, and I see a fleeting look of hurt cross his face. A minute later it's gone, but he doesn't fool me for one second. If Nibs has any sense, it won't fool her either. At this point, though, I seriously doubt that she does have any sense. I try to make eye contact with her, but she avoids me. Whatever her problem is, I'll get it out of her later.

Quickly changing the subject, Brayden says, "Nan was just about to tell us what happened in the cave."

"I'm sure the deputy does not want to hear about that."

"I *do* want to hear about that."

"Okay, then, here goes. I knew it was going to come down to Michael and me. This battle was to determine the fate of the tribe. It was about that all along, from the very beginning. I was not here, so he came to me when I was in the military. I only knew that I couldn't let it happen again. He is the same darkness that took my mother, Nibs's mother, and so many countless others. I can't imagine my world where all of you do not exist. I imagined in my mind's eye the medicine shield that April showed me how to create, and it was like this force, an ancient force, flowed through me, creating this intense power and light. I believe that neither Michael nor the darkness he embodies was able to handle that much light." I shrug. "That is as much as I know."

The three of them gape at me with something like awe.

"Okay, guys, you're making me uncomfortable. Can't we talk about my ring instead?"

We all look at each other, then burst out laughing.

"So now what?" Nibs asks when the chuckles die down.

"Now we get on with the business of living," I say, "Won't that be wonderful?"

"Yeah," Brayden says, and we won't have to be glued to each other's hips anymore." He looks at me. "Though I kind of enjoyed that part."

"And we'll get to sleep in our own beds," Daniel says. "That will be nice."

Nibs looks at him and says quietly, "I know we're not in danger anymore, but would you stay at my place one more night?"

You could have knocked us over with a feather, but no one more so than Daniel. He's so shocked all he can do is nod his head.

After Nibs and Daniel leave, I take care of my fiancé and tuck him for the night. I'm bone-tired, but it seems sleep will have to wait a little while longer. No sooner does my head touch the pillow when, *whoosh,* I am out of my body.

I hear the drumbeats and the chanting of women's voices.

As I get near the circle, I recognized my grandmother and the Ghigau. Many of the women's faces I have seen in Dreamtime. Everyone is in ceremonial dress, and when I look down, I see that I'm in my beaded white buckskin dress and full Ghigau regalia. When I reach the circle, the Ghigau speaks to me in Cherokee.

"Granddaughter, did you think we could let this day pass without a celebration?"

"I am grateful to my grandmothers and to the women who gather here. Thank you."

"We have gathered here to celebrate your tremendous victory over *this* evil. There will always be a battle between the dark and the light. Remember to always feed the light. It is just as important to celebrate the victories and joyous occasions as it is to grieve when it's time. Balance, Nanye'Hi."

"Yes, Grandmother." I sense a change. This the most the Ghigau had ever spoken to me.

"Ah, you feel it. It is time for me to rest, Nanye'Hi."

"What will I do without you, Ghigau?"

"You will still have one grandmother here that will serve as your guide, as will others. Teachers will come and go, as will spirit animals, throughout your lifetime, serving you as you need for your growth and the challenges to come."

The Ghigau pauses for a beat. "There is a different kind of change coming to the People, Nanye'Hi, you must be ready for it. We are well pleased, Granddaughter."

As the Ghigau starts to fade, I say, "Ghigau and Grand-mother, thank you for all you have done. You will always have my gratitude and love."

Grandmother puts her arms around my shoulders and leads me to the fire, where I'm given a gift–a silver ring shaped into two wolf heads. One with a light stone, quartz maybe, and one with a dark onyx stone. I understand that it is a reminder always to feed the light wolf.

In the morning, I stretch my arms above my head, and for the first time in what seems a very long time, look forward to a normal day. I look at my hands. On my left is my beautiful horse-inspired engagement ring, and on my right is the one given to me by the Ghigau.

"What do we have here?" Brayden asks.

"A very precious gift."

30

At Long Last

Dear Diary,

Grandmother told me that it's time to start keeping a diary so that you, the new Ghigau, will have clues and teachings to go by from this time in history. I don't have a clue who you might be, but I am hoping you will be my daughter. It is my deepest wish that I will be here to guide you and help you along your path, as will your father. If it is the wish of the Great Spirit, you will have family around you and to support you. I'm so new at this that I can't imagine being able to teach anything to anyone, but here goes. From my heart to your heart, may you always be blessed with as much love as I have been in my life. Love will sustain you.

Life is pretty sweet right now. No evil person is running around the village threatening to kill me, or any one of the tribe, including my newly

*established family. The People seem to be faring
well, and my wedding is a week away. Brayden,
my husband-to-be, is busy remodeling his place;
he is determined to make it the perfect home for
us. I insisted on us living apart until after we're
married. It's probably a silly request considering,
but I want our wedding night to be special. And
besides, a girl has to have her boundaries.*

*Nibs is my Maid of Honor, April, my bridesmaid.
April has turned out to be one of those friends that
grow on you a little at a time. She's so accept-
ing of what is and offers unconditional love to the
world. She is a great healer in her unique way. It's
wonderful to see her and Nibs establishing such
a strong bond. They have a lot in common, more
than Deputy Daniel, that is. Three of us are going
wedding dress shopping in Fayetteville today, and
I am surprised by how much I am looking forward
to it. I know I should probably be writing more
about Ghigau stuff in this diary, but I can't help
myself. Life is good.*

———◦◉◦———

This one must be a hit; I think as I step out of the dressing
room to stand in front of a four-way mirror.

I receive the correct amount of *oohs* and *ahhs*, followed
by the appropriate sniffing one would hope to hear while trying on a wedding dress. I look in the mirror and stifle a gasp,
for I don't recognize my reflection. Before me is a woman,
all grown up and obviously very much in love and loved.

This woman is beaming. I look past my reflection and see Nibs and April with their thumbs raised in approval. I'm getting ready to turn and face them when the air around me shimmers and warms; Grandmother is weighing in.

My daughter's daughter, you are beautiful.

"Thank you, Grandmother," I murmur.

"Is this the one?" Nibs asks.

"Yes. Yes, it is." I smile at them. "Now it's your turn."

Nibs and April start shifting uncomfortably.

"Oh, come on. You've made it this far, and bridesmaid dress shopping can't be that bad, can it?"

I'm wrong; it is that bad. These two cannot agree on anything. After searching through several wedding dress shops in the greater Fayetteville area, we find two similar dresses that they both find agreeable. We're about to leave the shop for a celebratory lunch when a sudden wave of dizziness hits me so fast I have to grab Nibs's arm.

"Nan, what is it?"

"I'm not sure. I just got dizzy."

"Dizzy as in...?" she trails off, giving me the eye and sideways glance.

"No, physically dizzy."

"When did you eat last?" April asks.

"Not since last night," I say. "I'll bet that's it; I'll be fine when we get lunch."

Nibs is giving me a look, but she doesn't say much.

We stop at a local burger place, and I fill up on a burger, fries, and milkshake. All is well for about two minutes, then my stomach goes into full revolt. I take off running to the bathroom and barely make it to the stall before tossing my entire meal.

A second later I hear the door open, then Nibs asks, "What can I do?"

"Guess I've got a bug or something."

"Uh huh, why don't you come to the clinic tomorrow and just let me check you out, okay?"

"Okay, but I'm sure it's nothing."

Nibs gives me a pointed look. "Uh, huh."

After a very restless night, I wake up feeling just as queasy as the day before. In fact, as soon as my feet hit the floor, I'm running to the bathroom and vomiting.

I better keep that appointment with Nibs, just to make sure.

I decide on green tea rather than coffee, and I'm feeling hopeful when I'm able to keep down tea and dry toast. It's only three days until the wedding. Not the time to be getting the flu. Whatever it is, Nibs will have me in peak position for the big day. I feel better by the minute and go on with my morning ritual of yoga, smudge ceremony, and Ghigau stuff. As I go to the fence line to see the horses and Fabio, Magic comes to see me and stands directly in front of my face. This is his way to let me know that he wants to "talk" with me. Storm, Daisy, and Fabio stand next to him, also waiting. Hmmm. Something's going on.

"Good morning, my friends."

Before I get any further, Daisy comes forward.

"Oh, Daisy. Do you need something?"

I put one hand on her withers and one at her heart space, expecting to send healing. Instead, I receive a vision, as vivid as a movie. A little girl about two years old and with beautiful, wheat-colored hair is running in the field around the cabin with the horses. She's laughing at Fabio. Brayden comes into the frame and picks her up, circling her around and around so that she can "fly." Then I watch myself come out the back door, walk over and give them both a bear hug. I am very, very pregnant.

I am still slightly dazed an hour later when I walk into the clinic.

"How are you feeling?" Nibs asks.

"I was sick again this morning. Then I had some tea and toast and feel fine now. The horses showed me this morning."

"You're pregnant."

"Did you know?"

"I suspected, but let's just run some tests to cover all the bases," she says, already preparing the needle to draw blood.

"Okay . . . Oh, my God. Now what? What is Brayden going to say?

"Oh, Nan, you know better. Relax."

She's right. My Brayden will be happy, no matter what. This isn't the way I would have planned it, but these things rarely are.

I'm out feeding the horses when I see a tall, lanky man approaching. Though startled, I sense no danger from him.

"Can I help you?"

"Hey, White Girl, you still hanging out in graveyards?"

Though the voice is familiar, it takes me a few seconds to figure out who he is.

"Derrick! Look at you; you're all grown up." I rush over to hug him. "My goodness, you're a solid wall of muscle."

He smiles. "That's from the logging mostly. Helped pay for school."

"Have you seen Brayden yet?"

"No, I came here first. I sent him a text. He said to meet him here."

Right on cue, Brayden comes around the corner, his face lighting up when he sees Derrick.

"Hey, Cuz!" Derrick said.

"It's so good to see you. Thanks again for agreeing to be my best man." Brayden moves towards Derrick, giving him a handshake and a shoulder grab.

"There's nowhere I'd rather be."

Derrick fills us in on his life as the chef at a swanky restaurant in a Las Vegas hotel. I get the feeling that there's so much more to tell. I feel some heartache there and loneliness, which is confirmed by the subtle but pointed look Brayden shoots me. I know he'll talk with him later.

It hits me so fast. One minute I'm standing there talking to Brayden and Derrick, and the next I'm lying on my back in the grass looking up at Brayden's very worried face.

He picks me up like I weigh nothing, yelling at Derrick to call Nibs.

"Quit fussing, and don't bother her. It's just the flu."

As I say the words, I push the guilty feeling to the back of my mind. I'm not ready to tell him; I haven't even had a minute to process it yet. Plus, I tell myself there is still a chance the test will be negative.

Brayden has me in bed, propped up with pillows when Nibs comes in.

"Oh, Derrick, it's so good to see you," she says, giving him a quick hug. She turns to me. "And how's the patient?"

"Nibs, she fainted," Brayden says.

"It happens, sometimes," she says, her eyes flicking over me.

That's when I know for certain.

Brayden looks from me to Nibs and back again. "You too think you're so subtle but you're not fooling anyone. Will you please stop talking in Morse code and tell me what's going on?"

When we don't answer right away, I feel Brayden tense up like he's going to storm.

"Nibs, please. It isn't normal to faint with the flu, is it?"

"Well, maybe if you have a *really* bad case of the flu." Nibs smiles, earning a glare from Brayden.

"I swear to God, Nibs…"

"Don't worry, Cuz. She'll be all better in about six months."

Nibs turns to Derrick, who is smiling. "Let's get out of here, brother, and catch up so these two can talk."

I take a minute to gather courage. "Just so we're clear. I've been on the pill. The whole time."

"What pills, what are you talking about?"

I see it when he gets it, and I feel the warmth spread across my chest. No more talking now, just Brayden's arms around me while my face is repeatedly kissed. There was never a happier man in the entire universe.

He places a hand on either side of my face, "My Nan." Then he places a hand lightly on my belly. "My baby. What could be better?"

From the back of my mind comes an overwhelming sense of joy and the tickle of laughter.

Congratulations, Nanye'Hi, with a heart as big as the sky.

"Thank you, Grandmother."

"How is she with all of this?" Brayden asks.

"Pleased. But it's a good thing we're getting married, Cowboy, or I'd have to get the shotgun out."

The next two days are, along with morning sickness, happily filled with family, friends, and celebration. Derrick bunks with Brayden and takes care of the food. April, who's staying with Nibs, handles all the decorations and helps with last minute details. The only fly in the ointment is the continued iciness between Nibs and Deputy Daniel. In fact, aside from an occasional check-in to see how Brayden's doing, Daniel has made himself scarce. Finally I can't stand it another minute and decide to stick my nose in where it doesn't' belong.

"Okay, Nibs, I've been more than patient, and way too considerate of your privacy, for way too long. Where is Daniel, and how did you two leave it?"

"We didn't leave it anywhere. When we got back to my place, he stayed on the couch, and when I got up in the morning, he was gone. No note, nothing. I haven't heard from him or seen him since."

"Where could he have possibly gone?" I ask.

"I have no idea."

This is serious, I know he has a lot to deal with. Especially the part about being the son of White Owl. I hope he makes it back, not only for the wedding, but for Nibs. She's hurt, and that I don't like.

I step outside on my deck and run back in to get my jacket. The sun is out and glorious, but the cool fall air has a nip in it. This is the last time I will do my morning ritual as a single woman. Brayden's face appears in my mind, and I get that same warm honey feeling I get when Grandmother's close. I take a deep breath and begin my yoga practice. When

I finish, I enter the Dreamtime. The quiet is astounding, almost palpable. I see the beautiful meadow, the trees, grass, and animals of Dreamtime, but nothing is moving or making any sound. Just as I start to get alarmed, Grandmother speaks.

My daughter's daughter, they honor you.

"Thank you, Grandmother."

We are most pleased. Take every opportunity for joy in this life.

"I can't believe that I'm going to be a wife and mother."

And yet, here you are.

I feel her energy and spirit fading, "Grandmother?"

I will always be with you, Nanye'Hi, and will watch over your children.

"I love you so much, Grandmother."

With a heart as big as the sky.

As I get ready to close the Dreamtime, I start to feel something heavy and dark on the outskirts of the meadow. It reminds me of Michael. My heart starts to race, and I want to force myself out of the vision but know I must stay with it.

Not today Nanye'Hi. Today is a day for new beginnings, joy, and celebration. There will always be time for duty.

The Great Spirit and my grandmother have excellent timing. As I leave the Dreamtime, I hear two rather excited bridesmaids bounding out to greet me.

"Enough with the Ghigau stuff," April says, "It's time to get ready for your wedding."

"For once, I agree. Get moving Ghigau," Nibs says.

As Nibs walks me out the back door and under the beautiful arbor Brayden made, I'm aware of the entire tribe surrounding the deck. I briefly glance at White Owl, who looks every inch of Medicine Man. But it's Brayden who takes my breath away. He's wearing a black suit with cowboy boots and a cowboy hat, his smoldering eyes going right through me, to my very soul. Derrick stands to his left. On White Owl's right stands April. Everyone is here; almost. Out of the corner of my eye, I see Daniel at the back of the crowd and can only hope this day will be a turning point for him and my best friend as well.

Nibs makes a sound like she's clearing her throat and I squeeze her hand. I step forward to Brayden as the air around us warms and shimmers. We are all enveloped in that warm honey energy of my grandmother. Brayden gives me a quick nod, and I know he feels it too. White Owl looks overhead like he might be expecting to see her.

We are here Nanye'Hi, Grandmother says.

"Dearly Beloved, Osiyo." White Owl says.

And so it begins.

The End

Afterword

The Cherokee tribe was organized into seven clans—
the Deer, Longhair, Bird, Wild Potato, Blue, Paint,
and Wolf. The clans each had a purpose for the tribe,
and the Wolf Clan was the largest and fiercest. They were the
tribe's warriors and hunters, learning at an early age to pro-
vide and protect. The men and women fought together side
by side. The women often chewed musket bullets so that they
would inflict greater damage.

Nanye'Hi (Nan-ne-hi), (Nancy Ward), was born of the
Cherokee's Wolf Clan in 1738, at Fort Loudon, Tennessee.
She was raised to hunt and fight, and to be a warrior. She
had one son, FiveKiller, through an arranged marriage to the
Chief's son Kingfisher, by the age of sixteen. When she was
eighteen, she became a widow during great battle with the
tribe's enemy, the Creeks. During this battle, she took up her
husband's rifle and fought until the battle was over and the
Cherokee were victorious. The tribe and warriors honored
her for her bravery and bestowed her with the tribe's greatest honor, "Ghigau" (Gee-ga-u), the Beloved Woman. The
Ghigau's power in the tribe was second only to the Chief.

Her voice was the one to say which prisoners lived or died and held tremendous weight over the tribe's policies. Her counsel was the one the Cherokee people would seek in all spiritual matters. Her voice was the one that acted as an emissary for the tribe, speaking directly with the Great Spirit on their behalf.

Nanye'Hi remarried French trader Bryant Ward and had one daughter, Catherine. Bryant Ward did not stay in the Cherokee Nation long and returned to his white family living in Virginia. In those days, many white men were legally able to marry both Indian wives and white wives, because the Indian marriage was not seen as a legal institution. Sadly, in these circumstances, most white men would simply walk away from their Indian wives and children. According to some old written reports, Nancy Ward and her children would visit the home of Bryant Ward and his white family. She would not stay long and was always well received.

Nancy Ward was an amazing woman, fostering peace, treaties, and even keeping her village safe from attacks by the whites, due to her political standing with the U.S. government. She was also recognized for introducing the first cattle into the tribes after saving a white prisoner, Mrs. Bean, from being burned at the stake.

The Trail of Tears was the Cherokee term for a series of forced relocations of Native Americans in the United States, known as the Indian Removal Act of 1830. The removals included Native Americans from the Cherokee, Muscogee, Seminole, Chickasaw, and Choctaw nations. They were forced from their ancestral homelands in the southeastern United States to areas west of the Mississippi River, designated as Indian Territory." (Jahoda, G. (1995), *The Trail of Tears; The Story of The American Indian Removals 1813-1855*. New Jersey: Wings Books.) Nancy Ward's life and the lives of my incredibly resilient ancestors serve as the inspiration for *Three Full Moons*.

The Author

Carolan Dickinson is a psychic medium, bestselling author, teacher, and soon to be licensed professional counselor. One of her favorites gifts is the ability to see the unique qualities and talents of each person and help them find the best way to express them. As a psychic, she will get to the heart of the matter quickly and uncover the most urgent need. Carolan believes that one of the most critical missions she has in this life is helping others learn how to connect and communicate with their own spiritual team of archangels, guardian angels, and deceased loved ones. When she is not working, writing, or teaching a class, you will find her in a yoga class or walking and talking with the Archangels.

Website: https://carolandickinson.com
Facebook: carolandickinson
Email: carolan903@gmail.com
Instagram: @carolandickinson

Acknowledgment

I am extremely fortunate to have a long list of people to be grateful for, both heavenly and earthly. To my friends and family, thank you for your love and support, and a special thank you to my sister Gina, who always believed in this story. I am convinced that we all have a spiritual team that works with us in every aspect of our lives. I also send my love and gratitude to my very enthusiastic ancestors whose guidance breathed life into Nan's story. Alyson Gannon, thank you for the Psychic Sit-ups and helping me find my People. Andy Byng, (Arthur Findlay College Tutor, mentor, and medium extraordinaire), thank you for teaching me that the most important story ever told is the one told by the departed.